THE LUMINIST IS a warm dazzle of a first novel – a profoundly human story of shadow and light fixed in the searing simplicity of David Rocklin's diamond-bright prose.

SUSAN TAYLOR CHEHAK, author of *Apocalypse Tonight*

NOT SINCE *TINKERS* have I read a book which, in its sheer beauty and mystery, has carried me off the way *The Luminist* has. Every sentence is a small miracle; every character glows with a complex elegance, as if seen by candlelight. David Rocklin's lush rendering of raw, unstable, colonial Ceylon will be etched in my memory for a long, long time. Superb.

MYLÈNE DRESSLER, author of *The Deadwood Beetle*

IN THIS EXTRAORDINARY debut, David Rocklin takes us to the heart of photography's unlikely origins through language that shimmers like the art of light itself. As creative obsession fuses with political crisis in colonial Ceylon, the result is one unforgettable story. *The Luminist* is a gorgeous evocation of era, place, and human passion.

AIMEE LIU, author of *Flash House* and *Cloud Mountain*

THIS BOOK IS one of those few in which an author's specific sensibilities nourish the text, as Abraham Verghese's multi-geographic heritage and his physician's life inform *Cutting For Stone* and Andrea Barrett's fiction, from *Ship Fever* to *Servants of the Map*, owes its density and savor to the botanic and historiographic facts that beguile her. David Rocklin's *The Luminist* is a weave of legend and history, science and art, politics and domesticity that are symphonic themes in the main title, the story of an enduring and forbidden friendship.

JACQUELYN MITCHARD, author of *The Deep End of the Ocean*

CEYLON OF THE 19th century is more than the setting for David Rocklin's richly imagined and deeply moving novel. It is the central character, a world no less alienated and scarred than the people who inhabit it. That Rocklin chooses to capture the rawness of those lives through the nascent lens of photography is even more impressive, lending the novel a lyricism that comes as both a shock and a comfort.

JONATHAN RABB, author of *Shadow and Light*, and *The Second Son*

Library of Congress
Cataloging-in-Publication Data

Rocklin, David, 1961–
The luminist : a novel / David Rocklin.
p. cm.
ISBN 978-0-9790188-7-9
(alk. paper)

1. Single women–Fiction.
2. British–Sri Lanka–Fiction.
3. Social classes–Sri Lanka–Fiction.
4. Sri Lanka–History–19th century–Fiction.

I. Title

PS3618.O354465L57 2011

813'.6–DC22

2011004506

Hawthorne Books
& Literary Arts

9 2201 Northeast 23rd Avenue
8 3rd Floor
7 Portland, Oregon 97212
6 hawthornebooks.com
5 *Form*:
4 Adam McIsaac, Bklyn, NY
3
2 Printed in China
1 Set in Paperback

For Nina, Ariel and Kavanna,
always and forever.

Acknowledgements

I AM DEEPLY GRATEFUL TO RHONDA HUGHES, KATE SAGE, Adam O'Connor Rodriguez, and Liz Crain of Hawthorne Books; and agents extraordinaire Christy Fletcher and Melissa Chinchillo of Fletcher & Co. You willed this book to be better, to be sold, and to be seen. Thank you for making the dream real.

A heartfelt thank you to Susan Taylor Chehak. Without your mentoring and your friendship, this book would not have made its way into the world.

To Dr. Nadeem Hasnain, for his graciousness in reviewing the manuscript in its nascent stages.

To Julian Cox, for his assistance with the Getty Museum's photographic collection, and for directing me to the kindly staff at the Royal Botanic Gardens, Kew.

To Gloria Luxenberg, who told a twelve-year old boy he could write.

To my family and friends, too numerous to mention. Thanks for understanding whenever I seemed to be far away.

To Starbucks, for the perfect blend of writing space and chai tea.

The Luminist was initially inspired by an installation of Victorian-era photography at the Getty Museum in Southern California. The character of Catherine Colebrook is very loosely suggested by the life and work of Julia Margaret Cameron, one of the first photographic pioneers. Her pictures of children were especially haunting, at once warmly immediate and bittersweet; those lives are, after all, lost to us now. What followed – research into colonial life in Ceylon, the traditions of Victorian photography, a plunge (inadequate, I'm certain) into the religions, cultures and customs of India – really began there, with photographic relics and writerly imaginings about the woman who made them. Though the novel deals with matters of history and the origins of photography, I have taken broad liberties with each. My apologies for tampering with these worlds in the interests of fiction.

DEEPALETE

DERPALETE

ripe

el R

ibo

Vaddie

gam

ndele

oads

BO

pitty

iruwa

Morotto

Pantura

Moligode

Caltura

Caloemodere

Barbaryn

Bentotte

Hosgodde

Balapitimodere

Amblangodde

Hiccodé Oya

Dodandove

Mahamoder

Galle

Katjawalle

Cagalle

Goyapan

Belligam

Madura

Dondra H.

FOUR GRAV

Naghagedre

Rospe

Dambadiniya

Bandawe

Girioulle

Paraw

TOOMPANE

ERRIS

PATTOO

Oddo

Amoor

KANDY

Allutge

Tunuesall

Allow

Molligod

ATTENOSWERE

Ganga

rewa

Gongam

Koegamowa

Ballapanne

HEWAHETT

Ambapusse

Maruwene

Hanga

rokett

FOUR KORLES

Aranderre

Gampol

OODDAPALATA

Pasellawa

Minuangodde

Atelle

DOLLO

Collagode

Aluanwelle

BAGE

Ramb

Yeni

godde

OODDA

Havelle

Seetawaka

Disahawelle

Dumbulla

Pedolalle

Thuawell

BOOLAT

Eseuo

HEWAGAMA

GAMME

KORLE

SALPITTY

Kotta

Halpitty

Oya

Hackgulle

KORLE

Vitorowitte

Atlants pk.

Kirigul

Horona

Namba

pane

KOROWITTE

Idengodde

R. Medwal

Gillemalle

Horton Pt.s

RAYGAM

Halmalgame

Ratnapoora

Paragalle

Denewaka

Openake

Alutner

Wau

kagode

Pattiwelgame

Balangodde

Roekelle

SAFERAGAM

Dilgode

Kalla

pitty

Jakewille

Kapagode

Agrasmouri

Haycock H.

Natoon

pitty

Opale

Dangalle

Colona

WALLAWITTE

GODDE

Cadougal

MORV

Welletre

Maplegamma

Morvoke

Walpitty

Diatore

Orele

game

SOUTH

Ringe

Bellig

Olivatte

Mangwelle

Halma

Walove

Baygam

Argoragam

Cogodde

Tolhane

Goyapan

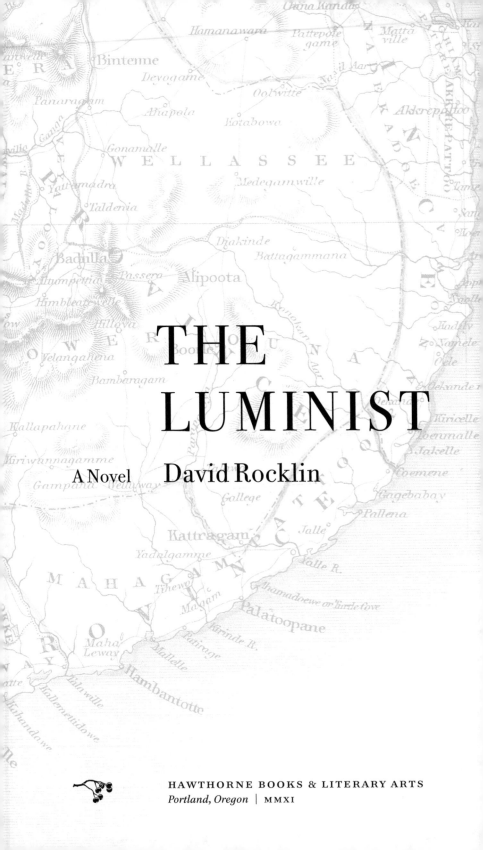

THE LUMINIST

A Novel   David Rocklin

HAWTHORNE BOOKS & LITERARY ARTS
Portland, Oregon | MMXI

Introduction
Jacquelyn Mitchard

PHOTOGRAPHY IN ITS INFANCY WAS A DANGEROUS GAME.
As they do now, practitioners of the mysterious art,
named from root words that literally mean "drawing with light,"
went into the darkness to do it. But in the 19th century dark-
room, they worked by candlelight, coating glass plates with
flammable substances, breathing ether, mercury, and ammonia,
because the necessary absence of light also meant a lack of
ventilation. They got stains on their hands from silver nitrate,
and to remove them, used the even more toxic potassium
chloride. Matthew Brady, who made the images most of us call
to mind when we picture the battlefields of the Civil War, had to
kneel or lie down in his field tent to do his processing. Sweat
streamed, eyes smarted and muscles ached from hauling water,
chemicals and the camera and plates, which were both bulky
and heartbreakingly fragile. Such was the potency of this infatu-
ation that we modern-day purists, who bristle when we pass
a smoker's miasma in a parking lot, have to wonder how much
these pioneers understood, or cared, about the damage that
they inflicted on themselves. We ask ourselves if the majesty of
the experience was so great that, like Marie Curie's fatal
obsession with radiation, they went forth, no matter what.

Photography comprises the bright, tensile thread in the
sweep of David Rocklin's novel, *The Luminist*, drawing tight
a narrative that shifts between the prejudices and passions of
Victorian England and those of colonial Ceylon. It binds the

destinies of Catherine Colebrook, the proper wife of a fading
diplomat, who rebels against every convention to chase the
romance of science through her lens, and Eligius, an Indian teen-
ager thrust into servitude after his father is killed demanding
native rights.

Thus, this book is one of those few in which an author's
specific sensibilities nourish the text, as Abraham Verghese's
multi-geographic heritage and his physician's life inform *Cutting
For Stone* and Andrea Barrett's fiction, from *Ship Fever* to
Servants of the Map, owes its density and savor to the botanic and
historiographic facts that beguile her. David Rocklin's *The
Luminist* is a weave of legend and history, science and art, politics
and domesticity that are symphonic themes in the main title,
the story of an enduring and forbidden friendship. Catherine and
Eligius must each struggle with internal forces that inspire
them and societal pressures that command them. Uprooted to
Ceylon with her adolescent daughter and her newborn son, a
twin who survived his brother, Catherine is expected to do good
works and host luncheon parties to further her husband's
career. All the while, her turbulent soul, in part informed by the
loss of her child and her inability to keep his likeness, embraces
photography with the fervor of alchemy. Eligius, named for the
patron saint of metalworkers, is trapped by the strictures of his
class. Hired as a laborer by British gentry, he is shamed and
excited by finding the intellectual fulfillment he aspires to in the
Colebrook home, not his own.

So different, Catherine and Eligius are twinned in torment.
She loves her old and failing husband, her moody daughter,
and her lonely young son, yet all of them impede her obsession.
Eligius is duty-bound to his widowed mother and ailing baby
sister; his father's comrades urge him to rob his employers, the
usurpers of his nation.

Still, his relationship with the Colebrooks deepens, and
the bigotry of the oppressed cannot survive. Catherine's
beautiful daughter, Julia, becomes Eligius' confidant. He sees

that Catherine's husband, "the old lion," despite his upbringing, brings on his own ruin trying to do the right thing. The British matron, raised to a famous reserve, invests photography with a holy power. The separate peace, however, has a price. Catherine is an outcast, Eligius a traitor. Yet their photographs draw more attention, and attract more and more patrons, when, at virtually the same moment, the tide of armed revolution breaks over Ceylon.

Rocklin's is a bold landscape, against which an intimate drama is poignantly played out. *The Luminist* recalls *Out of Africa*, and Karen Blixen's bond with her house manager, Farah, from whom she learns how little she can control, but their relationship is not in vain. It comprises a doom made glorious, a failure in the midst of grandeur, a loss imbued with hope.

Just in this way, our minds recall in every detail the photo snapped at the moment of pain, while all the lovely scenes seem to run together.

THE LUMINIST

I.

Ceylon, from whatever direction it may be approached, unfolds a scene of loveliness and grandeur unsurpassed, if it be rivaled, by any land. The Brahmans designated it by the epithet of Lanka, the resplendent, and in their dreamy rhapsodies extolled it as the region of mystery.

SIR JAMES EMERSON TENNANT
Ceylon: An Account of the Island, Vol. I, 1859

Must we always object to science, that it leads its servants to doubt the immortal soul? No, this is my prayer: enlighten my mind so that I may be enabled to see more clearly the illuminations of mortal Man, and behind it, the immortal Light.

SIR JOHN HOLLAND
Preliminary Discourse on a New Mechanism of Portraiture, 1835

Imagine, arresting beauty at the very moment beauty comes into being and passes out of the world. Imagine if life could be held still.

Letter from Catherine Colebrook to Sir John Holland
February 22, 1836

The End of This

THE NOISES OUTSIDE HER WINDOW WERE OF WIND AND the near sea, of clay chimes kilned to crystalline tones. Natives not opposed to Britishers had strung them at odd heights from the thatching of her bungalow roof to ward off demons during her pregnancy. Their sound filled her sleep and informed her dreams.

Ewen and Hardy nestled against her still-swollen midsection. Before, when the pains of labor had ruled her, this would have filled her heart.

She took her babies into her arms and bundled them. Folding the letter carefully, she brought them to the carriage and placed them next to her. At the flick of her reins, the old bay stumbled into motion.

She gazed at her newly-arrived sons and tried not to think of the future.

THE RIDE TO the Maclears' home in Table Bay was not ritual, yet her passage through the Cape of Good Hope's sifting littorals possessed equal weight and hollowness. She struggled to think of the right word for this, her second foray along the sea path to the lonely Dutch outpost of stone imposing itself on the African sky.

Her sons jostled alongside her. She wanted simply to place the letter in Sir John Holland's hand and leave, and be whoever it was that she would be tomorrow.

When the bend in the road opened onto the sea's turquoise at the mouth of Agulhas, she thought of Sir John's lecture. That night at the Maclears' he'd marveled at how the Cape marked the place where a man traveling from the equator ceases traveling southward and begins traveling eastward without ever having changed direction. The world changes without changing. Wondrous, he'd said, his shock of white hair a cloud above his face.

The world is capable of such things, she thought.

The road was rutted. Ewen cried out. Catherine brought her children close and told them that they traveled over the same dirt and lichens, past the same protea, as the Voortrekkers who fled the sea to escape the rampaging Xhosa, and found peaceful vistas inland where they grew their rye and gathered their wool. Boys, she thought, are fond of narrow escapes and bloodthirst. These are the sorts of things they will remember as men, when they find themselves soldiers or surgeons: once as a child, they made believe they were brave.

She regarded Hardy's face for the first time since the mote of light slipped from his eyes.

They passed through the port market, a slipshod constellation of many-hued fruits, dyed cloths, hung meats, animals braying at the blades of the butchers, macaws on horsehair leads, natives porting crates to and from ships on callused feet, swearing under their breath in Capie and broken English.

The Maclears' home stood next to the Cape lighthouse, atop a red rock jetty. Its view of the whalers and tall mast ships was the envy of the expatriates. A line of carriages filled the road at the base of the house. Porters brought the parcels of voyage from the front door. Sir John's departure on his star map travels was imminent.

The Maclears' servants fell silent at the sight of her binding her horse to the low boughs of a fig tree. She was late in her forties, but still possessed a severe, weathered beauty. She was unadorned of jewels or those impractical satchels other colonial women carried, and all the more striking for it; there was nothing else to consider but the shaded hollows of her cheeks, the quartered mango of her lips, the expanse of her slender neck.

She'd pulled back her brown hair and fastened it with mother of pearl sometime in the long night, but strands had come loose to brush her skin. She was swathed in local cloth, shod in sandals, uncaring of her appearance.

She took her babies to the front door.

Sir John came shortly, still wet from bathing. A towel was loosely draped about his neck. His eyes were crinkled with age and recent sleep.

Early, she realized. In another time, I would think a visit at this hour quite inappropriate.

"My lord," Sir John whispered when he saw Hardy.

She hefted her babies higher against her chest. Ewen protested, but she needed a free hand to extend the letter.

"I hope you remember me," she said.

Inside the house she saw the Wynfield boy, George, portraitist at seventeen and already of some renown. He would be accompanying Sir John to fashion a painted record of their travels. The sights and ports of call, the map itself.

"You know who I am," she called out to George. He was intent on his canvas. "Your father and my husband are allied in Ceylon."

"I am aware, madam. Your Julia has sat many hours watching me work. A delightful creature. I've spoken of her to my father."

"I should like to commission you to paint my children."

He regarded her from across the expanse. He could not see clearly. "Of course," he said.

Distantly, she felt herself bleed.

"I am so glad to see you before you leave South Africa," she said to Sir John.

"We met some months ago, did we not? You're Catherine Colebrook."

He could not look away from her boys.

He will remember, she thought. What I ask will be tied to this moment. He will carry it with him.

"I'm grateful that you recall. It is important that you understand, I am not mad. I am a woman. We let go of nothing." She declined his offer of food and a doctor's attention. "I have a daughter. A little younger than George Wynfield by the look of him. She's alone and afraid."

"But you are not."

"The worst has passed."

In time, she returned to her cart and her home in the Cape. The shanties around the port were coming to life. A steady current of vendors made their way along the water. They sold fish and shells, flowers and exotics fresh from the tethered boats newly arrived from places she once imagined she'd visit. Here and there she saw the other European expats, their easels, open pages of poetry, unfolded letters of distant news and regrets passed across months at sea. They sat in makeshift tents, hoping to sell their foreignness and continental birth for food and the means to remain far from home.

She'd extracted promises from the scientist. That he would pray for her. That he would read her letter and remember her.

Feldhausen
Cape of Good Hope, South Africa
February 22, 1836

To the kind attention of Sir John Holland:

My name is Catherine Colebrook. We were first and recently acquainted at the home of Thomas Maclear, Astronomer Royal here in the Cape. I was most fortunate to attend his party in your honor some months back. You spoke eloquently of the comet Halley and her path among the heavenly bodies, and of your curiosity at the application of Lyell's geographic principles to mapping the celestial. Ever so briefly, you shared the first murmurings of a nascent science. The ability to arrest a moment of the world, on types of tin and copper.

Crude, you called it. But the beginning, perhaps, of something wondrous. I am certain you recall how forward I was.
For I was at this gathering without my husband Charles, an eminent barrister and man of letters. We are here in the Cape these thirteen months so that he might recover his fragile health – oh, stalwart man that he is! Even now he is in Ceylon at Andrew's request and that of the John Company, attending to matters of importance to the Crown, beyond the ken of a woman like me. Soon we will be journeying to that land to join him.

Much has transpired since we met. For these past nine months I have been with child until just yesterday. Twins. Two boys, Ewen and Hardy. They are with me as I write to you. I held Hardy as long as I could.

This would, to any decent woman, bring to mind our Father's admonition to abide our deficient minds. We cannot grasp all that He does. Were I truly as decent as I have long thought – I attend church, I pray there and elsewhere, I accept unquestioningly the existence of my soul after I pass to dust – I would seek solace in the answers we faithful believe we already possess. Yet all that comes to mind, all that now remains with me, is your presentation of the science of images. Of arrest. To hear you is to understand that currently, this science languishes in the confines of possibility. Impending, perhaps, but no more. This I cannot endure. God blessed me with a moment worthy of holding. A mote of light in my Hardy's eye. There, then gone. Light is a capricious thing. Perhaps God curses me now, with my frail and fracturing memory of it. Its contours, its size and precise hue, my own shadow within it. All leaving me. I have begun my own inquiry. My modest bungalow here is filled with daguerreotypes, tintypes, all manner of that nascent science you described. It is remarkable what can be acquired at the bazaars. They are precisely as you said. Crude. Lifeless. They hold nothing divine. They cannot be the end of this. I wish to correspond with you. Let

me assist in finding what can be. I don't know where I will be.
Ceylon, for the foreseeable future. A man of Charles' stature is
required in many ports. For myself, I remain ill with the
effects of my sons' emergence. Soon, I shall be restored. In
truth, composing this letter to you is curative.you will find me
indefatigable, Sir John. This I promise.

Yours,
Catherine Colebrook

JULIA MET HER at the door to their bungalow. She was still and wary while the chimes made their hushed music. Behind her, a gracefully folded linen lay on a table, next to a basin of water. "I bartered for a sheet at the bazaar," she said. "I hope you find it suitable."

Her hazel eyes were rimmed red. Her oft-brushed hair was matted against her scalp. She tried to stand as tall as her mother, but her shoulders were rounded with lost sleep.

A mother should not weigh on her child, Catherine thought. She took up the cloth. White as blanched bone, soft. "You are a blessing to me."

Julia's jaw clenched. "You shouldn't be up."

"I'm well," Catherine said. "We must pack."

"Travel? Oh, mother. Your health."

"We are expected at your father's side. It's right, to be there."

"Mother, you brought Hardy with you."

"Fetch the priest, Julia. The Anglican. He is all we have to choose from in this place."

"I'll go if you lie down."

"Very well. You're a good daughter."

"Mother, where were you? Where did you go?"

"To have time with him. To say one day that I showed him the sun and the sea."

Julia left, satisfied. Catherine returned to her bed with her sons. Nursing Ewen, she unfolded Charles' letter and read the parts directed to her. The rest – Council doings, musings on the amendments needed to align Ceylon's regulatory infrastructure with the needs of modern commerce, the map he'd enclosed; all that he rebuilt himself by – she would leave to him.

Say you'll come, he'd written. *And if you will not, raise our children. Julia, and the child who has arrived since last I saw you. I will send money quarterly. Do not send our children to Ceylon. This is no country for the motherless.*

In a week there would be a ship, and the clouds and the sea storms blowing south to southeast, and she would not hold any of it forever. Each day she would pick up a moment and sacrifice the one before it. Each day something fell out of the world.

The priest arrived at dusk, redolent with the night-blooming flowers that grew along the sea road. By then she had lain Hardy in a separate bed fashioned from sheets of washed cotton that were patterned with all manner of woodland scenes befitting a boy. Boys, she imagined, longed for forests to explore. To wander through, with the sun always overhead, broken by leaves into bits of light. Boys needed to look for signs of hiding light.

"I wish to bury my son," she told the priest. Julia sat at her side, rocking Ewen. "His name was Hardy Hay Colebrook. He never breathed."

Aipassi

EACH MORNING OF ELIGIUS SHOURIE'S LIFE, THIS HAD been the world. The women of Matara cooked what they foraged and mended what the village's men hadn't torn beyond redemption. The youngest children mewled from their huts, in thrall to hunger and the cholera that swept in with the previous summer's monsoons. The older ones who survived such things by Kali's grace communed with their futures. Girls painted errant mendhi and dreamed of betrothal. Boys gathered near the banyan trees where their fathers met each morning to smoke before breaking themselves against the flesh and bone of the country. If the men spoke at all, it was of the taxes. Which of them would lose their hut next and leave Matara behind, to beg on the streets of Port Colombo.

Things had begun to change after the colonials' celebration of their new year, 1836. There had been no particular day, no one moment. One night, he simply noticed what he hadn't before. That his father Swaran, still in his servant tunic, ministered tirelessly to books of colonial laws, the Britishers' paper reasons for being in Ceylon. The man who walked with him at Diwali and mimicked the chatter of monkeys to make him laugh, now read feverishly through the night hours that once belonged to endless bedtime conjurings of Ceylon's past, its gods and hymns. His father could make so much come with nothing but a candle and a bit of broken glass to magnify the light into a nova; just outside the circle that illuminated them both, the night would move.

It frightened Eligius to see that there had been something in his father that he'd never guessed at. A burning to exchange his life.

One night his mother told his father that she no longer knew him. "I want to make things different for you," his father said. "It's in their words." His eyes were so bright; he was a man in terrible love with an imagined better day.

He gathered the totems that shaped love for his father. The pieces of glass, split free from discarded lihuli bottles at the sides of the drinking men's huts. He brought the glass to his father, and before his father could protest that there was no time for childish diversions in this coming world, Eligius moved the glass until the delicate candlelight shivering in his father's eyes grew across the pages. Then the Britishers' words bowed beneath a sun of his making.

His father smiled. The first in who knew how long. "Ah, I can see them so much better now. Shall I tell you what they mean?"

After that, Eligius didn't leave him alone at night anymore. Outside their glassed light, the night moved for Matara, but differently for them.

While he stayed up late by his appa's side like a man, the colonials' words came to him. Over the last of winter he learned the secret heart hiding in the language of English law. That they'd come hundreds of years before as merchants and warriors who showered the Mughal Jahangir with riches and rarities until India's arms opened wide. "In whatsoever place they choose to live," the Mughal decreed, "in whatsoever port they arrive, let none molest their peace and prosperity." One trading post became legions, became the East India Company, a nation within their nation possessing the power to tax, to make war and peace, to send India's wealth across the sea.

Spring 1836 came. His father told him that in Aipassi, the colonials' October, the East India Company Governor and its Court of Directors would meet to renew the Company's Charter, and with it bend India into the ornate, locked gates of empire.

Their neighbors' lives still turned simply from season to season. The taxes, the villages lost to the currents of the Britishers' expansion; these newer maladies were no different than the old diseases and droughts that came on the tides of passing time. They didn't seem to notice that this new world was an unreadable sky stretching over their country.

His father called Matara's men together at the nirayanam, in the colonials' April. He told them he'd go to the East India Company Court six months hence. He would argue for the Charter to be amended in accord with colonial law, for the lagaan to be lifted, and for a greater Indian voice in their own affairs. The Director he'd served had allowed him to study books of English law. For what reason, if not to invite Indian ideas?

The village men laughed at him. Matara's leader, its grama sevaka, called him naïve and even dangerous. Eligius didn't believe his father was dangerous, but he thought his mother did from the way she held her pregnant belly when his father read statutes aloud, as if she were swept up in a surging crowd.

Chakran came to Swaran on a summer evening and asked him to explain it once more. "Tell me again. What are you trying to do?"

His father spoke to the grama sevaka all that night. Nothing more than words, but words weighed more than the sea when a man has lived too long in quiet grief that his life must, and won't, change. That was what his father said later to his wife, his Sudarma, while Eligius listened to them from the next room, his cheek pressed against the cool wall. "These words, Swaran," his mother worried.

This is how Matara begins to hope, his father said to her, like a lover.

When he stole a glance, Eligius caught them kissing. He realized he'd begun to hope as well.

Then the rains came, then the fall again, and then the first day of Aipassi, 1836, when Swaran said that he'd read enough. It was time to speak.

ON THE MORNING of Court, Eligius sat in front of his hut, watching the dawn light wash Matara's landscape with gold. It was well past the usual hour of the men's departure from the banyans for the Overstone fields and the John Company quarry, yet still they paced restlessly in the rain-promising air. "Eligius!" one of the neighbor women called. "For your appa Swaran, and all of us! Tell Sudarma to give thanks for a good man!" She clasped her hands together.

He returned her anjali mudra. One more prayer. Another frail light joined to the multitude.

Sudarma came out into the street. She made a fire like the other women. Navigating herself onto her haunches, she melted ghee, then poured a cascade of reddish grains into a heavy pot. They hissed against the slickened iron before bursting.

He held up a shard of glass and sent the sun where he pleased. For a moment he lost himself.

Sudarma's hands flew to her belly. Her face cinched up. She clutched herself as if the plateau rising from her might break open. "Restless today. Like you. Another few days, I think."

"Will he stay?"

She smiled her quiet smile; when she was happy, her smile chimed in him. "I'm not so sure it's a boy. Go to your father. Tell him the men are still here, and the women all pray for his success at Court."

"Yes, amma." He went inside, where Swaran madly displaced ragged tomes of British law.

"Appa, the men haven't left. I think they're waiting to go with you."

"Is grama sevaka among them?"

Eligius peered outside. "Yes appa, I see him." Chandrak was easy enough to spot. Tall, lean, dark as charred teak, he shared a jar of lihuli with the men congregating around him, who waited to see what he would do. A leader in Matara, revered among its lower-born, he had elemental, wanting eyes.

"Keep your mother company," Swaran said. "We're almost ready to leave."

"Are the men coming with?"

"I'll ask it of Chandrak. We will see." He chose from a sheaf of papers. "Put these with the charter."

Eligius took his father's notes outside, reading them silently and allowing the stone-on-stone noise of them to fill his mouth. They were nothing like Tamil, which moved like a quiet tide to shore.

"Just like him, I see."

Chandrak eyed Swaran's notes without comprehension. Kneeling near Sudarma, he poked at her cooking fire with a stick. "How old are you now, Eligius? Fourteen?"

"He'll be fifteen soon," Sudarma said. She put her dull knife to the slope of an onion.

"I was a year at the foundry in Sufragam at his age, pulling black oxide from the ground."

Eligius heard his father sighing at books the way laboring men like Chandrak sighed in the colonials' endless fields.

"I had to break rocks against my body." Chandrak ignored Sudarma's smirk. The muscles on his forearms twined. "Look at my hands. A man like your father, who does nothing but pour other men's coffee, doesn't have hands like these. Such hands break men but make leaders."

He's more of a man than you, Eligius thought as his father emerged. Anger passed through him like rings of warm light.

Chandrak raised a fist. The murmurings of the men fell away. "Swaran, why do you think the Britishers will listen to you in their language or anyone else's? We've talked and talked and still I don't see. Becoming like them does nothing but hold you apart from your own."

"If I know nothing beyond pouring their coffee, grama sevaka, why should they make time for such a man? But they have made time for me today." He removed his glasses and wiped his eyes. He was no older than Chandrak, yet to Eligius he'd aged terribly in the last months. "We cannot settle for shouting at their gate. We must walk through their doors. I ask your blessing."

"If their soldiers come through Matara, what would become of us if we followed you? The answer isn't in those books, Swaran. We can put nothing between us and them but men and the promise of what men can do."

The others grunted assent. Some of them bore limbs torn from the banyan grove ringing Matara.

"Do not come if you intend to cause trouble," Swaran told them. "I'll go alone. My son and I. I would do this even in defiance of you. We will die if we remain this way."

"Come." Chandrak extended his hand. "Why are we fighting?"

Swaran took it. "I'll go with you if Sudarma wishes me to," Chandrak said with a wink.

Eligius saw his father pull his hand back, with some effort. Chandrak's grip was field-strong.

He stood, taking his father's notes and the East India Company's charter. "I'm ready, appa."

Sudarma spilled pieces of onion into the simmering ragi. She guided her knife back through the bulb, her hands precise, her fingers slivering near the promise of blood. "Go because you're men of Matara who know each other all your lives. And if not for that, then stay in the fields and do nothing."

Swaran kissed his wife's forehead. She gazed up at him and put both hands on her stomach, but he'd already turned to face Chandrak and his fellow villagers. "To have you with me would be a blessing. Among these Directors, there may be an honorable man. He is new. I don't know him to say that he will listen to me, and make the others listen. But there is time enough if I fail for you to tell me how wrong and weak I am. Then we can see how well your way works."

Chandrak conferred with his fellows. "We'll go with you."

Eligius carried his father's most precious notes. They fluttered in the breeze he stirred as he ran across the road towards the jungle. A ribbon of runoff water passed beneath his feet and he stepped in it, bursting the reflection of the sun.

Matara's women called after their men. Admonitions to be safe, to come home when it was done, to tell them how it was.

"They think your father's ideas will save us," Chandrak said when he caught up with Eligius. Swaran walked ahead, alone with his thoughts. "And if he fails, what they already suffer will be blamed on him, as if it was always his fault. This is the way of the world. You shouldn't grow up weak and believing in nonsense. Do you understand?"

Eligius stared at the banyan limb in Chandrak's hands.

"Now we have everything we need," Chandrak said.

Dimbola

CATHERINE WALKED ACROSS THE GROUNDS TOWARD the small cottage where the crate and the letter from Sir John waited. It was October 1836. The natives called it Aipassi.

When she'd first disembarked the *Royal Captain* in January of that year, touching the hewn stone of Ceylon's Port Colombo dock caused her to despair her reunion with Charles. How could she explain Hardy to a man who understood only the simple calculus of legal theory, calendar days, nautical distances?

She'd spent the prior four months studying Bible verse and struggling to puzzle out her emotions in the impossible leaning of the sea. On the day of her arrival in Ceylon's harbor, Julia had come to her cabin weeping that there was a body floating freely atop the waves. In another moment she'd heard its impact against the ship's hull, like the hesitant knocking of a child at a parent's closed door. That was Ceylon.

Matters needed time, she'd thought.

Charles had come in a solid, if ordinary, carriage piloted by the maid he'd written of in his letter, and so she'd looked this Mary up and down, searching for signs of the new life. A sturdy, quiet twenty-three year old, Mary carried herself that day and all days after with the bearing of a bricklayer and the air of lessened expectations common to servants aligned with mid-level households.

Charles looked older. Sick even still. His ivory beard was thicker now. It blanketed the prominent jawline she had watched soften with age. His burly frame had thinned considerably. She wondered what Mary was feeding him, or whether he was closing himself off in a room amongst the chaos of his books and papers. But his eyes were so full of hope for her devotion that she'd kissed his hand and ignored the milling natives just outside their carriage, with their language of melody and unmapped terrain, their skin like burnt chicory. Charles needed her filial kiss. Men must feel necessary.

She'd found nothing in Mary's demeanor, nothing in Charles' quiet embrace upon hearing of Hardy, nothing in the wordless mien that settled upon them during the journey from Port Colombo to Kalutara and her new home, nothing in the quiet non-intersecting circles they followed in the months after, from which assurance could be drawn that this was the life she was meant for. This was home.

From all appearances, Charles' life in the house he called Dimbola scarcely extended beyond the single room he'd established as his study, and in which he'd arranged his considerable library. The rest of the house felt empty and in need when she'd arrived. Sparse furnishings, a disorder to the English amalgam of rooms and functions, a lack of cultural flourishes – art, namely – by which their guests might come to know Charles' achievements. It had not surprised her that during his long sojourn in Ceylon without her, Charles had not attended to details best left to a wife. Still, Dimbola suffered a malaise that she quickly set about dispelling. Mary kept order. She kept the children fed and occupied, allowing Catherine to reclaim her role as wife and architect of a socially presentable colonial life.

Soon after her arrival, she'd discovered the cottage while searching for an old cachepot. The structure was nothing, and treated as such. Mary stored her mops and buckets there, alongside the remaining crates, odd chairs and tables, the items her new mistress and master had brought to Ceylon.

In it Catherine found saris, wraps, the detritus of Indian women hanging in the gray space of an alcove. They were covered in a patina of dust, their hues no more than suggestions of what they once were.

Left by servants, she decided. Women long since vanished.

By early spring, their arrival had lost the luster of the new. Charles returned to his books and laws, Mary to her grumbling and cleansing of her betters, Julia to her writerly musings and complaints about the life abroad her parents were surely withholding from her.

Catherine returned to the cottage each day.

It held no furniture or fixtures. It walls were bare. Its ceiling had been rent open by storms. Yet its vacancy was of a different sort than the main house. The cottage didn't feel empty to her. It felt free. Charles' persistent quiet, the maid's taciturn labors, Ewen's pronounced need; none of it reached her here. In the cottage, possibilities turned in the breeze of the near sea.

The crate and the letter from Sir John arrived by ship's post in September. Mary brought them to her master with no regard for Catherine's name as intended recipient. A message from a man journeying on the largesse of her new master's superior, to her mistress? Inappropriate was too gentle a word.

Charles was a quiet rain after Sir John's delivery. He punished Catherine with silence, unanswered entreaties over dinner, a closed study door.

He didn't understand, nor could she expect him to. She knew this. He hadn't witnessed her in the Cape. Had he known that she'd infused a far away man with hope for the resurrection of her child's first and last day, he would have hated her for needing such things.

She moved the crate, unopened, into the cottage.

Weeks passed. Colonial Ceylon invited them to dinners and a party in Andrew Wynfield's honor, to fete the imminent completion of Ceylon's first grand church, the Galle Face. At Charles' direction, Mary selected a dress and provided Catherine with the hour by which she was expected to emerge, ready. There were instructions pinned to the russetted bodice. Topics about which

Catherine was to be learned, others about which she was to be silent. A map provided her with the location in Charles' library where a book might be selected, should she desire a supplement on the laws her husband had drafted.

Charles didn't speak to her on their carriage ride to the Galle Face.

Near the port, their carriage joined a queue. They were greeted by Tamil children from the Galle Face's newly inaugurated Religious Tract and Bible Class. The children sang lyrics from the Acts while invited Britishers walked a pebbled path to the church entrance.

Charles let himself out and strode off, leaving Catherine to the preachings of the children.

A procession of Bishops led the invitees through a sculpted metal portcullis. Above the entry was a round window embellished with flowing tracery, and through it Catherine saw the grand gable of the roof, the coffered ceiling that swallowed all but traces of the many flickering candles, clustered columns, the topmost ribs of the nave, and the piping and roseglass of the sainted windows. Everywhere she saw the scars of expansion.

The exterior was mapped in cages of scaffolding. The columns pierced the underside of the sky. They were yet to be carved, but soon their snowy marble would be expertly relieved in flower garlands gracing Christ in His infancy.

Inside, the Directors' wives remained at the rear of the sanctuary, where they expressed admiration for the native children's mastery of their prayers and spoke longingly of London boutiques. They asked Catherine to chair a lunch where charities would be formed and decisions made. She was requested to draw up a menu for their inspection.

She saw Charles in line, waiting for Andrew to acknowledge him.

Between the wives she saw the open door, and if she moved slightly to her left, a glimpse of Ceylon's curtain of trees, its contours and slopes, its painterly last light. Behind everything, far from sight, the cottage and the unopened crate.

The wives invited her to their table. She politely declined. Despite Charles' stare, she remained in the doorway, where the air of this country could be heard and felt.

The evening ended. They returned to their plantation. She could take no more.

"I am grateful you brought us here," she said, unbidden, the following morning. She'd dressed herself and Ewen for the missionary Ault's service in the shadow of the Galle Face before locating Charles in his study.

She'd come to invite him without knowing why. He had never shared her faith and did not believe in the time church attendance thieved from other pursuits. It was a familiar dance. She asked him to come, he refused. But she felt the need for her husband to sit with her as other husbands did. She wanted him to know the breadth of her belief. There was no other way for him to know how that belief had begun to falter in the Cape, and she with it.

Upon his refusal she made to depart but lingered over his books. Perhaps if she delayed, if she touched them, she might discover why this constituted prayer for him.

"It seems this silence between us persists," she said. "Shall we declare it done?"

"If you wish."

"I wish for my husband."

"Your husband is here. This is what my life is now. Is it enough for you? A man not given to frivolous poetry. I cannot be other."

"Nor can I. Yet we love each other." She tapped his papers. "An immutable fact."

"A law, I suggest."

"Agreed."

His first smile since the port. "Know that it pained me, Catherine. I didn't want to leave having just learned you were with child. But I tell you we will have a life here. The one we want, among English society. Now we have declared the silence between us done. May we also conclude the melancholy I see in you? Just as your journey here, tell me there is a ship and a map to bring you to a state of contentment, and I will pay your passage."

"You are poetic despite yourself."

"You inspire matters I didn't know I was capable of. Come, let me show you something of Ceylon."

He led her out onto the grass. "My predecessor on the Court called this estate Dimbola. A suitably exotic appellation. But look there. Look at the curve of the land to the trees and the sea. Do you see the borders of this country? There, where the land meets the Arabian and stops. Tell me you see the beauty in these things so that I may be sure of you."

She let moments pass. She devoted herself to the curl of the land into the weave of jungle and sea. "What resides in the crate," she began, "is somehow of me, as all of this is now of you."

She could feel him turn inward. Their years had taught her. A sudden distance in his eyes, a stiffening of his stance. But she did not stop. "Odds and ends left from the Cape, sent to the Maclears' because they were the most important Britishers in the area. Sent via Sir John because of the shared connection to Andrew. Andrew does not underwrite charity. He has affiliated himself with two great men."

"Why speak of it," Charles said tersely.

"I must have your blessing."

"What am I asked to bless, I wonder."

"Something has captured my attention. You know what sort of woman I am. Remember the story of my mother?"

"Off with you to Paris. The café windows."

"Then you know how it is with me. Perhaps you'll be piqued. Whatever resides in the crate is of science, as well as beauty. It must be. It lacks even a name at present."

His distance widened. It began at the edge of his eyes. She

took his hand and willed him to know her heart. *Your illness is not frailty. Look at us. In Ceylon, so you may structure the Charter that will bring an unruly country into civility and English law. You sit at the elbow of the governor. You are not fated to be less than other men. You have married a woman fated to want what isn't here. I am sorry for that.*

"Your place is at my side," he said. "You understand the importance of this."

"I do."

"Then take care not to hurt yourself opening that damned crate."

It was October. Aipassi. She opened the letter first.

I enclose what exists to the present in this quest of ours. Nothing lasts. There are others working on matters of chemicals, surfaces, and the contraption itself. Reijlander, chiefly, in Sweden. Archer and Talbott. I am in correspondence with them. Through me, so shall you be.

Presently, I travel to Alexandria. I hope to reach Ceylon by year's end and will send advance word. Though truly the sky is the same everywhere, I wish to see it from all the hemispheres and all the outcroppings of the world.

I enclose instructions and materials. I know what they yield to me in form and function. As for what they yield to you, Catherine, I can only hope that it will be enough. What shall become of your days now, I wonder. Perhaps I shall hear of it in your letter to me. May they offer comfort, if nothing else.

—Sir John Holland

With the letter, Sir John had enclosed images. A tintype of a silvery shroud encircling the harbor at Pretoria. There was a sailboat in the foreground. There was the sea, washed to silver by the setting sun.

Not enough, she thought. There is nothing from life here.

Through the cottage door, she saw the burning lamps of her home. Dimbola. It was the dinner hour. Mary would see her empty chair and feed her family. She would tell Julia and Ewen to pray and ready themselves for bed. Charles would close his study door.

Her dress bound her too well. She shed it and for a moment she let Ceylon's breathing liturgic winds find her. Then she went to the alcove and selected a sari of washed red. Moving beneath its loose weave was of no consequence.

She unpacked the crate of its parts. Oddly incandescent paper. Small casks of exotically named chemicals. Wood cut into spindles, dowels, a box. A black cloak. Hinges and small mirrors. There were instructions. How to assemble, what to do next. How to approximate what had been done, where to look for what could be.

Above her was the punctured roof of the cottage. Stars, blackness, the sky Sir John deemed the same, everywhere.

She began to build with no sense of what it would be. She only knew that the world was falling away. *Each day of my life must be this.*

From Life

ELIGIUS FOLLOWED HIS FATHER ON A WIDE PATH ALONG-
side stands of palm trees and sawgrass. Swaran led them on an
ascent of Prinsep Hill's pinnacle. To the west was the sea, rounded
at the shore where it swelled into the white defilements of the
colonials' construction. The East India Company, the Galle Face
church, Court Directors' homes and plantations, all blemishes
from a plague swiftly traveling inland, borne by the Britishers'
ever larger machines.

In his years, Eligius had seen simple machetes give way to
axes on wheels, pulled by bison and then by elephants and
then by something else, some infernal wheezing metal cart that
ate a swath through the neem and banyan trees and spilled red
mangoes onto the ground like blood. The colonials felled everything in their path to make way for more of what they wished
India to be: the breadbasket of London. Yet the azure sea
persisted and the jungle always grew back to fill the cavities of
whitewashed stone and stained glass with fruit and birds and
flowers.

From Prinsep, Eligius could see the roads open to them.
The East India Court lay to the west, near the Galle Face.
An easterly route would take them away from Port Colombo, away
from the waterfront homes and inland plantations devoted to
cotton, indigo, jute, and the ever-craved coffee. North would
take them to the other villages outside Colombo and Mulkirigala,
to slums just like Matara filled with stagnant water that spread

sleep amongst the newborns. A little further and they would find what remained of the elephant temple. Sudarma had often brought him there as a child, despite the day-long trek, to see the shattered gopuram canopied by the treetops. Bearing him in her arms as if he were nothing, she would point to the burnished copper rendering of Lakshmi on her lotus. She would tell him how Lakshmi showered the faithful with gold coins, and how the temple elephants, cousins to the clouds, showered her in turn.

They trekked west until a crescent of the sapphire sea emerged at the horizon line where the jungle gave way to the outskirts of Port Colombo. Following the road, they passed the Overstone plantation and the men laboring in its fields.

"Look at them," Swaran whispered. "I don't want these men's lives for you, meri beta."

Eligius watched the workers cut the ground open, seed it and sew it shut again with tools brought from across the sea. Once, these men were the sellers and buyers, the beginning and the end. They were the circle of the world; so his father said. Now they were oxen pulling blades across the dirt for their betters.

They emerged from the jungle at the Court building, near a throng of angry men. Hindu, Punjabi, Sinhalese, Tamil, Sikh, Vedda – Eligius saw every caste, every group. They'd all come to see if chants of protest could make the colonials stop what they'd been doing since the first Charter Act gave the John Company sovereignty. Men in dirty clothes and soldiers in uniform paced their respective sides of the bars, eyeing each other warily.

Swaran avoided the other Indian men. He approached the gate and bowed to the closest guard. The guard waved him over. "I am presenting a bill of concerns to Governor Wynfield and the Court of Directors."

The guard gestured to Eligius.

"My son."

"And me." Chandrak stepped forward. "A servant of no great importance."

After conferring with his superior, the guard opened a door in the gate and ushered them swiftly through.

A brick flew past Eligius' ears. "Tell the Britishers to pack their things and leave," a man's voice cried. This stirred the mob up, and they began to surge towards the gate. The man who'd screamed was at the front of the crowd. There was a long stick in his hand. A thick cord of braided horsehair sliced the air with an audible hum as he turned it upon himself.

The crowd began to chant in time to his self punishment. He smiled as his back grew slick with sweat and blood.

"I am Ceylon," he said, his teeth grinding against the pain. "I am Ceylon. Tell them."

The guards pressed themselves against the gate, bracing it. More fusillades launched from the crowd. Mangoes and kavas burst against the bars, raining pulp across the tended grass of the Court garden.

Eligius turned his back on their anger. Brushing bits of fruit from his shirt, he felt as if his trembling heart were visible to the world.

The court building itself looked much like a plantation, with its columns, its walls the color of ripe coconut meat, its polished glass. The Rees flag billowed on sea winds. The sculpted grounds made a mockery of the anger he'd come through. Even the breeze gentled once past the gates.

A parade of strutting peacocks scampered aside as they approached the carved ebony doors of the Court's entryway. Before knocking, Swaran drew palmfuls of water from a stone basin. Lotus blossoms floated aimlessly, cut from their roots.

A Sikh doorman regarded Swaran's petition without expression. His chubby face had cracked from the sun. Rivulets of perspiration crept down the folds of his neck, slipping beneath the banded collar of his uniform. "It is more today than yesterday," he said, opening the door wide. "Every day they get louder. When this door closes, you won't hear them at all."

The room beyond was marvelous to behold. All of Matara

could have fit inside its ellipse. Its walls were covered with clean
white paper embossed with raised images of acacia. Windows
opened wide onto an expanse of tall sugar cane fields and
the stone edifice of the Galle Face church. The windows were
bordered with enough cloth to stock a bazaar. Gathered in
loose folds with links of golden cord, the cloth breathed with each
gust of sea air.

On any other day Eligius might have run from wall to wall
like a child delighting in his flight. He might race along the
room's perimeter and imagine running across the sea to strange
places.

Across the expanse from them, a Hindu servant struggled
to remain upright as the boy riding atop his shoulders bobbed
up and down, his small red head snapping with the jerkiness of
his mount's gait. "Horse!" the young boy screamed. "Lift me up!
Up!"

The servant obeyed. He hefted the boy high in his arms
and paraded him past windows. When the boy tired of this,
he demanded his horse once again. In an instant the servant was
hopscotching in a mad circle.

"No." A woman's voice.

Ewen halted his exultant flight. He began to cry at his
mother's tone.

Something else disturbed Catherine's view of the prosce-
nium, the marble, the frescoes and the light suffusing the
Court's expanse in descending sparks of dust. An instant before
the Indian boy, the contraption's keyhole was making dervishes
of the strolling men. Cups and saucers lost their mundane
structure and became the obelisks of London, the surrounding
dust like that city's silverwashed fog. Faces came undone from
the men and women who possessed them. Faces were geometry.

The contraption, with its mirrors and polished glass,
brought resolution to the world like nothing else in life. It isolated
the possible. She saw moments in the eyes, in the filament
creases around mouths. There, a happy marriage. There, a

thwarted plan. Aspects that were daily lost to careless memory might still be found somewhere on each one passing through her vision.

Then the Indian boy came within her view and remained. He stood stiffly next to an older Indian man. His father, perhaps. There was another man with them but he felt peripheral; he was sinewy and hard, as if he'd been broken from the ground and put to a whetstone. The boy, who appeared to be Julia's age, had skin the color of milky tea. He wore trousers and a tunic. The clothes gentled his lean physique, made him less a part of this strange country.

When he looked at the man who held reams of papers and an open book, she wondered if the boy was the sort who watched his father tirelessly, to become the one she found in her camera's view.

The boy turned to face her camera. He tilted his head, regarding it and perhaps the suggestion of the woman hidden within it. When he moved, he opened a patch of pale watercolored sky in the window behind him. His shadow cast across the polished floor.

She was about to bark an order for him to move away but she could not. In that unlikely face, in the void of sound or motion, the space between her and her dead child came to her.

The Indian boy's shape against the Court wall was a moment that she could not name. It stepped forward from life and meant to remain, but she could not understand why that should be so, when Hardy had come as a moment already passed.

"No," she finally said.

Eligius saw her emerge from under a dark cloak. Despite the earthen sari adorning her, this woman was colonial. There was no mistaking the empire in her.

Regarding him from across the foyer, she returned beneath the cloak of a spidery apparatus that filled Eligius with a queer dread. The thing stood on black legs, smooth and lucent in the twitching gaslights and filtering sun. Five feet high, most of its body was hidden away beneath the black hood that reminded him of the draped macaw cages he marveled at as a child.

A British girl of Eligius' age stood alongside the hidden woman. Her hair was golden, her face made turbulent in the mottling light. She fingered a glass pendant around her neck. When the afternoon sun struck the dangling shape, bubbles of color spilled across the blue-veined marble floor.

A Cingalese servant girl hurried past, bearing trays of sweet meats and pastries no larger than hatchlings. The British girl's pendant light adorned her, then fell away.

"Whose water do you draw?" the servant whispered when she reached Swaran.

"We're here to address the Court," Swaran said.

"You may wait in the chambers, but be sure and remain at the top of the stairs, where it's dark."

Eligius glanced back. The woman was out from under her cloak and standing at a window with the girl, facing the Galle Face and the sea beyond. The boy played in the shadow of wall frescoes depicting forgotten colonials.

The servant led them to a set of whitewashed doors. Inside, they took seats in the uppermost row. At the bottom was a dais, a lectern and several tables. Colonials congregated in groups like clusters of nettles, festooned in their finest linens and silks. The men tugged at brilliantly hued sashes fixed around their throats while they raged at each other in something approaching verse. Their voices rose and fell while white boys carved into parchment with the sharpened quills of native birds. Their handiwork was rendered with such speed, it seemed that the boys were charged with the task of arresting the men's words no sooner than they were aloft.

Eligius couldn't understand much of it, but the comings and goings fascinated him. Like the bazaars at Kaveri and the port, pockets of commerce unfolded in corners. Hindi women held up flowers and cinnamon satchels. While they waited to be noticed, their eyes wandered to the men bringing the council members steaming tea and plates of clove loaf.

He pitied them, to be seen by their women this way.

One at a time, Britishers emerged from the dankness to approach the dais. They presented their wants. Rights to their neighbor's well, levies on tobacco imported from further than twenty five miles to Ceylon's markets, news of growing unrest in Madurai and whether the directors might impose a limit on servants brought in from that part of the country. "They bring able backs, but contempt for their betters," an aggrieved man said.

The directors sat at a long table under another Company flag. Though they listened, decisions seemed to come from one man, Governor Andrew Wynfield. He cut a robust figure, with broad shoulders and a piercing glare that he trained to imposing effect upon those who stepped forward. The other men seemed older, heavier, trapped by their station. This man was stronger than they were.

One director sat away from the others. His head was bathed in waning light from the ring of windows above him. He held a thick woolen overcoat tightly under his chin, like a blanket. His free hand stroked a beard of brambles and moonlight. A beggarly old lion. The Governor leaned to whisper to him after each solicitation.

Swaran got up and slowly descended towards the dais. Those conducting the business of the rich paid him no attention as he passed.

Eligius felt a guilty wave of embarrassment for his father. They'd walked a long way. The brown stain of Ceylon's mud roads covered him. His clothes were festooned with leaves and windborne dust that clung to the soft cloth like gray rain clouds.

Swaran approached a lectern. His bearing was regal despite the barely disguised mirth his appearance provoked among the colonials.

"You must be Swaran Shourie." The governor read from a document. He held up a hand, silencing the room. "You have asked for the floor and it is yours, though only for a moment. We are about to adjourn."

"I am here by right of the people," Swaran said. "The southern provinces and all their villages, Wynfield sa'ab."

"By right?" Governor Wynfield smiled. "Was there an election I should be aware of?"

"There are issues you should be aware of, sa'ab. Matters more pressing than where your servants come from."

"Your tone, sir."

"On behalf of Ceylon, I ask for leniency on the lagaan. The tax. I have studied the charter by which the Court and the Company gained sovereignty, and I believe the tax exceeds its bounds. I have the citations to your laws."

Wynfield's smile had not left him, yet something within it hardened like pottery in an artisan's kiln. "We have been over the same laws. It is a closed matter."

"There must be an open forum, sa'abs. The Charter is to be renewed for another twenty years. It cannot be, not as it stands."

One of the directors leaned forward. "Speak of it in the proper way, Swaran. It is a matter of respect, or else say nothing."

Eligius saw his father's hands tremble.

"Your Zamindari system forces us to grow only what you need," Swaran pressed on, "with seed we are forced to buy from you. Your lagaan takes us into debt, so we cannot afford to sow the fields. Having nothing to grow, we have nothing to sell and no way to pay this tax. Our markets are full of Indians bartering scraps of themselves to each other while we lose our lands."

"I have little sympathy." Wynfield held out his teacup and waited. In an instant, a Tamil servant stood at his side, refilling it. "Ceylon's poverty was a matter of record long before we accepted stewardship, at no small expense of the Crown's time and capital. Your people are free to work and raise the money to address their arrears. The fields afford them such work."

"Why should they work the fields?" Swaran's voice was

shrill. The Indians in the chamber cast their eyes down. "What do they gain?"

"Outrageous," one of the directors blurted.

"The simple task of amending the Charter has begun," Wynfield said. "When it is ready, you will hear of its terms, and I will look to you to convey those terms clearly to the people who appointed you."

Swaran stood helplessly. "The people will not accept this."

"The laws," Wynfield said angrily, "suggest that they must. Do they not?" He turned to the bundled old lion. "As the scrivener of their drafting, please speak to our rights under the Charter."

Eligius pulled back as the lion's gaze found him.

"I've read everything–" Swaran began.

"They are ample," the lion said quietly. "They are clear and unambiguous, Swaran."

"This is not your country!"

Eligius spun in his seat. Chandrak was bounding down the steps towards the dais. "We are not all weak men!" Chandrak shouted. "If we fall, so shall you!"

"Who is this man?" Wynfield stood as soldiers left their posts at either end of the dais. They headed towards Chandrak, bayonets leveled.

Swaran's head bowed. Eligius tried to see his father's face through the crush of bodies suddenly swarming the Court floor.

The soldiers caught Chandrak by the arms and hair. Pummeling him with the butts of their rifles, they dragged him through a side door. "So shall you!" Chandrak's cries echoed through the chamber.

Wynfield came to the edge of the dais as the directors cleared the hall. "You bring talk of rebellion in here? Rest assured, you are no longer welcome, Swaran. If you are seen again, you will be arrested."

"I did not speak of rebellion–"

"Further discussion is pointless. You will leave here. Now."

Eligius watched his father gather his papers. He wanted to

speak, but his words had fallen into a deep hole. Did his father feel this way, at this moment? As if he was drowning within himself?

"Is the boy your son, Swaran?"

The old lion stood from his seat with difficulty. "Tell me your name, boy," he said when Swaran tucked away the last of his notes in silence.

"Eligius." He watched his father trudge back up the hall steps, towards the servant entrance.

"Merely to pass through the mob outside took courage for you both," the lion said. "You have a Christian surname. Are you Christian?"

"Hill country Tamil. My family came from the north long ago. I was named for the missionary Ault's predecessor. He helped my mother when I was born, or I would not have lived. My mother had a fever."

"It's a harsh world for the young."

"I was weak when I was born. I am strong now. My mother said to me, 'Stay. You did not come all this way only to go back now.' And so I did."

"A splendid story."

"Why didn't you listen to my father? He worked hard to speak with you."

"Walk with me."

The great foyer outside fell into shadow as a cloud crossed its windows. For a moment, Eligius felt a glow upon him as he left the Court hall. Then he felt its recession from his skin, leaving only the old lion's cold hand. "I hope we meet again, Eligius. I would like to think there will be other things to remember me by."

Governor Wynfield came to the lion's side and led him away. "There's trouble," he said curtly.

Ahead of them, Swaran stood in the court doorway, frozen before a sea of screaming men just beyond the gate. The shapeless rumble of voices rose like heat. Eligius couldn't understand what they were saying, the men hurling themselves against the bars again and again.

Papers spilled from Swaran's hands as he left the doorway for the courtyard beyond. They caught the sea winds and hurtled upward.

"Appa!"

Eligius followed his father into the courtyard, where Chandrak lay on the hard stone near a cluster of carriages. An undulating circle of soldiers beat the cowering shape of him. His left leg bent grotesquely.

Matara's men were at the front of the mob, crying Chandrak's name, and Swaran's.

Eligius heard his father's voice now. A strangled, guttural wail. Wading into the teeming courtyard of soldiers, his papers swirling away from him, Swaran walked unsteadily towards the men around Chandrak. He paused, bent to the ground, then shambled on.

Eligius broke into a run when Swaran raised the banyan limb.

A young soldier with a blemished face pointed to Swaran and shouted something. His words were pulled up to the sky with Swaran's papers. Three other soldiers leveled their rifles at Swaran. The volley of thunder silenced the crowd.

There were lights. Tiny burning flowers spat from the dull metal barrels. Bursts of red opened Swaran's skin, his chest and head, leaving gashed holes all over him.

Thin plumes of smoke rose from the soldiers' rifles. The angry embers of their barrels faded.

The crowd ran hellishly then, in every direction. Swaran stood motionless in the courtyard. His expression was quizzical and concentrated, and so familiar to Eligius, who had been watching him for months as he grappled with the colonials' laws as if trying to grasp the fraying threads of a dream. He crumpled to the ground next to Chandrak.

"Help me!" Chandrak cried as he pawed at his own

wounds. A bullet had rent his left side open. "Take me home!" His cries were a boy's, suddenly afraid of the world.

Eligius knelt to his father. He slipped a hand beneath his head and tried to lift him away from the stain of blood spreading across the cobblestones. For a moment it was just him in the lifeless glass of his father's eyes, just the still reflection of him against the sky. Then there were soldiers behind and above him, pulling him away.

After the Rain

ON THE FIRST ANNIVERSARY OF SWARAN'S DEATH, THE whole of the world gathered itself in a gray winding sheet. Eligius spent nights counting the clouds sailing across the gaps in his roof. Fat drops filled his hut with music.

The rains had come for Ceylon. It was Aipassi, 1837.

On the evening of Diwali, the sky finally cleared. Matara's women brought their cooking pots out into the cool air. They called greetings and compared felled walls. They lit fires. The women who had pinches of curry and onion raita for their muthai kothu parotta spared some to those who did not. They sent their children out to fetch water from the well at the base of the trail to the sea. The echoes of spatulas pounding against skillets followed them down and back again.

After dinner, a neighbor boy, Hari, came to see Eligius for his English lesson. Already families were leaving their homes to join the processional of lamps to the sea in celebration of the harvest holiday. They took the path down the cliffs, their frail diyas forging flickering ribbons through the jungle.

"Hari, hurry." Eligius jostled the boy's shoulder. "We're leaving soon."

Hari returned to his English lesson. "And they gathered at shore to bid farewell, and set her to sea, asleep. The Lord's hand did hold hers, held her tethered to the deep, until she was no more than brine, than air. Then the Lord bade her, awake, and held her no more, and to the dark sea bottom, Gretel fell."

"Your English improves each time."

Sudarma baked chapati over their fire. She turned a lump of dough, careful to fan the plume of sweet smoke away from their doorway. The bread's cooked skin crisped to a golden shade, like the colors Eligius saw against the mountains at twilight when the cliffs became light itself.

She was smiling. It was a hard smile, as if she'd tasted bitter root. Sometimes she resembled Swaran, the same vanishing point in their gaze.

"It's time," she said.

He accepted Hari's offering of palm oil and told the boy to keep the book. "When I see you next, tell me what you think of her end."

The procession of his neighbors grew heavier. They carried their diyas as if those fragile lights were burdens. To him, the lights were the only beautiful thing he knew in Matara.

"I remember when your father asked you the very same question," she said. "About that poem. What would you say now, I wonder."

Eligius took his lamp and began the walk. Sudarma followed him, shifting Gita in her arms as she rolled a bit of cloth between her teeth for wicks. She wore her white garment; she was still a mourning wife and always would be. It dragged the dirt like everyone else's, yet the baubles she'd adorned it with were a gaggle of stars tumbling through their village.

"Maybe colonials prefer an Indian who knows their dead Gretel," he said. "For myself, I don't see the use in poems."

"May I walk with you?"

Chandrak came up alongside them. "I've missed too much, not having a family."

Sudarma bowed her head meekly.

"Eligius," Chandrak said, "you are the man of your family. I will respect your wishes."

"It doesn't make a difference to me where you walk."

He strode ahead, ignoring the open stares of his neighbors. He tried to fill his vision with the lights all around him.

Where the land ended in a rocky jut overlooking the sea, there was one well-worn path down to the beach. Some of the women did an impromptu karakattham, dancing with pots of uncooked rice atop their heads.

He took his mother's hand. Together they picked their way down the slope to the beach, where the fishermen tied their skiffs for the night. Chandrak followed them.

The men stripped off their clothes and left their sandals on the rocks. They waded into the frigid Arabian Sea with their lit diyas held above the tide.

Sudarma picked a spot on the breakers and sat. Some of the cut stone bore the stamped legend of the John Company. The letters had been shallowed by the lapping water. "You offer Lakshmi our prayer," she said. "You're the man of our family tonight. I'll stay here, where Gita and I can see you."

He scrabbled to the water's lapping edge. Chandrak followed. "You were braver than I was that day," Chandrak said. "I wanted to tell you that. Your father would be proud of the man I see now."

"Don't speak of him. It's for me only."

The last of the twilight's color drained away. It was hard to see the other men. Only their faces in the golden fog cast by their lamps.

"He and I were different," Chandrak said. "But we wanted the same thing. I still do."

"They shot because of you."

Chandrak's eyes were on him. They made him afraid of his own anger.

The voices of those shepherding their prayers out to sea were high and sweet. Laughter and curses at the cold mingled easily with their requests for good health and streets whole enough for carts to travel.

"They shot because of all of us," Chandrak said. "Because

of our skin and our language. Because we live at all. Yet, I beg you to forgive me, Eligius. Let there be something between us. If not fealty, then calm. At least that." He took a small glass bottle from under his tunic. When he uncapped it, a smell like rotting tamarind briefly infected the air. He held the flask up for Eligius.

"No."

"Take it into the sea and leave it there. That I shouldn't find it." His eyes were wet. "Swim fast. It won't be as cold. Pray for peace for Sudarma. A woman alone."

Carefully, Eligius drizzled scant oil into each diya, lit them and set them atop the tide. He slipped out of his clothes and lowered himself into the water. Frigid waves punched the air from his lungs.

He uncorked Chandrak's bottle and listened to its contents empty into the water. Then he crushed the frail spun glass in his fist. His blood greeted the salt sea.

He kept one glass shard, then let the others go. They caught the cold stars as they sank. Arranging the remnant on the diya, he turned it until the flame light was magnified.

So you can see, appa.

He propelled the diyas forward with a push of his hand, creating gentle waves that swept them toward the other lights scattered over the surface of the sea. *Health for my mother. Health for Gita.*

The tide's return from shore took his lights away. *A better home.*

Some diyas were extinguished by the waves. Others were so small that he couldn't be sure of them anymore. His lights floated among the many. He couldn't tell them apart. Soon even his appa's light folded into the black tide. Nothing of them seemed memorable.

He thought of the girl at Court that day. The way her light lingered after she'd gone. The way the soldiers' lights didn't linger at all as they found his father again and again.

That I do not always live this way.

He returned to shore. Sudarma sat near Chandrak. She stared at the sky while Gita slept against her. "How far did they get?" Chandrak asked.

"They didn't burn long," Eligius said.

HE LAY AWAKE all that night, listening to the runoff water split the ground outside his hut. It was as if someone had laid a strip of the murmuring sea down Matara's middle.

Chandrak came to his hut in the morning. "You deserve more than the fields." A grave man, relating a grave fact. "I've spoken to your mother and made arrangements through the missionary at Port Colombo."

"You have no right to speak to anyone about me."

His mother slipped a tunic over his head, let it fall, tugged roughly at it to test the strength of her mending. He grabbed it, ready to tear it to pieces and throw it at this presumptuous man's feet. His pulse pounded beneath the skin of his temples.

"It was your father's," Sudarma said. She gently moved his hand away and smoothed the fabric. "He served a colonial family. Now you serve another. Your father was treated well. Maybe they'll treat you well."

She handed him some bread and a battered diya. "This was my grandfather's. I've kept it for you. Do all that you are told to do. If you don't come home with rupees, I will not allow you to stay here."

CHANDRAK KEPT AT his heels, so he picked up his pace. His father's tunic felt like thorns against his skin as they passed through the jungle.

Chandrak led him to the opposite end of Port Colombo, where the clock tower rose above the crossing of Chatham and Queen streets. The East India Trading Company's fleet began at the southern shore and extended out to sea like a cobblestone path of sails. The schooners closest to port waited for scurrying Tamils to unload crates of the colonials' motherland needs: tins of smoked beef, pipe tobacco, linens and woolens, grand carriages and bicycles for the children. A separate line of workers loaded the ships with satin and muslin, salt, indigo, wild birds for the London and Paris zoos. Amid the bustle were the repatriating Britishers, their pockets overflowing with bits of Ceylon, boarding for the long voyage home.

Two families, British and Indian, waited on the docks in the shadow of an immense clipper, the *Earl of Abergavenny*. The Britishers stood on one side in their finest clothes. Servants wielded parasols against the misting rain their children insisted on playing in. The other family stood stoically as the rain made suggestive skins of their garments. Both families watched the eldest of their children walk the gangway, the Indian boy after the English boy.

"The sad truth of our life among them," Chandrak said. "Disease, schooling, culture. Then comes the moment when their families have to send their children back to England or risk losing them to our hazards."

"And the Thevar child?"

"A servant, I'm sure. Where they go, he follows."

Chandrak paused before an open crate of canned fruits. "I am only a pauper," he told the mate overseeing the crates' unloading. His English was broken and pathetic. "But what I wouldn't give for the food of my betters."

The mate, a hirsute man darkened to a burnished red by the sea sun, picked up a jar of apples. "Am I a do-gooder, then? Bound to give tithes from the pockets of my employer?"

"No, sa'ab. It's a hard life."

The mate smiled. A bit of curdled yellow glinted between his rotting teeth. He tossed Chandrak one of the jars and bade him a good walk.

Chandrak twisted the lid off of the jar and dipped his fingers into the syrup to pluck a slice. "Where were we?" He licked his fingers, then held them out to the falling rain to be washed clean. "Oh yes, the Thevar child made to follow his better. And now my display disturbs you. At least tell me this much. You thought I was stupid. So did your father. I'm an articulate man when it serves me."

"About the servant, his life isn't his own. About you? I didn't think you were stupid and neither did my father. He thought you didn't care."

"Any day, the Court directors could move the whole of the southern provinces further into the jungle, if they thought a crop of coffee would fare better where our huts stand. Do you care about this?"

"I think it's wrong. But I've seen enough of men who think words change the world. Go on and tell yourself how smart you are – you'll bleed just like my father. Nothing changes."

"It's not me you should be angry at. They do this to us, Eligius. With their laws."

The colonial family bade farewell to their eldest as he climbed aboard ship. The child's mother stifled sobs with an embroidered kerchief.

"I don't know the law," Eligius said, "nor will I ever want to again. I know what I've seen. Men throwing stones and rotted fruit at the Court gate. What good does any of it do?"

"Hiranyagarbha made stones first. As he made more and more things, like any good craftsman, I believe he got better at his task. He made man last, and manmade laws, and laws make consequences for men. Not just us. Them. They will bring the consequences on themselves."

A constellation of rain glistened on Chandrak's forehead. His breathing came harder, faster.

Eligius glanced around nervously. Were the colonials standing across the street watching? Could they understand Chandrak's words? To be seen speaking in anger in their Port, Indians were jailed for that.

Chandrak's voice fell, as if he knew what Eligius feared. "Stones draw blood. Blood changes law. Laws draw maps around nations, and create them, or destroy them. Now see, we've found the missionary. More of this talk another day. Calm your-self, boy."

Tall and gangly, the missionary Stephen Ault was known to most of the southern provinces. He lived, it seemed, to convert them and to funnel the charity of right-minded colonial women who donated blankets and books describing the ways of Christianity.

Eligius followed Chandrak down the length of Port Colombo's dock, along the sea. The waves pushed against the wood stanches, swaying the planks beneath. It felt as if the world strained to turn over.

Ault stood in a swiftly moving line of servants wending its way to the ship's captain. At their turn, each servant called out the name of the family they represented. The captain searched through neatly stacked piles of letters and parcels while the colonials sat shielded inside their carriages, waiting for words from loved ones across the sea.

Ault came to them with a slim parcel of letters. "First to my parish for an umbrella," he said to Chandrak in slow, rudi-mentary Tamil. "Then to the boy's employer in Kalutara. Tell the boy to put these under his tunic so they'll stay dry."

"What need do we have for an umbrella after hours in the rain?" Eligius asked in English.

"How wonderfully you speak! Let me explain. For you, arriving in the appearance of need is expected, and so you shall. For me, it would not do to look as bad off as I otherwise am. You'll learn, if it's in you to learn. Now, no more dawdling."

They left the docks and crossed Chatham, slipping from tree to tree in an effort to blunt the rain and rising wind. Briefly they shared the canopying fronds of a palm with a Britisher and his young wife. She struggled to keep the crinkled ruffle of her dress out of the downpour while her husband turned her away from two young beggars. Starvation and sickness bent their bodies. Their backs filled with wheezing breath, pressing the accordions of their ribcages against their parchment skin.

They were redolent with the manure they offered to sell for fuel. "Come, yaar, four lakhs of rupees…"

"There's a break in the rain," Ault said. "Quickly now, before another cloudburst strands us here."

They followed the missionary across Chatham to a muddy corner, where the monsoons had eaten a gorge into the street. A bridge fashioned from hemp and planks of unshaved wood spanned one side to the other. Down this far from the Galle Face, the buildings reflected none of Port Colombo's relentless gentrification by the British. Still chained to the beginning of the century, the storefronts and rooming houses were constructed from cheap stone and wood gone wormy from the seasons.

Ault's squat tenancy lay at the end of the block, among tobacconists and spice sellers. Its door opened upon a room scarcely larger than the huts found in Matara. The walls were porous stone that bled seawater. The floor was littered with candle drippings. A wooden cross hung from the wall near a small sketch of a man in priestly vestments, holding two fingers up to a blazing star.

"Father Paul Tanford," Ault said. "He founded the school in which I studied. In his name I came to this jungle. The day I arrived, I felt lost to England. It's been twelve years, and I fear your people remain unknowable to me." He opened his umbrella in the doorway. The rain had thinned to a sheet of cold pins.

Ault gestured to Eligius' parcel of mail. "Can you read as well?"

Eligius turned the top envelope over as they walked. The sender's hand was imprecise, and it took him a moment to discern the author, Sir John Holland. Catherine Colebrook was the recipient.

"Service is one of the paths to the divine in your faith, isn't it?"

Ault was looking at him. As if it concerned him, Eligius thought, whether I crumble. "Is it such a terrible thing to help your family when they need you? Put those envelopes back in your tunic, so when you present them to the memsa'ab, you'll be seen as concerned for their condition."

Their path took them out of the jungle at Kalutara, where they followed the sea to a small hill rising from a swath of cultivated fields. There the Colebrook estate stood, like all the colonial homes he'd seen before. Yet there was something about it that spoke of wildness and neglect. Blight twisted much of their fields. A tenacious ivy had overtaken the walls of the main house, erasing the demarcation between it and the ground. The hill it rested on sloped down to a river. Churned by the rains to brown rapids, it had flooded the entire frontage, up to the veranda wrapped around the base of the house. The property was thick with coconut, casuarinas, mango, and breadfruit, but they were under water to the base of their trunks.

He could see the problem from the gate. The Colebrook estate was a basin, high at either end and dipped in the middle.

A flotilla of wood had been hastily erected to span the flood. The planks led to the side of the house, where a canopy of billowing sheets had been erected. From the gate, Eligius could see rows of chairs facing forward toward the veranda and a canopied stage.

"Your memsa'ab," Ault said, "lives on superlatives as if they were her daily bread."

"I don't understand."

"Flattery," Ault said. "It will see you through when matters grow dark, as matters are bound to do. Remember to present her with the letters. As I knew nothing of you, I've not told her of your ability with English or your abhorrence at what it is you will be doing. It's best that you find your own place."

Eligius hesitated at the gate. "Did you know my father?"

Chandrak watched him.

"Yes," the missionary said.

"Did you bring him to these people?"

"To the people who lived here before. I've known your village for many years. I help where I can. I thought he might find something of worth here. That happens in the strangest places, I've come to realize. If not him, then someone else. But what of it?"

The back of Eligius' neck was stiff from the cold rain, but he couldn't rub it, or return Chandrak's warning gaze, or move at all. To act was to tilt the world somehow, and then he would not be able to put it right.

"I can remember how he was before the books and laws, when he was a man like other men in my village. He was my father. And then he wasn't. The other men listened to him speak but stopped calling him to the fire. My mother hardly looked at him. Everything that mattered got lost."

"The boy is upset," Chandrak said. "Let me speak to him. For his mother. It will help things."

Ault dismissed them with a wave. Chandrak led Eligius away from the missionary. "There's a greater good to be served," he told Eligius. "I will tell you what you need to know about these people, and you will listen."

"No, grama sevaka. I just want to go and come home with rupees."

Chandrak's hand tightened until a warning of pain blossomed in Eligius' arm. "Do you know they want to stamp England across India's brow? The households they're creating, like the one your father served, are English households. No matter that Ceylon lies just outside the window. In their homes, it's the role of the dutiful wife to govern her family's days and nights, their meals, their sleep, their social obligations and their cleanliness, and yet not be seen to govern anything, or else their husbands look weak. Do you understand this?"

"Yes," he said grudgingly. It wasn't so different from his own home.

"Your memsa'ab's husband is infirm. She has two children, and with all this to manage and never enough to manage it with, she must maintain their position. A servant who helps his memsa'ab with such things is a great blessing. You will be a servant they depend on. Tell me you will do this."

Eligius nodded. He wanted to leave, yet something of Chandrak's anger felt familiar, a once-inhabited room violently rearranged.

"I ask you now, be a man like your father. He served them so he would always know how it felt to bear these bastards on his back. It gave him strength to be the man he was."

The rain left tears on Chandrak's cheeks. "Go. Send your heart away and walk through their gate as if nothing mattered."

He turned from Eligius and shambled into the gathering storm. The soldiers' guns had made a ruin of him. His wearying, tilting gait carried him away from the estate onto the muddying road.

Ault waited impatiently at the gate. "What is so bothersome to you? I really must know, or else think of you as a boy too selfish to be concerned with his family, especially where the father of the house has met with such an end. Now tell me or else put this childish sulking aside."

"I don't want to be here," Eligius said.

"Is it that I knew your father? Does his shadow stretch over the kindness of Christian labor?" Ault considered him a moment. "I think your father simply learned to have hope that things could be made better, and hope became important above all else. Above soldiers, above dying, above you. What can anyone do for such a man?" He opened the Colebrooks' gate.

Send your heart away.

Eligius entered. He heard the gate close behind him, and the sound of Ault's departing over the pebbled road. Outside of it all, the day moved.

To the Gates of Empire

AFTER GRACE, MARY SERVED THE WYNFIELDS FIRST. Charles and Andrew sat at the far end of the lunch, engrossed in conversation. Catherine sat across from Lady Wynfield, who shared stories of her son's exploits with Sir John as they followed the threads of the star tapestry.

"Rangoon, last we heard. In any event, our visit. For I well recall the difficulties setting up a home. Charles should soon be paid sufficiently to afford some furnishings."

This caught Andrew's attention. He ceased his discussion with Charles. "Great work lies ahead." He offered Lady Wynfield a withering look that shrank her in her seat. "Great reward accompanies."

"Hence our visit," Lady Wynfield said uncomfortably. "Andrew, may I?"

Andrew shrugged.

Taking Catherine by the arm, Lady Wynfield led her outside to their carriage. Catherine paid scant attention. As they made their way between rows of empty chairs, she could not get Charles' expression out of her thoughts. Proud, at times arrogantly so, a man who suffered no one. Summarily silenced by Andrew and humiliated by Lady Wynfield, and he responded as if he expected such treatment. As if he harbored no expectation of better.

Lady Wynfield removed two canvases from their carriage. She unveiled them in the house. "My husband's sponsorship of

yours is a matter of some discussion amongst Ceylon society,
you see. Politics, like nature, cannot sustain a vacuum for long."

"My husband is an accomplished and well-considered
man, lest you see him otherwise."

"Otherwise?"

"Dependent. Place-seeking. In need."

"You as well, madam. The women with whom I am
acquainted speak of you. I wonder, are you as attuned to their
speculations in that matter?"

Catherine was silent.

Lady Wynfield unveiled the first painting. A perfectly
adequate rendering of Julia while at the Cape. A girl of fourteen
poised on the precipice of understanding and intending the
communication of beauty. Her smile, the curve of her lips, her
loosely pinned hair; George had acquitted himself well with her.

"May I again suggest a luncheon?" Lady Wynfield leaned
Julia's portrait against the wall. "I chair a group of Directors' wives.
We function as, shall we say, a far-flung adjunct of Christian
good works. We sponsor the transportation of children from this
savage country to the continent in times of cholera or malaria.
We help the edifice of the Galle Face rise. I wish to invite you to
organize such a gathering. To do so is to inoculate your husband
from needless gossip. For him, shall we say. Here, perhaps this
is a painting to hang elsewhere. Obvious reasons, of course."

She unveiled the second painting.

The infant bore the wings of angels, a quiet smile that
spoke of serene rest. It bore Ewen's face, and therefore what of
Hardy could be salvaged.

The light was wrong. The wrong shape in the eye, the wrong
density, the wrong compound of tear and flame. She'd done
her best to relate to George what she recalled and he had missed
everything.

"Perhaps you can hang this in that shack out there," Lady
Wynfield suggested.

Catherine thought about it. Failures resided in the cottage now, but hope did as well.

She saw, through the window, figures standing at her gate. Oddly, one – tall, lanky, perhaps that missionary? – held an umbrella above his own head while the smaller one stood in the rain, as if the deluge were home.

Something in the space between the figures and here, the house and its quiet, felt familiar.

She placed the angel on the floor, next to Julia's portrait. "It belongs in here," she said.

ASCENDING THE PLANKS, Eligius crossed the Colebrooks' frontage, passing the gray whiskered monkeys that squalled on the banks of the flooded yard. At the canopy, he was met by a young English woman. Her clothes were as simple and workman-like as her harried, unkempt appearance. "You're the servant?" she asked in clipped Tamil. "From Ault?"

He nodded.

My mistress sent me to see who you were." She turned, then stopped to see if he was following. "What are you waiting on? The rain's ready to blow the sheet out to sea! Is that how you want your memsahib to meet you?"

"No," he answered in Tamil. "But I have letters. I was told to present them to Colebrook memsa'ab."

"There's time enough for that." She climbed up onto the veranda and bade him to follow. Her face was creased and puffy, her hair a nest of knots. "Take hold of this pole and stretch the canopy taut. I'll have the other."

She walked towards the corner opposite him. Her gait was that of a shuffling elder, stooped and fussy, as if forever racing the rain.

Together they pulled the poles to opposite ends of the veranda. The canopy was little more than a series of old sheets hastily sewn together. It stretched at the gapping seams but did not tear when the wind pushed up and under it, threatening to yank the poles from their hands.

He glanced at the audience that had gathered to fill the seats. Thirty, he reckoned, maybe more. To a one they looked none too pleased that a maid and a local stood between them and a drenching. He recognized some of the men from the Court. Their jowls and mutton chops, starched collars and dour expressions, seemed cut from the same cloth. The women were dressed in their finest, yet appeared morose over having to hide their resplendence beneath umbrellas and shawls.

The girl he'd seen in the Court foyer, the spinner of light, sat in the front row. She wore a dark dress buttoned to her neck. Her hair flew freely in the wind. Stray strands clung to the moisture on her cheeks. The men all stole glances at her when their wives weren't looking. From her secret smile, Eligius wondered if she didn't know precisely her effect.

One of the men seated behind her tapped her shoulder, then whispered something. She smiled. "Who should open the play?" she said quite loudly, drawing the attention of those under the sheet. "Why, that would be my luckless self."

She was staring at the veranda. At him. "Does he know his role, Mary?"

The maid holding the other pole shook her head. "I haven't given him the playbill to hold, Miss Julia, for fear he'd drop it in this ocean."

"He looks capable enough."

The girl ascended to the veranda. She selected from a stack of bound papers on a small table. "Tell him to hold it just so." She opened the playbill and pointed the text to the center of the veranda. "Make sure my mother can see the pages. Should she forget a line, he must be there, but not obviously. She is not to be seen as needing, which is not unlike asking the sun to be discreet in shining."

He stifled a smile and waited for Mary to butcher the translation, then took the papers from her hand and held them towards the veranda while struggling to anchor the pole. The cover of the playbill startled him with its audacity. A woman lay under a flowering vine. So vivid was the rendering that she seemed in tormented motion beneath his fingers. A winged naked infant drew a cloth over her. It whispered to the woman the way the man had whispered to this Julia, with a smile and a thief's heart.

Leonora, it said. *Translated by Catherine Palgrove Colebrook. London: Longman Brown, 1827.*

"Such fascination with my mother's work," Julia said. "Why, one could mistake him for a reader."

Mary related her words. He thought about saying something to let her know that he could read, that he could understand. But the gulf between them felt like the best vantage point from which to see her. He responded in Tamil.

"He's embarrassed to be in your presence while holding an undressed woman," Mary said.

The restive audience quieted. Julia took her place in the middle of the veranda, her hands raised for silence. She glanced at the book Eligius held, then smiled. "Friends all, I know you'll join me in wishing my mother health and happiness, for evermore."

She walked off to polite applause. In a moment, the woman he'd seen at the Court, hiding beneath the spider's curtain, strode towards him. Her eyes fell to the open text. "Don't let's curse the rain! For isn't it just a part of God's covenant to remind us of the flood, and to renew us? Do you believe this?"

Governor Wynfield was seated closest to Eligius, with an attractive woman whose hard features and disapproving gaze remained intent upon Catherine, who basked in Leonora's funerary lament for her missing lover. "Endure! Endure! yet break the heart, yet judge not God's decree. Thy body from thy soul doth part. Oh, may He pardon thee!"

She bowed to light applause from her audience. "It speaks to your hearts that you ignore this weather and support the efforts of brave souls like Stephen Ault as he struggles to shine the light of Christ across this shadowland. I apologize that my husband cannot be among you today. He saves his strength for the good works of the Court, and with the favor of peers like Governor Wynfield, a new charter for the John Company and a new body of laws shall be his legacy to Ceylon and to England."

"Hear, hear," Wynfield said.

"And I apologize as well that because of these storms and the failure of this land to produce a bumper crop of worthy servants, our tea and cakes have not arrived! Words cannot convey my sorrow."

Eligius saw Lady Wynfield exchange bemused smiles with the other wives seated near her. Their silent condemnation continued while Catherine greeted her guests and collected donations. Unfailingly, their expressions and manner molted into mocking winks when she passed them. Eligius wondered if any of them cared for her at all.

Mary gestured to him to let the pole down. He did, and was promptly showered with a cascade of collected rainwater. He heard Julia laugh, but did not look. He didn't want to be one more man turning to her. Instead he busied himself with folding the sheets.

After an hour, the last of the Colebrooks' guests departed for their own estates. Catherine returned to the veranda, sifting rupees in her hands. She shooed away her maid's efforts to shelter her from the rain. "So few. Christ will have to pick and choose from the afflicted, it seems."

"Let the new boy take the money to the missionary," Julia said. "No one should have to go out in this."

"I will see to it myself. You're young and the world grows trustworthiness on trees. No, I have something else in mind for the boy." She gestured to the flood water.

"Mother, he is only one boy."

"And I am but one woman, in a man's world to boot. Yet look

what I have done. Mary, help me get this across to the boy. Does he see Holland House?"

The name sparked him. He opened his tunic and gave over the letters, with Sir John Holland's on top. Mary took them quickly and kept them beneath her umbrella.

Catherine eyed the top letter without comment. "Does he see the need afflicting the cottage?"

"The servant's house," Mary told him. "Near the eastern fence line."

Across the floodwater, there stood a separate structure. Though it was built from sturdier elements, it was in no better shape than the battered huts lining his street.

"Tell him he is to clear a way to Holland House in plenty of time for our esteemed guest's arrival," Catherine said.

Eligius waited for Mary's guttural translation before reacting. "Am I to fix it?" he asked Mary. "All of it?"

Catherine smiled at him. "I can see it on his face, he understands. This is his land. These are his rains. I'm sure he'll see a way clear, eh?"

Mary led him to the middle of the plank path. He stepped away from her parasol, letting the softening rain feather his skin. From there the hut the memsa'ab called Holland House could be seen more clearly. The rains had separated wall from wall, roof from gutter. They'd brought the yard's mud to the bowing door in a curl some three feet high, and now the yard had become so saturated that the water ebbed like a captive sea.

"What is so important about this hut?" he asked Mary.

"Your memsahib gets many letters. From many great and important men." Disapproval dripped from her lips. "Now it seems we're dedicating part of the house to her pursuits. Or pursuers. Have it as you will."

So her allegiance was to the sa'ab of the house, he thought.

The youngest Colebrook ran giddily down the planks to latch onto Mary's leg. She wrapped a protective arm about the boy's shoulders.

Ewen stared up at the dark boy surveying his home.

"You're angry," Mary said. "Maybe this isn't a place you're meant to be. Maybe a field's the right spot for you. Ewen's afraid of you."

"It's easy enough to see how this happened," Eligius said. "And I can see as well what's to be done."

"You don't rise to bait, do you, little fish?"

"May I see the memsa'ab?"

Mary smiled. "You're a smart one, I'll say that. See that you keep your wits about you. Dimbola will tax your senses."

"Dimbola?"

"Their name for this house and the land, to the sea."

He followed her back to the house. "He wished to see you," Mary told Catherine.

Catherine stood from her chair on the porch, where she'd been sitting with Julia, examining the contents of Sir John Holland's envelope.

"Does he understand his task?"

"He said so, mum."

"My pay," Eligius interrupted. "It is to be ten rupees. I want to be sure of this."

Reluctantly, Mary translated. Catherine's face grew taut.

"It doesn't bode well, does it?" she said.

BEFORE HE BEGAN working in earnest, he asked Mary what Holland House held that couldn't wait for Ceylon's winter rains to pass.

"Her pride," Mary told him, "and the attentions of a far off man."

Seated on the plank walkway, he plotted where to begin. Dimbola lay like a valley, right to the door of Holland House. It would be necessary to level it, to coax the grounds in a different direction.

Julia watched him from a gazebo at the western fence, on a modest bluff above the rainwater. Already he'd learned that

Mary had a caustic tongue and the arrogance of the all-seeing unnoticed. Ewen was a blur of childish need. The memsa'ab was yet unknown to him, but through others' eyes came the vague shape of a woman spoken of only at a distance. The sa'ab of this house was a man to be pitied.

Yet it was the barest of looks from Julia that needled his heart and made him want to walk away from here even as the world whispered consequences: Gita, bathed in another of her inevitable red fevers.

He set to work.

The water could not simply be spirited away. What was needed was what he'd watched Matara's men create, to drain the village of rain and refuse. A catch basin.

He found some planks the storm had pulled free from Holland House and plunged them into the water until they stood like the headstones behind the Galle Face. Then he dug at the accumulated mud while across from him, Ewen chased after a small peacock. Its wings bent at the water as its childish tormentor drove it from the banks into the brackish eddies.

Over three hours while his dam took form, the yard still remained under water. Miserable, he considered the immensity of the task before him and could think only of his hunger. What kinds of food lay in the main house? He wagered that the feeble sa'ab sat before a feast of fowl and good bread, and fruit carted in from the recesses of the country where the rains fell most sparingly. Money was no object to a director. The Colebrooks' table was certain to be piled high with excess. What was hunger to them? Something for the servants to remedy when summoned, something that a child could endure until the last peacock was rousted.

He worked deep into the day, through dizziness and cramps that doubled him over. All the while the rain fell, making a fool of him. Julia watched from the interior of the gazebo, paper tablet in her lap.

Under his incessant labor, a ditch formed that split the yard in half. He caught his breath while tracing the falling rain in the water's reflection, from the ashen sky down to him. As the funereal afternoon light waned, Mary called to him from the veranda. "There's food, if you've a need."

He climbed out of the flood and ran down the planks to the house. Clots of wet mud slid from his body. He held his crusted hands in the rain, letting the storm wash them clean, then accepted Mary's offering. Coconuts, sliced mango, some bread; all showing their age. Nothing that couldn't be gleaned from the land surrounding the house. He hid his disappointment and ate. When he finished, he took some more bread and wrapped it in his tunic. Looking up, he saw Catherine at the window of the house, watching him.

SHE WAITED UNTIL the sun fell below the cradle of trees before emerging. Through the afternoon, she'd watched him work. Charles had asked for tea and she'd bade Mary to respond. Julia sought respite from Ewen's ever-presence and she'd shooed them away. Nothing else beckoned to her as this, the hope that Holland House might be reclaimed by the boy who left the confines of the day she'd first seen him, to turn up before her eyes once again.

Crossing the walkway, she stood above the waves pulling against Eligius' dams. Mary saw her and ran down the planks. "Is this what you call work?" she shouted. Ewen pulled up short at her tone.

Julia set her paper down. She watched implacably.

"You've done nothing! If anything, the Colebrooks' home drowns in deeper water."

Eligius waded to the gate and his second dam. His legs burned. His back felt as if it had been hollowed and filled with molten iron.

"Mary," Catherine said, "enough."

"Your memsahib is doubtless very angry–"

He pulled the wood slats from the ground. The waters

rushed to the gate, now the low point in the yard. Their flow became a flood; the trapped rainfall thundered out, carving the ground alongside the road to Dimbola. It carried away weak vegetation. Even the slats of his dam were borne down the hillside towards the sea.

Ewen dangled his feet in the onrush, cackling delightedly as his legs disappeared to the knees in a froth of mud brown.

Eligius stood at the gate, watching the last of the rain depart. It only took moments for the yard to clear itself. A few pools remained in the aftermath, like mirrors atop the ruin of the Colebrooks' lawn. Ewen performed a mad dance through the heart of them, spraying mud and rain everywhere as Mary called out halfheartedly for him to stop. "Come on, then!" she yelled to Eligius. "Do you want to dry off, or stay like that?"

He glanced worriedly at the memsa'ab. She stood by the cottage's ruin of a door, heedless of the mud overtaking her feet. Silently, she gestured for him to follow the maid.

Something in her eyes unsettled him. An incongruous returning hope.

He followed Mary to the rear of the main house. There he found himself inside a colonial home for the first time.

The entry they passed through led into a dank hallway lit only by a single shuddering gaslamp. Having no ventilation save the door, the hall was thick with noxious fumes that left the floor greasy with soot.

Mary led him past a room that smelled of lingering sickness. The fireplace was stacked with old wood and uncollected ash. There were books on the wall, their spines embossed with the lofty words of the Court.

The sight chilled him. Unbidden moments joined him in the dankness. His father, breathing life into old colonial laws. Bright roses spitting from gunmetal. Himself, in his father's emptying eyes.

"You're getting water all over the floor," Mary snapped, "and who do you think cleaning it falls to?"

She took him to the scullery. He knew it immediately by the smell. Caked pots, buckets of rancid vegetables gone to oily black, meat on a butcher's table, its marbled flesh infested with flies.

"Servants," Mary said, "don't see the filth their betters live in. They don't smell their stench. Servants concern themselves only with what's to be done."

She stacked a single cord of wood atop the iron grate in the scullery hearth, then packed it in with crisp dead palm fronds. Striking a match, she lit a fire and bade him to sit. "I've no place for you to wash, and you aren't about to walk through the house shod in mud. Let it dry and cake. That'll do for you."

"It is no different at home. I'm used to it."

"No doubt."

She left him. He stripped to his loin cloth and sat close to the fire. The wood was relatively young and green at its core. Its smoke was faintly pungent. The fire would last a bit longer.

He draped his clothes across a stone seat to dry. A sound made him spin, his hands swift to cover his immodesty. Ewen stood in the doorway, dripping wet from the storm. He was naked and carried two towels. Raising one, he rubbed his face frenziedly, then handed the second towel to Eligius.

Eligius peeled ribbons of mud from his skin as he dried himself. Like a sheet of woven silk, the towel was the softest thing to touch him since his mother's hand. How long ago that had been.

He stretched his sore muscles, willing the heat of the fire into them. The boy sat down next to him and aped his every move.

I should hate you, Eligius thought as he regarded the boy. I should stand at your gate and scream until you leave.

He wiggled his toes. The boy did as well, delighted with the game. They held their hands out, fingers spread, until the light glowed through their skin and the veins could be read like words. Smiling, the boy put his arms out to Eligius. He wanted to be held. To be lifted.

Eligius leaned close to the boy. "No."

Ewen's eyes went wide with shock.

Eligius dressed quickly and left the boy in the room. His clothes were warm and stiff. They crackled as he walked back down the hall. His day was at an end, and with it his station as the holder of poles, the ditch digger, the keeper of charades that the Colebrooks did not smell and did not invite ridicule from their fellow colonials. That their child did not view him as just another Indian to ride.

He followed the sounds of muted conversation to a dining room, where the family sat around a table picking at plates of the meat he'd seen in the scullery. It was enough that they brought their appetite for beef to Ceylon. That they consumed it heedless of its condition sickened him. Didn't Britishers have the wealth of empires at their disposal? Wasn't this sa'ab one of the chosen, charged with the colonials' stewardship of India? Yet they lived the lives of near-villagers.

"Mother," Julia said, finally looking up from her plate. Like the others, she ate as if she were a starving Peshwar.

Catherine set down her fork and its speared coal of meat.

"My pay," he said to Mary.

"He's inquiring about the rupees," Mary said. "I'll tell the boy that he may first return the extra food he secreted into his pockets. Does he think I'm blind? Very little goes on in this house that I do not see."

It was all he could do to stay quiet while Mary wrestled her words into Tamil. "The food is for my mother and sister," Eligius told her. "My sister especially. She is sicker every day. This is why I am here."

Catherine stood at the sound of footsteps. "Charles. We've saved food for you. How goes your work?"

The man she called Charles put his hand on the back of a chair, steadying himself as he sat. Only then did he look up at the Indian boy before him. His face grew still as air before a storm. His hands trembled.

Eligius trembled as well. I remember you, he thought. Old lion.

His eyes were so like Ewen's that Eligius thought he might hold out his arms to be lifted.

Mary started to translate, but Charles interrupted. "I understand, and so does he. The food or the rupees. It cannot be both. Or else how will he learn the value of honest labor?"

Julia began to protest. "It's not fair, father. You agreed to –"

"Let it be food."

He'd spoken in their English. "In the time it takes me to bring rupees to market and buy the food, Gita might die. But I don't believe the food I have amounts to ten rupees. I shall take more. My family has seen too much loss."

He stood and waited, and wondered if this god of theirs – sometimes a baby, sometimes a man who simply bled and died, like other men he'd known – would pull the world out from under him. It would be such a simple thing to do to a servant.

"There is something memorable about you," Catherine said.

IN ALL, MARY gave him enough food to last into the next day. Some bread, some beli fruit, and some wrapped lamb battered in coconut milk and chick pea flour, a reasonable effort by her at kamargah. All covered in another of those wondrous cloths he'd dried off with. "Your memsahib's got more that needs doing," she told him at the gate. "There's the rest of the yard, and the harder chores, and of course her postings, which must go out daily. She's an irrepressible correspondent, that one."

"With Holland."

"Him. Others. Disciples and divines, the missionary always says. Her letters fly to and from Dimbola like these bloody insects."

"I will do all of these things for rupees, or for food."

"My, we're a cheeky one. I can see I'll wear myself out keeping you in line. The most important task lies with Holland House itself. The whole thing ought to have washed out to sea with the mud, if you ask me. There's repairs to be done, and plenty of, if it's to be ready for his arrival. Now go home. No doubt she's watching and wondering what we're talking about. The wife of a director can see conspiracies in the blowing of leaves."

He glanced back at the house, but saw nothing in the darkened windows. Dimbola was so still; it arose in him a childish contemplation that the day had been a dream.

THAT EVENING, CATHERINE braved the mud. She crossed the yard and closed herself up in the cottage to consider the day's events. The boy could be provocative; Charles and Mary especially heated at the sound of his voice. To them he was surly and entitled. He withheld his appreciation of English to mock them or worse. Perhaps he'd think overnight on what this colonial family did not have, how it lagged others, and not return.

She busied herself with tucking Julia's portrait in the cottage alcove – Julia had shown scant interest in it – and examining her failures under the light of the crossing moon, but she could not stop thinking about the boy. Strange, that they'd first encountered each other when neither knew the other's name, and now this. A cleared path. His footfalls in Dimbola. The shadow she'd seen at Court, emerged from a bloody day to life.

She found the Court image among the faded moments that she'd tried and failed to hold. It was nothing but a stain on paper to anyone else's eyes. Little more than dust. Yet she could find everything in its murk. The ampitheatrical lobby of the East India Court, the elusive, glimmering light, the boy's silhouette, prone and quivering in the streaming sun. His gray shadow across the marble floor like a spill of ash.

She drove a nail into the cottage wall and hung the paper from it. A rainwashed inference of structure and a boy, now with a name. Eligius.

The Night, Moving

THE CLOUDS PARTED JUST ENOUGH TO LAY A SLIVER OF moonlight across Eligius' path, easing his way. It was late when he reached his hut. His mother and Gita were both asleep on his mat. For a moment he thought his mother had fallen into sleep clutching a dead child. Then Gita's distended belly filled and fell, and he could breathe again.

He set the food on his mother's altar. Tiny seeds covered the altar top amidst a fine, pungent powder. Ajwain; his mother had been grinding it to medicate Gita's bowels.

He felt foolish and impotent. The man of the house, whether he wished it or not, and he'd failed to do as he was asked. Food was fine enough, but what did it matter to a child who could no longer keep it down?

"Know that I'm here, Eligius."

Chandrak came from Sudarma's room. He was half dressed. The withered root of his leg quivered until he shifted his weight off of it. His hair was tousled, his shoulders rouged with scratches. The scars across his left side formed craters atop his skin. Sudarma's scent, cardamom and citrus, radiated from him.

"I present myself to you with respect for you and your father," Chandrak said. "Your mother and sister need two different sorts of men. Let us each be men for them, you and I. Or would you rather she beg in the streets of Varanasi with the widows? Wake up and speak to him, Sudarma. I'll dress, and then Eligius will talk of his day."

"This can't be," Eligius whispered to his mother as Chandrak withdrew to Sudarma's room. "This is Swaran Shourie's home. You have no right."

"Swaran is dead, meri beta."

She ignited a thin reed of incense and plunged it into a cup, releasing a veil of sweet smoke that washed the hut clean of musk and sweat. "From the time you were born, I've had a vision of you. You're somewhere else. Somewhere beautiful, watching the lights the way you do. Now I see that I was never supposed to have the men others have."

"Make him leave."

"Sometime I hope you'll tell me what you see in the light that holds you the way it does. I think you wouldn't get so lost if you had a father. I think I wouldn't worry if I had a husband. Ay, my child, don't despise me for wanting. We all hate what we turn into. You may still. You won't be alone. I see women staring at their babies as if they were strangers. Men watch the sea and wish they didn't have to return home. Your father and I thought that we'd escape the worst of this life. But days drift over us. I've done things I never thought I'd do."

Chandrak came out wearing a clean shirt and pants. "Come with me to the fires, Eligius."

"Go with him." Sudarma watched from the doorway as Eligius followed Chandrak into the street.

Chandrak stepped between banyans. He left the road behind. "Come. This way."

"But the fires. And the soldiers. It's past curfew."

"We'll make our own fire."

He followed Chandrak to a clearing hewn from causarina and breadfruit. There were two other men waiting silently. He didn't recognize them.

"You brought food only," Chandrak said. "What about money?"

"I had to choose. Gita starves–"

"Tell me about them."

"I don't understand. Who are these men?"

"What did you see of their house? What do they have?"

"I won't go back." The sound of his own voice disgusted him. A child's plea. "Every minute I'm there, I'm shamed. I'll work in the fields. You have no right to be in my home with my mother."

"Let me deal with this boy," one of the men said.

"No."

Chandrak took Eligius by the arm and led him back into the jungle. "It's unfair of me to expect so much of you without warning, Eligius. But I have a reason. I know you better than you think. You hate them. You remember Swaran dying at their hands, and if you could, you'd do something. I tell you, you can. I see so much of him in you. I ask you now, picture their home. What did you see?"

"Furniture. A rug. Gas lamps."

"These are big," Chandrak blurted impatiently. "Think of small things. Personal things."

"I know what you're asking. I won't steal. It's enough that you make me work for them—"

There was only the briefest shudder of air; Chandrak's slap made no sound. His open hand snapped Eligius' head back.

"They're murderers," Chandrak told him. "We've tolerated them for too long. Not striking back at them, that is your shame. But you will strike, and I'm telling you how. You go back. Remember what they have, anything that can be taken a little at a time. For now, that's enough. When you prove to me that you're a man, I'll tell you of the great work we've begun. But hear me. You will do this for your father and for me. You will watch them and I will watch you."

He left Eligius amidst the swaying boughs. The undertow of the men's murmurs sank beneath the hiss of air-stirred leaves.

Picking his way back to the road, Eligius hesitated. There was the fire, and the men's talk of the fields. There was his hut, where the shapes of Sudarma and Chandrak twinned in the doorway.

He turned away from all of it. This night, Matara breathed new truths.

Somewhere else, he thought. Better to find the way there.

BY THE TIME he made it to the Colebrooks, the moon sat low above the sea, plating the visible world in blue. Its light made jewels of the raindrops falling on him as he sat against a thick tree outside the gate. It would be dawn soon. He would be smarter for the next day's work. He would eat only when obliged to by the demands of his tasks, and take back as much of the colonials' money as he could. Gita needed more than omum powder to keep her from the valley.

He would watch and remember. But would he speak of it? Was Chandrak right?

Lost in his thoughts, he didn't notice the figure standing at the gate, an alabaster doll in the cold moonlight. Julia's pale skin disappeared beneath a fan of hair.

"Why are you here? My mother will not pay you more just because you beat her to the sunrise."

Her haughtiness hid something. A restlessness. She was not at ease, and it made him smile.

"Don't pretend you don't understand me. I was at the table, or did you forget?"

"I did not. I brought home the food and returned because I wanted to see the lion's mouth before I slept."

"Are you insulting me?"

"No," he laughed. "It's a place. The highest point in Ceylon. You can see every corner of the sky from there. And since it was more than halfway, and it was already so late…"

"And I think you're lying. I think you're as insolent at home as you are here, and they wouldn't let you through the door."

"If you wish." He bundled himself tighter.

"Did you know there would be trouble that day at Court? I always meant to ask, had I seen you again."

Shifting position, he turned his gaze towards the sea.

"I suppose," Julia said loudly, "you've no interest in why I chose to come out here. Certainly, I could have noted your presence with the same indifference you now display and returned to my bed. Well, enjoy the water."

She spun on her heels and took a few steps. "If you must know," she called, "I felt you deserved something more for the work you did."

He stood and walked to the gate. "Come back. Please."

"If it matters so much to you."

She held out a thin chain. The glass bauble he'd seen at the Court caught the moonlight and flared, sending its shards across his chest. "You cannot speak of this to mother," she said. "It wasn't right that you should simply receive food. We should all receive food, just as we should receive the next day. This is all I have. I cannot take her money. She knows it too well. But I am told by men more worldly than I that you steal from us and sell our goods at bazaars. If so, I hope you're paid well."

The bauble spun at the end of her chain. He raised it level with his eyes. It fashioned the moonlight into a calliope of white clouds that overlay the trees, the sea, her.

She was walking away. This time there was no hesitancy in her step. She'd done all that she'd come to do.

He found that if he held the bauble just so, he could throw tiny lights deep into the Colebrooks' yard, to the gazebo even, and set them dancing with a flick of his wrist. He imagined Julia watching him with the queer mix of her ilk's imperiousness and the odd wakefulness that had brought her to the gate.

A bit of his light found Holland House. Clearly there would be other tasks. The letters, preparing the yard, perhaps anchoring the pole again while the memsa'ab held forth. He felt certain that Holland House was where he would find himself most often. Then, he supposed, the Colebrooks would have no further need for him. By then Gita might be healthy, and he would find a new way to show his worth at home.

Someone was in the cottage doorway.

He quickly covered the bauble with his hand and looked again. The clouds came and took the moon away. Now he couldn't be sure of what he'd seen – a figure standing behind a chair in the open doorway. All was night. He couldn't discern anything.

He settled back against the tree and waited. In time he closed his eyes. Soon he was aloft over a land too dark to see.

Mother and Child

HE LOOKED UP AT THE SOUND OF FEET WHISKING through the dewed grass. Mary stood over him, bowl in hand. "Bring it into the house when you've finished. There's a mountain of mud to be cleared, and more yet when you're past that." She left him the porridge without a word on finding him just outside Dimbola's gate.

He ate the thin mixture of cracked rice and milk, then began shoveling the mud away. Gradually, the sun broke through and stirred some warmth in his blood. It felt good to be alone, testing himself against the weight of his country. The glass bauble tapped against his chest in gentle time to his work.

At mid-day, the memsa'ab emerged from the house carrying a parcel of letters. He grabbed his tunic and put it on, tucking the bauble within.

She handed the letters to him. "Take these to the missionary in Port Colombo. He will show you how to post them."

"I remember the ship."

Mary stood nearby. "Do I need a translator?" Catherine snapped at her. "Clearly not."

Mary slunk back to the house.

"While you're in the port," she told Eligius, "the missionary should give you some materials he's received on my behalf. You are to bring them back here. Leave nothing behind."

She deposited a small sack in his hand. "See to it that these rupees make it to their destination. The captain of the postal vessel is an acquaintance, and who can say when I might visit his ship myself? Be sure that my first question will be about his business with you today."

"I will not steal your money," he said. *You know it too well.*

AFTER POSTING THE letters with the captain, he hid the few remaining rupees in a fold of his tunic and went to the missionary's small parish. It was empty but for a departing beggar. "Ah," Ault said when Eligius told him of the memsa'ab's request for her materials. "I've been looking forward to ridding myself of these."

There were two casks the size of Eligius' torso. "How do I carry these all the way to Kalutara?" he asked.

"I have a cart. If your young back can load these drums, I'll take you. It won't cost you any more than what I hear jingling in your clothes. Come now, give freely to God's servant. On your memsahib's behalf, it's the most tithing she'll have done in months."

The remaining rupees went for Ault's cart and an elder donkey to pull it. Eligius loaded the casks and they were on their way before noon. "What do they hold?" he asked as Port Colombo's uneasy queue of battered and new, Indian and British, slipped below the skyline of trees.

"Salts of some kind." Ault absently turned a single rupee over in his hand. "They came from London. She has them shipped, I believe, from a gentleman there."

"Holland?"

"He and others. William Henry Talbot. Oscar Reijlander. Exotic name, that. Your memsahib maintains a steady correspondence about this endeavor of hers."

He thought of Mary's cluck of disapproval over the acquaintances her mistress kept.

"It does no good to ask our Lady Colebrook what she wants or seeks," Ault said, as if to himself. "Nor to question her tenacity. Such is her doggedness to find whatever it is she needs to find. Good graces be damned."

"What is it she's doing?"

"I haven't the first idea. I wonder if even she knows." Ault placed the rupee in his breast pocket. "Mind your path, Eligius."

For the sake of the cart and its contents, they took the low road through the valley and arrived at Dimbola's gates by early evening. Ewen was acting as a lookout. When he saw them, he ran into the house crying Eligius' name.

"The child has taken to you," Ault said.

Catherine met them at the gate. Ault climbed down from the cart to greet her with a kiss of her hand. "Such a difference now that your Red Sea has parted. It seems that the servant boy has met your expectations, eh?"

"He is a spirited boy," she said, "and not without competence. Indeed, I find I have more uses of him than there are days. Such is the life of a director's family."

"How true."

"I wish for the boy to remain here during the week. He may return to see his family on Sundays. It is a holy day for us, though I don't expect him to understand that. Please do inform his family of the new arrangement. If there is a problem, I should like to know of it now, so I can find a suitable replacement."

"I will tell them." Ault turned to Eligius. "I hear no objections."

She watched him. And waited.

Eligius' mind made shameful short work of it. Forces in his life now were beyond his understanding. He needed to find a far place such as this Dimbola from which to make sense of them all. "When you are there, please see about Gita. How she is feeling. Tell her and my mother I stay to earn as much as I can for them."

He unloaded the cart. Ault bid his goodbyes and left him behind. It was that easy. The shift to Dimbola as the place he would see most often was done.

Catherine surprised him by lifting one of the barrels herself and carrying it to the house. He took one and followed her.

They passed through the front door into a dark foyer.
A stairway at the rear, next to an arterial corridor, wound up to a
second story marked with a dwarfed brown chest on which a
series of grotesque figurine candlesticks stood. Their charred
tapers had wilted from overuse. Above him, a black iron can-
delabra hung precariously from a cobwebbed chain. Dust motes
rolled in the breeze ribboning the house, up against the
wainscoting and across the stone floors like earthbound clouds.

The visible rooms were crowded with ill-fitting odds and
ends. There was a study, its interior dim with old cigar smoke.
Despite the gloom he could make out the ivory of a stuffed owl
under a glass conical, and next to it a humidor and a pinccone
cachepot.

The room across from the study was a riot of flowery bro-
cades and impractically soft settees that bore the imprint of
recent occupation. A tea service sat on a low round table littered
with balled pieces of paper.

He understood none of what he saw, only that the
Colebrook estate bore its once opulent clutter like fruit left on
the vine to rot.

Mary took up a corner of the area rug, a faded expanse of
brown and white obelisks woven in heavy woolen thread. "How
do I move this with your bloody dead weight on it?"

He stepped off, shifting the cask in his aching arms. She
pulled the rug out of the foyer and down the hall.

"This way!" Catherine's voice bellowed. Ewen and Julia
stopped what they were doing to wander after her.

Eligius followed the sound of Catherine's passage and
found himself in a corridor of paintings. They were as vivid as
the textured cover of her stage tragedy, only rendered in oils
of gold, green and black. There were girls and women, and wise-
looking men of learning held in place by scalloped wood
frames. The characters in these paintings all stared past him at
some point of reverie in the middle distance.

Catherine set her cask down at the end of the hall, beneath

a painting of a child with wings as white and stilled as the owl in the study. "Did the same hand render all these paintings?" Eligius asked.

"Bravo," Julia said. "How did you know?"

"They just seemed related. And the light looks the same. As if they were all painted at the same hour."

"An acquaintance of our family. He fancies himself a portraitist of religious awakenings and wealthy colonials. They're called gouaches."

"May we proceed?" Catherine snapped. It angered her to spend time on George's work, such as it was. "Are we quite done educating the boy on our paintings?"

Julia and Mary exchanged uneasy looks. Ewen kept his eyes glued to the cask in Eligius' hands.

"Look at me," Eligius whispered to the boy. Surprised, the child gazed up. Eligius studied his face, plaintive and pale, and then the painting above the door. The winged child in the painting resembled the boy before him, so much so that he could not help but stare.

"Stop it," Ewen said softly.

"He is a reticent child," Catherine remarked. "Not given to flight. And that painting, I shall say that it lacks grievously of life and leave matters at that. Now, let me ask you something on the subject, as the kind of boy you are means something to me. You know of our Lord and his son?"

"Let him be, mother," Julia sighed. "I wager he'd prefer rupees to religion."

"He speaks English. He is named for a servant of God, did you not say so to my husband?"

"I did."

"Then by all means, answer my question."

"I learned a little of it," Eligius told her. "The child was born under a thatched roof, like mine. He grew, then died." He shrugged. "At least he was able to live for a while."

"Indeed. A child of your poverty of experience would see it

that way, eh?" She took a heavy ring from the thick folds of her sari. A long, skeletal key dangled from it. "It is evident that you are not close, either to my God or yours. You have not been found in this world. I wonder if it matters to you at all."

Her family stood in an uncomfortable silence.

"Are you worth the effort it takes to look for you?" she added. "Perhaps that is the better question."

"I'm not hard to find, memsa'ab. I stand among barrels and paintings. At this moment, it seems I'm easier to see than the child god you speak of."

"He should be dismissed for that," Mary said. "Feeding their family isn't reason enough for a servant's manners with these lot."

"That is because they don't know there is more to hope for." Catherine slipped the bony key into the lock and pushed the door open. "Place your cask in here, then come to the cottage with me. I want you to see something before another ill chosen word leaves you."

It stood on black legs. Five feet high, most of its body was draped with the dark hood he'd first glimpsed in the Court lobby. A sheet of paper, its surface grainy and trembling with minute sparkles, lay in a tray next to the beast. Watery and dissolute though it was, he could see the suggestion of the cottage in it, with its door open onto the colorless world, and a chair, empty and waiting. It was like an unfinished painting, like an indelible dark twin of where he stood, only drained of life and light.

Catherine was at his ear. "Does it frighten you to know that this house contains matters you've never dreamt of?"

There were other occupants in this musty place she called Holland House. Trays, stacks of the paper, lines on the floor like sifted coal dust. In one spot on the wall, a rectangle where a painting might have hung above the peg and groove slats that had lifted under assault from unimpeded rain. Next to it, a single square of paper nailed to the wall. Odd textures besmirched its surface. He wanted to approach it, to see what lay hidden in these stilled waves, but feared to move with the memsa'ab's eyes so alight at his discomfort.

She directed him to look at the paper. To see it, she told him. "I remember you, you know. From the Court that day."

"You remember my father, I am certain. What happened."

"No. That is where you will find that I differ. I remember you. And you remember me. I see it in your eyes. The moment you saw me. The woman from Court, from under the dark curtain. Why are you still here? We, all of us, are bound to a terrible day. You could go to any colonial house. Do you wish to avenge your father? Do you blame us?"

"I am not such a man, memsa'ab."

"Then what sort are you?" She took up the image of the Court. "Every colonial has objects of value, and they fear your theft. Mine may not be jeweled or inlaid with precious metal. But I fear losing them. I have lost enough in my life. Perhaps you understand this."

"Yes."

"My needs are simple, Eligius. Do not profane who we are or what we do. Do not desecrate what is ours. Do not drink and expect to be welcome here."

"Mother, enough," Julia said. "What is it you want from him?"

"Does a boy who speaks English also read it?"

Catherine handed him a letter. He unfolded it. *If this be your life's work, I will continue our correspondence on the science of this. But this is not art, nor is it God. It is the merest shadow of life. Have you not held shadows long enough?*

The letter was signed by Sir John Holland.

He understands, Catherine thought. And he does not run.

"You serve a woman who wishes to prove those words wrong," she said. "But hear me on this. Do not let me become familiar with you now, only to yearn to forget you later."

She walked out of the cottage. "I cannot stand goodbyes,"

she called. "Tomorrow you will work and I will provide you food and a rupee perhaps. What more can a soul do?"

Mary took the letter from him. "She may take pity on you, but I don't. Be sure of that. As hard as I work, I'll not let your smart tongue in this house. Know your place. There are a hundred more just like you, less the cost and half the trouble, I can see already. But she's cast her eye on you, the good Lord knows why. I'll see you leave before long. Do you understand those words?"

"I understand."

"Children, to bed with you." She took Julia by the arm and led her away. Ewen lingered a moment. Eligius tolerated it.

"Ewen," Mary said. Ewen went to her, obedient. "Put out the lights, Eligius. It's your duty now, not mine."

THE NEXT MORNING he took to the roof of Holland House, cutting wood into rough planks with the only suitable tool he could find, a corroded machete. Hacking until his hands bled, he wondered if his father had wielded such an instrument in similar circumstances, before his life among the colonials sent him from Dimbola to the Court, to beg for crumbs and ash.

Repairing the roof was painstaking, tedious work. The machete was dull. He ran out of strength and worse, wood.

Before climbing down, he peered into the bowels of Holland House. The last of the daylight revealed the spider, patient and still, resting in the sun among his memsa'ab's bits and pieces.

That evening, he told the memsa'ab that more wood was needed, and a proper cutting blade, if she had any hope of keeping the sky out of her beloved Holland House. "I shall pray on it," she said and walked away after telling Mary to bring him some food.

He suspected that other Britishers were better off than the people he found himself among. The others' pockets were filled with gold, no doubt, and rupees fell like rain from them as they walked through fields of thriving coffee that brushed the blue canvas of the world.

The week wore on. He ministered to the roof as best he could. As time passed he took notice of the family's peculiarities. The sa'ab rarely asked him to do anything, even fetch tobacco for his pipe or a splint to light it with. When the pipe went cold, he simply sat as night fell over him.

Eligius was grateful for the sa'ab's isolation. He couldn't bring himself to look the old lion in the eye.

The memsa'ab doted on her husband, albeit in flurries and during daylight only. She brought him a bit of food – there seemed to be little more in the house than a body needed to get through the day – or a cup of tea and a word about the writing forever in the sa'ab's lap. Then she was lost to the task of composing her letters. She wrote several each day for Eligius to post.

"Place it on our account," she would say before dismissing him for the port. The expression he saw on the captain's face told him those words had been spoken too often.

The sa'ab couldn't abide bustle. The memsa'ab equally opposed stillness. Their marriage puzzled him, never more so than at night. At that hour there were no more tasks to busy with and he could watch these people. The sa'ab always retired first. He would put down his quill, bid goodnight and remain in the study. Not even his children drew near once he entered that frail, enveloping quiet. Julia would take up her book of paper and gaze about the house, while Ewen occupied some middle space between his parents.

The memsa'ab simply closed herself into Holland House with the spider, to do who knew what. Occasionally she brought the angel painting of Ewen in with her, then replaced it in the corridor deep in the night. The sound of the wood frame as she mounted it back on its nail seeped through the porous walls.

The days, the evenings, a bit of sleep and to the roof again. His first week among the colonials was strangely dislocating. He and his mother had a fraction of their space, none of the furniture, not even the food, yet he longed for the dirt floors and the bristling sleeping mat of his hut. He longed to hear Gita breathing in time to her dreams. Now his own last sights before sleep were white stone walls, a bench with his servant's tunic draped over it, a window through which he could see a smudged sliver of the jungle.

He wanted to go back to Matara and whatever awaited him there before the very notion of his village fell away, and he became just one more piece of clutter set aside and forgotten in Dimbola.

Perhaps that was best, he thought. Dimbola is a mad woman's empire. In such a place, it was better not to be seen.

EARLY SATURDAY MORNING, Mary interrupted him while he ran the machete blade over a whetstone in hopes of an edge. "I need meat for today. We're going to the butchers." She handed him a pail. "Mine shouldn't be the only back that aches."

Catherine was at the gate with Ault and Charles, who clutched at the corners of a heavy woolen coat as if it bound his bones together.

The missionary sat atop his cart. A Tamil unloaded burlap sacks onto the road. "Namaskaram," Eligius said to the worker. It felt good to use his own tongue. "What village do you come from?"

The man was older and burly. A lifetime of field work had been written into his skin. He stepped past Eligius without a word. Kneeling in the Colebrooks' field, he ground dead leaves to a powder between his palms.

"A man of Governor Wynfield's," Ault said. "A loan, with their compliments."

Catherine's face flushed. She wanted Charles to rise up to the insult but he merely gazed across the fields, as if the missionary's words were just another passing breeze. She did not inquire into his dealings with Wynfield and resented having to consider them at all. It was not her place to worry about money, or to defend him. Now, in front of servants, it was no longer possible to believe that the family of a Director flourished.

"We need no help keeping up with our fellows," she said stiffly. "A man who has devoted his life to affairs of state at home and abroad need never place hunt."

"I did not mean to offend –"

She cut the missionary off with an imperious wave. "I am in the wrong," Ault said, sighing. "I apologize without reservation."

"Charles, do you accept?"

"We are not at Court, nor are we under scrutiny from our friends and neighbors. Our coffee and cotton crops are poor. We need help, not manners."

"You are my husband, and I only wish to glorify you in whatever meager way a woman can."

"The matter is closed."

His indignation rose only for her. She relented. "The children and I are accepting his kind invitation to church, where I shall ask God's grace on this field and on your health. Won't you come?"

"Spend your time as you wish. I've work to do. I can either finish my work on the charter or Wynfield will finish it for me." A wry smile crossed his lips. "Have you seen our home, Stephen? It is enough of a church to rival any."

"My husband is in a quiet humor today. The work of championing this country and its people is a burden. Children, come! We have church."

Julia and Ewen ran from the house, dressed in their finery. They took seats atop Ault's cart.

"Some meat," she told Mary. "Something to fight the pallor in my husband."

Ault tugged at the reins and his donkey – gray as spent coal, bloated in the stomach, her hind quarters a landscape of weevil bites – stepped gingerly forward. Mary kicked Eligius' pail. "Will you be much longer in the clouds?"

In a moment they were walking along the well-worn ruts

in the road, following Ault's cart tracks to Port Colombo and the marketplace there. "Heaven forfend they should spare us the walk," Mary grumbled. She spat onto the ground. "Your countryman seemed morose, don't you think?"

"I greeted him but he didn't answer."

"It's a hard lot working for the Governor, I've no doubt. He's arrogant with his money."

He thought about what she was saying. "He gives the Colebrooks seed and a man to plant them?"

"The master doesn't make what these others do and don't think a maid doesn't know it. It's left to me to stretch their money and make them look a part of society, and do I get thanks? That's where they're most impoverished."

He had so many questions, but Mary's bitterness gave him pause. Everything about her – her bent posture, her headlong gait, her weathered hands – spoke of the harsh physical labor that informed her life. Yet he felt her need to speak unfurling like a sail. They were just two servants away from their masters, tongues loosening with the miles.

"I know that the sa'ab and memsa'ab make the decisions," he said, "but from what I've seen, it is you that runs Dimbola."

She straightened haughtily. "More so than any of the maids we'll see at market. More than should be my weight. 'Fortune doesn't always smile where she should, and sadness grows in her absence.' Ault says that. It's a place of sorrows we've come to, Eligius. Yet what right do I have to complain about it, or leave it? None."

"So what the memsa'ab said about their place with the others, like Governor Wynfield and his wife, isn't true?"

"She should watch her tongue around her husband. The way she hangs bits of honey on her words, she must think she lives among fools."

The road parted at a copse of trees, opening a crevice of color. Silks and muslins fluttered in the wind. The air carried the voices of merchants and the smell of butchered meat, like iron and sweet wine.

He worried about being seen by someone he knew. What would his neighbors think of him, toting a colonial's food past the hungry mouths of his family?

"I don't understand what it is on this earth that moves her," Mary said. "In my short time, I've seen her suffer with pains only another woman could know. There was no one for her but me. I've seen her tear at herself with worry for the next farthing for taxes. And now this. These casks while her husband withers. No one for me to tell but you. It's a funny sort of world, I'll say that. Who are you to me, but someone to pass by?"

The market was a heady swirl of cultures and tongues. Mary led him through the Indian-run stalls of spices and artisan offerings. They went to the colonial area instead. Underclass British maintained wooden stalls of vegetables, meats, fish and imported textiles from London. Women's fashion fought for space with slaughtered lambs, tallow candles and papers bringing news of the crown.

Other servants gathered around the butchers' offerings. The maids were younger than Mary, and not as severely bent by their work. They milled around the stalls of the apprentices, sinewy boys who wielded their cleavers against cavities of marbled meat and cages of bone.

Flirtation sparked from servant to servant. Giggles rippled like windblown leaves when one of the boys offered cuttings of lamb fat in exchange for a kiss.

Mary pushed past the milling girls to the front of the largest stall. "The Colebrooks have an order."

A powerfully built Britisher, his hair as bursting with red as the carcasses strewn at his feet, scraped his cutting table clean of innards. Bloody remains clotted on the sawdusted ground. "No more credit for your house," he told Mary.

The other servants hushed.

"The madam has a list." Mary handed a slip of paper to the butcher. She held her bucket up expectantly.

"Show me money or move out of the way. I'll not go without payment another month. A Director's family, broke as beggars. Shame."

One of the servant girls approached very cautiously, her eyes on the ground. "I work in the Trothers' house. Their hearts are good, and I know they would not object to a kindness."

Mary's hand swooped out of the air, snapping the girl's head and filling her eyes with shallow pools. "My house doesn't need your charity. Now let me get back to bartering. Maybe watching'll teach you what it means to drive a bargain. Don't slander us again."

The girl retreated in tears. Her fellow maids put comforting arms around her.

"Give me your rupees," Mary said to Eligius in his tongue.

He shook his head.

"Give them here or the Colebrooks go hungry. There's the matter of a sick old man and a child who need not miss another supper."

"I know what it means to starve."

"To be a Britisher and starve in plain sight of your neighbors, there's something you don't know. It's not our place to go without."

Eligius put his pail down. He expected the next slap was his and didn't want the embarrassment of dropping his servant's tool like a maid. "Should the memsa'ab need money, she can find a roof to patch, like me."

Mary's eyes narrowed. She fished into her pocket and brought out a small palmful of coins. "The list," she told the butcher.

"I'll give you only what this buys. Tell your madam her credit is done."

When he finished with them, their pails held stringy cuts

of goat meat, bony oxtail, and some fat for cooking. Still, Mary strode away from the marketplace as if toting a feast.

"Is this what becomes of me?" Eligius shouted at her. The smell of sun-grayed meat gathered around him. "I do servant's work so that you try to steal from me?"

"Had that been you in my place, forced to bargain with nothing in your pocket, would you be taking a servant's pity?"

"It isn't pity to help a neighbor. It is custom in my village."

"Your ways have no place. They'd bring shame on your employers, and that's the thing to avoid at all costs. Maybe pity's more acceptable when it's passed between the pitiable, but there's the matter of standing to consider here."

A fringed surrey passed by. Mary bowed her head until it was well up the road. "Almost a week I've known you," she said, "and all I've seen is defiance. Not a word of the servant who came before you in another man's house. Should I be blaming the quiet minds you're all said to possess, or are you just forgetting that I knew your father before these Colebrooks arrived?"

They were near the port. The Galle Face stood over the trees, its parapets swept by low clouds.

"Swaran served his sahib loyally," Mary said, "and suffered every indignity with restraint. He was exactly what he was supposed to be. He carried the sahib's children like they were his and took reading lessons with them, like a child. Never did he mention you or your mother. Once we shared some ale and he spouted nonsense about making laws like the Directors. Even that foolishness didn't soften the house in his favor. He was still expected to bow. Maybe he didn't deserve what he got, but there's a lesson all the same. You and me and everyone like us, we don't make a mark on this country."

A terrible heat gripped Eligius' heart.

"That's what it is to serve," Mary told him, "and above all, to serve her. Her casks and paper and godly designs. This is your life now, and what's there to do about it? If you walk away, you'll end up in the fields or with the men who leave their families at night and talk about trouble they don't have the strength to make. If you stay on at Dimbola, well, I wager it'll be the same for you. Why worry about the loss of a few rupees when there are such things to think of? Be about the business of getting what you can. The world is a wide window if you've got the courage."

They left the dried mud road for the paved streets of Port Colombo. Colonials passed them on either side with children in hand. Servants followed dutifully behind, carrying the day's shopping in heavy bags. The poor sat under the shade of jackfruit trees, waiting for alms to be tossed from the hansoms that rolled solemnly by.

"Learn this route," Mary told him. "It'll ingratiate you."

She crossed Chatham Street to the Galle Face. Its iron doors were open. She paused in the threshold of the church and bowed her head. This gesture seemed a world away from the ser-vility she'd shown the passing carriage. She appeared chastened.

A cloud of perfumed air as biting as crushed clove emanated from the open doorway. Rows of benches stretched into a murky fog of shadow and soft candlelight. The flickering lights were as innumerable as the stars breaking the night above the lion's mouth. Those who were seated in the rows – maybe one hundred, but far too few to fill the church – raised their voices at the behest of a man holding a cup of shimmering silver. Their tune was foreign but lovely, and somehow sad.

"Bow your head," Mary whispered shrilly. "She sees you."

The memsa'ab and her children sat with Ault in one of the rearmost rows. They'd turned in their places and were look-ing at him as if they'd never laid eyes on him before. Their bodies were aflame with the midday sun streaming through a stained glass fresco that filled the rear wall. It was of a woman. Her robes were held aloft by serving children. A ring of white light glowed above her head. The baby in her arms wanted it; its chubby hand sought it, perhaps to teethe on it the way Gita chewed on the charms adorning his mother's mourning sari. That the babe had its own light seemed not to matter.

The sun carried the woman to every corner of the church. Her colors bled across the faces of the faithful. Her garment, indigo where the light streamed through, lay over Ewen. Her skin became the gold in Julia's hair.

Catherine sat in darkness. The light passing through the frescoed child fell at her feet. Where she was, where the other Directors' wives and colonials far from home were, was a prayer house. The world was meant to be cut away from here. Pared down to the one thing. Money. Influence. Health. Love.

Something once within her had come undone since the Cape. Its absence had oddly multiplied matters. She could no longer reduce the world to the thing she needed.

The priest raised a cross into the dust-flecked air. Suddenly the church became the floor of the Court foyer, a canvas on which stars danced.

"Come on, then," Mary said. "We'd better be getting this meat home before the sun spoils it any further."

That night, Mary cooked the rancidness out of the meat by impaling it and holding it above the fire until it charred, then boiling it with parsnips and heavy pepper. The memsa'ab scolded her by name every time she and her children sneezed, while Charles laughed.

Their voices followed Eligius through the corridors where he sought refuge away from them. There was something terribly tedious about being forgotten at the end of a long hall, listening to the cacophony of a strange family. A servant, bemoaning a servant's life.

The light fell away as Mary snuffed out the gas lamps to save her employers' lungs. Ewen's whimpering faded over the minutes – a child's sleep that he would never again know.

He stared at the painting of the winged boy and tried to imagine him alive with light, like the woman of glass. He couldn't. He told himself that he might have been able to in another time, but that sort of sight was lost to him now.

Canvases

SHRIKES FOUGHT IN THE MORNING SKY. THEY PLUNGED
towards Holland House, then pinwheeled impossibly upwards
on drafts of agitated air.

Amma would call it a portent, Eligius thought as he opened
the cottage door to continue his repairs. Perhaps it was.
Perhaps there were those who could perceive life's most obscure
operations where he could not.

He opened the cottage door to continue his repairs. Julia
stood inside, as if she'd been waiting for him to find her. Next
to her was a table she had pulled to the center of the room, with
paper and quills fanned over its surface. A painting leaned
against it, facing the door. It depicted her, but younger, maybe
twelve or thirteen. In it she was dressed in a simple frock of rose,
sashed at the waist. A child's amused defiance played across
her lips. Something pleased her. The corners of her mouth
curved impishly out. Her right hand brushed her cheek. Her left
clutched at a necklace of beads dangling down to her belly.

"I take it out from time to time," she said. "It was painted
almost three years ago, on the eve of Sir John Holland's travels
to map the skies. His son George joined the voyage as a cartogra-
pher and portraitist. Before they departed, all George did was
paint. I sat in his studio at the Maclear residence in the Cape.
The scientist was taken with the skies, the painter with me, and
others. You've seen his work in our halls."

He endured her recitation of strange places and privileged

pursuits. These colonials were always dangling bait, relishing the opportunity to sigh their sighs and explain things.

She brushed a bit of dirt from the heavy frame. "I watched him paint during the day. At night everyone debated God and man. There was the man of science, this man my mother had only just become acquainted with while my father was off with his laws. Here, actually. Sir John saw the stars as real and fixed, and my mother listened to him as if he knew. She wanted certainty, I suppose. She spoke of God, in the way she should have spoken of my father. As someone she hoped would come back. None of it matters. The world, the parts I could and could not see, had come to me in the Cape. I couldn't be this girl in the painting anymore."

"Please," Eligius said. "I should not see this, or hear of these things."

"Why should any of this bother you?"

He didn't answer. The version of her in the painting could remain a girl, touching young skin that would never wrinkle, never bleed, and she would never not smile, never not be beautiful; she would deny time. He resented the girl before him. She would never know what it was, to be changed in an instant. She bemoaned trifles and conversation; no gunshots would ever fold her life onto itself.

"This is why you work on this cottage." Julia draped a cloth over the painting. "The scientist and young master George Wynfield are crossing the ocean, back to Ceylon. Sir John is to reside here until he completes his star map insofar as these skies are captured. And George, I expect, will not be a stranger. Maybe then there will be some life in Dimbola. Perhaps he will paint me again and show me around the world. He writes to me and tells me lovely things. I know he wants to take me away with him. My father and the governor have spoken of our marriage as if it is certainty itself. Perhaps I'll allow it. I should like at least something of me to leave here and become more than I am."

"If you wished to go elsewhere, would you be allowed to?"

She was quiet for a time and he waited. He could not hear the birds anymore. Perhaps they had settled their matter as animals did, and one of them had fallen to earth.

"I've seen what the departure of a child does," she said. "The madness of farewells. That's what my mother calls it. No, I could never ask it of her."

Outside, a carriage with curtained windows and brass trim pulled to the gate. A man in a suit and fine tall hat climbed down to open the carriage doors. Governor Wynfield stepped out, followed by his wife. Catherine and Charles met them at the gate. They began to walk together, toward Holland House.

"Take that bauble off," Julia said hastily said. "It was a gift from the Wynfield son to me. He told me of its birth in Venice. They shouldn't see you with it."

The ease with which she ordered him, as if nothing of him were of consequence, angered him. He tugged the bauble free and set it down atop the stack of paper.

She selected a feather quill and placed it over the bauble as Catherine and Charles stepped through the door, followed by the Wynfields. "Young Julia." Governor Wynfield took her hand and kissed it. "Every season you grow more radiant. Womanhood becomes you. Does it not, Rebecca?"

"It's rather early to tell," Lady Wynfield said.

"Can you not picture it?" Catherine walked to the far wall of Holland House and paced off its expanse. "People will come from all over to see Sir John's work, and your son's."

"And yours, I see." The governor paused before the image of the Court. "I should hardly see the point, honestly. Of what use is this, Catherine?"

"What better use of me could there be but to unify the works of God and man?"

The governor brought forth a rolled parchment and handed it to Charles. A rash of red appeared above Charles' collar as he glanced over it.

"I will be presenting this to the Court of Proprietors," Wynfield said. "I anticipate your assistance, of course."

"When?" Charles asked.

"In due time."

"I wish to review it with you. To be prepared."

"Now is the time to celebrate your wife's grand vision, and your daughter's artistry."

"Then I'll retire to my study and give it the attention it merits."

"I'll take you." Mary led him through the door.

"You are too kind," Catherine told Wynfield, "to encourage our artistic aspirations. Julia's, particularly."

"Can we not remember a time when we were as passionate about childish things? It is precious to behold. And then it is relinquished in favor of children and caring for a home. Let her enjoy these moments while she can."

"Or perhaps she shall be like her mother, eh? Unable to stop until she achieves something beyond that which is permitted her in the world of men."

"I would regret that, madam." He ran his finger across the image of the Court. "To embarrass your husband is not what a good mother inspires in her child. She inspires piety. Devotion to her children. She lives her life for others and leaves her interior musings to maids and diaries. A woman's security is her husband's standing. When that collapses, a woman learns that charity flows most freely to those who have abided by this man's world."

Jousting like this with her husband's superior, their antagonism palpable beneath the surface of civil discourse exchanged with the grace of a calling card on a silver tray, was a mistake. An indulgence that could be visited upon Charles.

She drew a breath. "I am a lucky woman, to be guided by learned men."

"Julia returns. Enough of this."

Julia entered with an armful of pages. She laid them on the

table. The paper shone in the sunlight. Its surface was roughened, like sand.

Wynfield stood close to her as she read from them. Catherine stared at the pages too, but there was disturbance in her eyes. Eligius had seen his own mother gaze at Gita that way, when her coughing became a wretched thunder in her small body.

She summoned Eligius to her side and whispered in his ear. "It is an embarrassment to me that this house is in such a state. Work faster, or I will have no choice but to find someone who can."

Sunlight poured through the open roof, washing over the quills, the paper, over Catherine and Julia and the governor. It made them things of considerable beauty, worthy of the Galle Face.

He stormed off to scrounge up whatever wood might yet have gone unfound. Toting the material to the top of Holland House, he began hammering with reckless defiance.

Watching him, Catherine regretted her words. Wynfield's dismissive arrogance, Julia's casual trespass; the boy had received what she could not loose upon them. It was no more her place to say what she thought than it was Eligius'. Her anger would have to turn elsewhere.

So be it, she thought. Anger drives the birth of all invention. Even God was born of fury at cold, at death, at what was always lost.

BY EVENING, ELIGIUS' back and arms had become raw from the sun. He'd labored until it grew too dark to see where the nails should be placed.

Another carriage pulled up to the gate in the fading light. "How they work you!" Ault called to him. "Come, fetch your mistress' post. Your memsahib will want to see this, no doubt."

Eligius found Catherine in the dining room, eating alone. Ewen, spent from his play, slept on the floor beneath his chair, an untouched dinner plate on the table.

The boy's scraps will come to me, Eligius thought as he handed the package over.

Catherine tore it open and laid its contents on the table. "We have little time," she said.

> *I enclose specimens of chemical novelty. Cotton, with the deathly attributes of gunpowder owing to a fascinating mix of nitrates, and collodion – a medical salve, and all that holds the guncotton's volatility still. The eternal stalemate between life and death, and in such simple vessels. Imagine! Their uses are as yet unclear, but what fun I've had at their expense.*
>
> *We embark tomorrow for Ceylon. Arriving two months. Such sights to show you. John Holland.*

"By the date of this post," she said, "our guests arrive in little more than a month. You see the paper this is written on? Is the rest of it still in Holland House?"

"The young miss had me take the paper there. I think she was to use it for writing."

"Fetch it. I'll deal with her later. This is not ordinary paper. It is of science."

"Don't be angry." Julia stood in the entryway to the dining room. "I only wished to show the governor how far I've come in my writing. Did I hear that Sir John is close?"

"Do not disturb my materials again. Do you understand?"

"Yes, mother."

"And your passages? I believe you were to start Corinthians tonight."

"I will."

"Come read it to me here. I feel for something gracious. Eligius, do as I have asked you."

He retrieved the paper and quills. On the walk back, he saw something on the top page. A shadow that didn't move when he removed the quill and the bauble.

He put the paper down on the dining room table for the

memsa'ab to see. She picked up the sheet and studied it. "Julia, to bed with you."

"Mother, it is early yet and I haven't finished."

"Now, girl."

Julia gathered up the bauble without a word. When she was gone, Catherine held a quill up to the shadow. It was as if the feather rested alongside its black self. The size and detail were perfect. When she took the quill away, its shadow remained in the fibrous weave of the paper.

"Show me where it was," she said.

He did. Standing in Holland House, regarding the table, then the walls, and the stars through the open holes in the ceiling, Catherine murmured to herself. Such joy in her eyes.

She told Eligius to take the image and keep it hidden under his meager straw mattress, protected by an old cutting board from Mary's pantry. "Tomorrow is Sunday. Your day to be with your family. On Monday, great work begins. Do you see the importance?"

He nodded, uncertain of this shadow now to reside under his sleep.

"You have been touched. It may not be a moment the world will ever know of, but you are different now than you were even a moment ago."

"Perhaps there is a better place to hide it than with me."

"You're afraid of it."

No, he wanted to say. I am afraid of who made it.

"No one will disturb it here because a servant's quarters are not to be approached by proper ladies and gentlemen unless there is theft. Do you see?"

He said nothing. She left him alone in its presence.

Deep in the night, he awoke from a fitful sleep to find Julia standing in his doorway. A candle illuminated the bauble around her neck. "I offer you a chance to ask for it back."

He shook his head. Her candle threw shadows against his

wall and against himself. A seductive fear gripped him that they would remain.

"What a strange, sad boy you are." She left the necklace on his table, then took her light down the hall.

Mendhi

THE CHIMING OF LITTLE BELLS STARTLED HIM. FOUR rupees tumbled down on him from Mary's hand. They spun to a halt next to his mat while she walked briskly away. He wondered if she'd seen the bauble Julia had left so openly.

He bought dosai at the port bazaar before completing the trek to Matara where his mother cooked and fed him. She tore a dosa into bits for Gita. "Tell me more of these people."

"They have a rug. Very big, but it's the only one they have. Their maid says they require her to move it whenever the sun lays on it too long for fear that it will fade. And the lamps give off smoke and grease."

He felt terribly weary. He wanted his mother to just know what he'd seen in only a week's time. He didn't want to have to speak, and what could he say? Hope of survival lay with him now. He had no choice but to abide in that house, where a shadow that didn't need light to live awaited his return.

The sight of the altar where Sudarma prayed for rupees to fall from the clouds seemed sad to him now. "The house they worship in," he said, "is bigger than any temple I've ever seen. It's like the light is part of its walls. Come see it with me."

"We've no need for these places." She mumbled some words to Lakshmi.

"What of Chandrak? Has he brought you anything? What do people say about us?"

"Don't let your head be turned working for the Britishers."

She stroked Gita's hair. "I see little of him. He is with men at night. They quiet down when anyone walks by. Three more of our neighbors awoke to the sheets on their doors. They say they won't leave." She tore her own food into smaller bits but didn't eat. "Serve these colonials well. Perhaps they will show you the door to a better life. For you, at least."

"They hold nothing for me. They're colonials."

She cut him off with a swat that was not meant to touch him. Her hand sliced through the air. "Do not be like these idle men, chattering about the British while their wives crush palm for a drop of lamp oil. When I grieve, I do it quietly and alone. No one drank with me when Swaran died. I don't need like men do."

He waited for her to stop trembling. The light shrank away.

"I dreamt of you last night." She took Gita in her arms. The child coughed gently into the folds of her breasts. "When I boiled your tunic to clean it of the colonials' demands on you, I heard the words of other countries. Fat clouds of steam hissed from your pockets like the long pipes of ships crossing the ocean. These things I see, they'll find you. It's as I told you. You will not always be here."

"I will never leave you," he said.

She hummed softly. Gita stared at him, at his eyes, as if expecting to find something there.

HE HAD JUST begun to dream when his mother woke him and brought him to the door. Men and boys waited in the street. Their bodies came alive with firelight.

"Come outside," Chandrak told him.

Eligius recognized one of the men. I am Ceylon, he'd chanted at the Court, his whip hand and the moans of the masses rising together. Tell them. I am Ceylon.

Sudarma cradled Gita in the hut doorway. He understood she could not help him. To be a man, he had to discover his place among the landscape of men's eyes and mothers' arms wrapped around their babies. Anyone reading a map was inevitably alone, in a foreign place.

Lakhan, a neighbor, exited his hut with his sobbing wife draped across his shoulders. He shook her free. She fell anguished to the dirt, a crumpled dove clutching a wadded paper. "A man tells you to go with him and you go! Where will he be when the soldiers throw us out like garbage?"

Eligius didn't need to see the paper to know what it said. Soon there would be clothes and pots in the street, and another family would be driven away from their lives. Before long, the soldiers would hammer a nail to the wall of his hut.

The men followed Chandrak to the clearing. No fire; the soldiers' patrols had increased. In the dark there was talk of Matara's men, and Devampiya's, and others. Who would come soon, who continued to place their trust in the colonials' grace. They spoke in insular fragments that Eligius couldn't understand, that traced back to other nights and other hushed meetings.

Men brought forth their sons and made them stand side-by-side. Chandrak led Eligius to the front and asked him to set an example for the other dusk outlines of boys. "Tell us what they have," Chandrak said, "that may be of value."

Heads nodded, sons after their fathers.

"Books." Eligius dropped his gaze so none would sense the flowers of fear opening in his veins. "Casks of salt. They have little."

"He lies." A man, not of Matara. Angry as only a stranger could be.

Chandrak put himself between the men and Eligius. "Are you protecting them?" Chandrak asked him in a low voice. "Don't put yourself at risk for them."

"I'm not."

"Just something, to secure your place here."

"But they don't seem like other colonials. Their things are old."

"Your father watches you always." He turned to address the

other men. "So here is what we must do. To be sure of this boy, we will go to their home. Tonight. Who is there, after all, but a feeble old man and women?"

Other boys spoke up about what they'd seen while working the docks and the fields. They recited the keepsakes that next time they would take. The rings and pocketwatches and carriage headposts that gleamed when the light caught them and made them precious.

Eligius thought hard of the Colebrooks' halls, the rheumy study and the space where he'd seen things that could be carried, but what value did they have to anyone else?

He thought of Catherine. She was a stern mistress but she'd paid as promised, and she'd captured some sort of otherness from the secret place in the world where such things hid. That meant something.

He thought of Julia in the gazebo, writing and smiling at nothing he could see. Her face forced the words from him.

"I know a place. Their church. The Galle Face, at the port. I saw inside."

He listened to their voices, to the scuttle of leaves and dirt beneath his feet, to the glide of animals across the boughs. He waited to see what manner of thing he had just brought into the world.

Chandrak shifted his weight off of his left side. He stared. Then he smiled at Eligius.

It was done.

THEY INSTRUCTED HIM to keep his eyes on the port road. Another boy watched the trees for colonials or soldiers. The sound of the church lock crumbling under Chandrak's brick seemed like thunder. Eligius exchanged terrified looks with the boy.

The church doors opened and the men scurried inside in knots of hunched backs and grasping hands. Some of them emerged immediately, bearing crosses, cups, pillows of blood velvet, and satchels of the colonials' incense.

There are rooms inside, he heard one man say. There must be children because look what I found.

The other boy accepted his father's gift, courtesy of the now-absent children. A doll with pitch eyes, its shell face cavitied by too much salt air. Take it to Sonia, the man said. They walked into the trees together.

"Here."

Chandrak held something out to him. "This is not to sell. It's for you to keep. Your mother told me of your games with light."

Eligius accepted the square of ornate glass. The size of Gretel's pages, it was framed in silver and laced with rivulets of red and blue. The rest of the glass woman and her baby emerged from the Galle Face in fragments, with broken piping trailing her pieces like roots. In moments she was gone.

He peered inside the church. A wound stood high in the wall where she'd been. Like the pane in his hands, it was lifeless in the dark. "When they see what we've done," he said, "they'll search every home."

"We don't have homes," Chandrak said. "We have mud huts. They'll find nothing. Come."

THEY MADE THEIR way back to Matara's outskirts, at the cliffs overlooking the sea. In the trees they lay what they'd taken on the ground. Some spoke of their desire to keep what they'd spirited away. Others wanted to sell their prizes at bazaar.

Chandrak told them to leave their hoard where it was.

Before dawn a man came. Corpulent and bearded, he conferred with Chandrak while appraising the pieces. They arrived at an accord, then shook hands and walked a short distance to a thicket of tangled tree limbs. In a moment they returned with two long boxes.

Chandrak raised his hands for quiet. "I've heard from Karampakam and Jaffna. All through the peninsula, we're becoming a movement, bandhutva. For this, we'll be blessed. If you take back what the colonials have taken from us, I promise you they'll fall."

He opened the first box and removed a rifle of silver and wood. Slipping a finger around the trigger, he aimed it at Eligius.

Eligius thought, *this is what appa saw*.

Chandrak shouldered the rifle like a soldier. "Now that you understand how well-placed you are, will you do this? Did Swaran raise a man as these others have?"

His hand came to Eligius' face. It sank deep, as if willing itself through to his heart. "Say yes, meri beta." There was little confidence in his voice. "I see it in you."

The bearded man approached. "You'll take care of this," he told Chandrak. "I see fear in his face. I think there are no men in your home. I think your good name will be swept out to sea."

"He's not my father," Eligius said.

There was more talk of buying powder and bullets, sending boys to other colonials' homes. The bearded man counseled them to steal what sold most readily. The most personal things. His voice was soothing. He laughed easily.

At home, Chandrak removed Eligius' tunic that held, somewhere, the ashen steam of ships. "Take anything you see in the Colebrooks' home," he said. "Bring it to me and we'll buy a rifle for our brothers. Few men have raised enough money, so we'll be considered important. Tomorrow, when the others see you, they must know I am a man who means to raise a man. They must see."

Eligius turned so that the banyan strip would lace his back. "Swaran, you are a part of history," Chandrak said, and wept.

The banyan's serrated edge fell. Soon Eligius' sight left him. His mother and Gita, awake now and cowering in the corner next to Lakshmi; all slipped below the surface of a warm, gathering dark. The beating became less of his flesh and more of sound and light. It slipped clouds beneath him and took him up through the holes in the hut roof. There was no pain. There was only a shadow of a feather in his hands. Its blackness seeped into him, weaving a stain of him into the walls of the world.

CATHERINE HEARD THE first cry well into the night. She was in the cottage, ministering over her latest attempt. A local girl, dark, diamonds for eyes and a boy's muscled shoulders. One of the many urchins who routinely came to the windows of passing carriages offering something forlorn and filthy for sale. A few rupees had purchased the girl's stillness over a long afternoon. Now the sotted paper yielded only a blot of dark space. Failure, again.

Wisps of silversalt had carried her off; she'd fallen asleep to the melody of her own breathing. The moaning infiltrated her dreams, of giving birth to a baby with a voice that twinned her own.

She awoke to the sound. It came from outside, like a whisper through the cottage walls.

Across the yard she spotted Eligius lying against Dimbola's gate. He could not speak to say how he had come through the jungle in his condition. It took her and Julia to carry him to his mat in the house.

He slept through the night and well into the next day, in a fever born of his beating. When he woke, Julia told him that he writhed as if in some kind of flight.

"Wynfield's soldiers are in your village," she said. "The church was ransacked last night. And your beating…"

He sucked in air, breaking the colors clouding his vision.

"My mother and I heard you in the night. You spoke of your father as if he was alive."

"Please. I don't want the soldiers to hurt my mother."

"It's done." Catherine stood in the doorway. "What happened to you ought have no place. It's savage. It cannot go unanswered."

He tried to sit up. The effort ignited a fire deep in his chest.

"I have lost yet more time. The roof remains a shambles. Is there wood? I can finish."

"You'll stay in bed. Let the other colonials drive their servants to the ground. But you'll not lay around idling away time." She placed a thick book on the mat at his feet. "I expect you to apply your heart to this. Tonight, I'll hear your thoughts on the passage I've marked."

Her fingers were red, like a maid's. She appeared as if she'd been scaling fish against rock, as his mother did at low tide. But his mother had never returned with her efforts still radiant upon her. She had never been touched by the madness slumbering under his mat.

"Julia, let him be. You too, Ewen."

Ewen rolled to his feet. He'd been lying still, pressed into the shadows enveloping the sleeping mat. "You never saw me." He giggled as he ran out of the room.

"Did you know about the Galle Face?" Julia asked. "Is that why you were beaten? For refusing to go?"

"I don't understand."

She lifted his blanket. The pane of glass lay against his thigh. "It was next to you when we found you. If you were a thief, you would have sold it."

She left him. He opened the bible the memsa'ab had given him. She'd circled a passage in soft charcoal. Fine black granules filled the separation between pages. Ecclesiastes. The word felt insurmountable. The rest of the passage chilled him.

When Catherine returned that evening, she asked him to read it aloud. Her lean face was near beautiful, with its fine cheekbones and high forehead. Her hair was wrapped demurely. Yet still there was something wild about her.

"I'm afraid," he said.

"I know you are. Do as I ask."

He opened the book. "Light is sweet, and it is pleasant to the eyes to see the sun. Even those who live many years should rejoice in it; yet let them remember that the days of darkness will be many."

She sat down next to his mat, on the floor like a child. "Its meaning?"

"Are the dark days here now?"

"To believe otherwise is vanity."

She reached fór the book. Now there was silver across her palms, embedded like stars. She had come to love the way it dusted her, like something from a child's wondrous dream. "The question that intrigues is how to hold the light higher, eh?"

Footsteps in the corridor interrupted her. The sa'ab's slow shuffle. "Is he awake?' Charles called. "How is it with him?"

"Better."

She lowered her voice to a conspirator's hushed whisper and read from the book. "Before the sun and the light and the moon and the stars are darkened, and the clouds return with the rain, and men are bent, and the breath returns to God who gave it."

This madness engulfed her. It slipped a crooked smile across her face and kept her from rising at her husband's approach.

"Julia tells me of her conviction that you are not a boy who would desecrate a church," she told him. "I can't say where this conviction comes from, but my daughter does not idly place her faith. Do not make a fool of her, or me."

"Are you reading to him?" Charles appeared in the doorway.

"No, my husband. I'm done for tonight."

"Well, he looks better. I'll say goodnight."

"As will I."

She had begun an education of his eyes; her shining hands had started it. Already she felt increasingly adrift from her known life, with only an Indian for company.

"Memsa'ab? I'm not afraid of reading. I'm afraid of everything changing."

"As am I. Perhaps we can find a way around that sad state."

She left him in a gray growing dark. It deepened with the hour. Gradually, the sounds of Mary's evening cleaning fell away. The clatter of dishes, the emptying of filthy water buckets into the yard outside his window, the strangely forlorn whisk of the rug being dragged to its morning spot. When all was still, he rose from his mat. His wounds had dried to taut seams in his skin.

The halls of the Colebrooks' home were quiet. It was as if the family became weightless at night. These people were nothing like the families in Matara. Even at a late, lonely hour, he always felt his village around him, like the stones Matara's mothers placed at the corners of their children's bedding to hold their babies down when the wind came in a flurry of fists against their huts.

He passed the watchful paintings on his way to the front of the house. At the window, he glanced outside and saw a figure at the gate. Chandrak's face shone in the moonlight. It glistened like the starlit trails left in the sand by molting crabs.

Eligius held himself very still. It's dark in here, he thought. The moon doesn't catch me; there are no holes in this roof. He cannot see me.

Chandrak remained at the gate a long time. Once, he picked up a rock as if he might hurl it. But he just held it, while gazing towards the faint light in Holland House.

Eligius glanced around the room for anything he could use as a weapon, should Chandrak come over the gate. It could only be the memsa'ab in the cottage, keeping company with her wood-legged beast.

When Chandrak finally left, Eligius crept outside. To his eyes, Chandrak had left the same black impression as, at that moment, lay under his mat. A mark on the air. But when he reached the gate, there was nothing.

The door to Holland House was ajar. Beyond it, pale light rippled as if disturbed by the breeze. He peered inside, careful to stay silent.

She sat on the floor, muttering to herself. She held a feather in one hand, the paper in the other.

A letter, he thought. From that man. Words, what to do.

She was trying to make it come again. Her hands were stained. In the available light he saw swirls of black atop her fingers.

Somewhere within, he thought, hides the name of this obsession she has betrothed herself to.

He went to the well and returned with a small cistern of water. Entering, he knelt beside her, took the feather from her hand, and began to rinse her skin of its stain. So much of it remained.

She was silent while he ministered to her with patient, careful fingers. "These shadows," he said. "To hold the fact of one, like the stone it came from. Nothing else matters to you."

Putting the letter down, she held her other hand out to him. "No," she said, marveling at the sound of it. Her blood set to words.

He tended to her. As flecks of never-born shade fell from her palm into the cistern, he wondered what became of such things as these, that came to the world broken or not at all, and stayed no longer than a breath.

A Boy Who Remains

REVEREND AULT SET DOWN HIS TEACUP SO MARY COULD refill it. "I'm told the soldiers have searched through the southern country and found no evidence to identify the perpetrators of the Galle Face's desecration."

Eligius hid his bruised face in the mid-day murk of Charles' shuttered study. There was some comfort to be found in the gloom that the memsa'ab always complained of. It reminded him of his hut in Matara. So little of the light found a way in.

"You left word with the villagers in Matara, then." Catherine raised her cup, sending Mary back to the scullery for the kettle and another muslin bag of tea. "Someone beat this boy terribly."

"I must report that I did not. There were no men in the village. Only women."

"Stephen," Charles said, "it's vitally important that you get word to Governor Wynfield and the other directors, that they are to come to me today. We have to discuss this. A fire such as this is slow to spread, but eventually it will."

That day, the Colebrooks found easy tasks for Eligius to do. He helped Mary cut cold pheasant for lunch, ground the bird's feathers down to a fine point so Julia might have some writing materials, cleaned the study floor while the sa'ab read a treatise on land rights that bore his name. They were tentative with him, and he thought that it was not all attributable to his injuries. Even Julia, who emerged from Holland House in the late afternoon and took her quills without a word, looked at him as if he were painful with light.

The full Court – nine men in all, ones he'd seen and some he had not – arrived at twilight to an inviting fire and trays of brandy in the study. "Stay near," Charles told him, "lest their glasses go unnoticed."

Of the directors present, most seemed aligned with the governor; they even sat on his side of the study. Two remained with Charles. One was older, rotund and pinched around his eyes. The other was a younger man, tall and thin, with a whippet's spastic alertness and a beard like dusted curtain cord.

Wynfield spoke first. "I have gone forward with my bill on the taxes to the provinces. It will come to a vote of the Court, then on to Parliament. I believe the roll favors me, my friends. I ask your support. Justice Newhope, I see you itch to speak."

The older director rose from his seat at Charles' side. "We've all heard of the havoc to the north, and it began with an exodus of the men. They bought arms and within weeks there were homes and trades ablaze. Trouble has found us. Should we now levy another property tax here in the southern country, upon men who could not meet the last one and show a penchant for outrage against the church of England? Is it not the height of irresponsibility to push them to their limit?"

"Surely Ceylon doesn't know of the occurrences so far north," Wynfield said. "Lack of communication plagues these people, but it can be a boon in such times. These are not related acts."

Charles leaned forward until he could peer out the study door. "Come here, Eligius."

Eligius brought a brandy snifter and stood in the doorway to the study. "Tell us," Charles said, "how long it takes you to walk to our gate from Matara."

"Less than half the night, sa'ab."

"It is not so much, then," Charles said, "to consider men trekking through the jungle, passing word to each village. Let me tell you my thoughts on this bill. Word will spread that our interests have been attacked in Jaffna, and now the port. A hike in taxes that they cannot bear that all the pawnbrokers in Madurai cannot fund? Governor, haven't we already given them reason enough to despise our presence?"

Their eyes drilled holes in the back of Eligius' head as he filled glasses and emptied pipe ashes into an urn.

"It is my wish," Wynfield said, "to avoid violence." He picked up a framed cartograph of Ceylon from Charles' desk. "But these men, these howling fools at the Court gates, stand on the precipice of a terrible day. Perhaps your servant can explain their conduct to me. Is this a holiday of some kind? Something for the men alone, that the villages should empty of them?"

Eligius remained quiet.

"Tell me, boy."

"It is not."

Charles clutched his heavy woolen coat about his body. It was as if he resided alone in a country of eternal cold. "Do you know where your fellows are, Eligius?"

He shook his head.

"If you know anything of the men of your village," Newhope said, "you must tell us."

"I was with my mother on your Sunday. The other men were still there with their sons."

"What were they doing?"

"Watching my beating."

"For what reason were you beaten?" Charles coughed, bringing a sodden handkerchief to his lips.

"No reason was given."

"There's been no end of trouble in the provinces," Wynfield said. "Men like these abandon their responsibilities to mere children. Or is there something else to their disappearance, boy?"

Eligius looked to Charles. The old man seemed intent on the map in Wynfield's hands.

"Hearing nothing to the contrary," Wynfield said, "I presume the actions of your fellows speak for you."

"Do you speak for all here?" Eligius asked.

"Don't be impudent," Charles said.

"Is this how servants conduct themselves in your house?" Wynfield asked. "Small wonder, your wife's distractions from her duties. I don't wish to see these walls continue to crumble around you, my friend."

"How dare you insult him in his ill health!" Crowell shouted.

"There's more to it than you know, sir."

Charles' eyes found his young servant in the corner. They filled briefly, then dried. "There is no need for that subject, Andrew. We are not speaking of me, but of the threat of violence swelling in this country."

"The subjects are linked, I'm afraid. A man of vigor controls his servants as well as his wife. He puts a firm oar in the water. Everything about you speaks of twilight at a time when our obligation to England tips the balance in favor of immediate and vigorous action here in Ceylon. A popular uprising gains traction and leads to rebellion. Commerce halts. Fields die. Taxes cease. To stop these incidents from becoming an issue, we must keep these people focused on working their fields and on paying their debts. Sad but true, it always falls to us."

Setting Charles' map down, he went to the door. "We are apart on so many things now, Charles. Have you noticed? Let us find common ground on at least this much. The affairs of her Majesty's colonies must be equal to their cost, and thus far we have much ground to cover. Her fleet, her trading company, her exports. India is a bride with an insufficient dowry."

He tucked the bill into the lining of his overcoat. "I've drafted an amendment to the Doctrine of Lapse. Where the absence of a feudal heir triggers the natives' forfeiture of villages now, we will broaden it to include villages where the men are missing and delinquent taxes continue. Parliament has responded favorably."

"I knew nothing of this," Charles said.

"It is a service we will provide to Ceylon. In a jungle-covered country like this, diseases of the most malignant character are harbored. Year after year they reap a pestilential harvest from this thinly scattered population. Cholera, dysentery, fever, and smallpox all appear in their turn and annually sweep whole villages away. Gentlemen, I ask you. Can we stand by and do nothing? I for one say no. I have seen enough of the moldering dead. If a village comprising two hundred able-bodied men is reduced by sickness to a population of fifty, can those left behind cultivate the same amount of land? No, gentlemen, it falls to us to clear it away and make something of it. These people have to adapt to us, not the other way around."

Wynfield rose to leave. His loyalists rose with him. "You have some time to study this as you wish. But not long, my friends. I expect your answer soon. This cannot wait."

"You have my word," Charles said as Newhope and Crowell stared at him.

"Excellent. My best to your wife and children. Please, have Catherine send her bill of needs to my staff for the celebration in honor of Holland. As sponsor of his voyage, it is only right. Let your maid walk through the market untroubled."

Eligius glared at Wynfield as he left. Charles waved him over and handed him an empty brandy snifter. "Watch yourself, boy. While you glare at one, another sees you and marks you for trouble. There is too much you don't know to be so impetuous at such a dangerous time."

"Why doesn't anyone believe me? I don't know where the men are."

"Your wounds are likely all that keep you from being arrested in their place. Now go about your work. Let us alone to talk this out."

Eligius left the study. How uneasy Newhope and Crowell appeared. How uncertain. He'd never seen a colonial without their attendant arrogance. These men breathed the same anxiety as the men of Matara did around their fires while their ranks thinned and the trees rang louder with new voices each night.

And the sa'ab; he looked ashamed and small. What could such men do to move the governor? Did they even want to? In the end it was just Indians losing their land. A common enough occurrence.

He left the study door slightly open. From the dining room, he heard enough to know that Charles was behaving irregularly in the eyes of his friends. Once there'd been a different man, said Crowell. Newhope reminded him that he was ill, not dead. Would he not rise to Ceylon's defense, as the man he once was?

Only when Newhope suggested that they contact the Court of Proprietors in London did Charles speak. He asked them to give him time in the same tone that he'd employed with the governor. A kind of prayer. "Let me study this in concurrence with the laws on the subject," Charles said. "Perhaps there are mechanisms we can employ."

Mary interrupted his eavesdropping. She handed him a bucket and mop. "Ewen took ill."

He went to Ewen's room, grateful for the task. It was better to sop up a boy's vomit than to hear these old men talk.

In the evening, Charles and Catherine asked him to sit in the dining room with the family. Mary remained in the kitchen, making it clear with her cacophony that she didn't appreciate a servant's elevation to the dining room while there was food set out on a tin in the scullery.

Catherine took her husband's hand. She asked Julia and Ewen to join in a prayer, for Eligius. "It is a sad thing," she said, "to be in the presence of someone who has never realized joy."

"My life doesn't have room for such thoughts, memsa'ab."

"I'm beginning to understand that, child."

"Tomorrow I want you to speak to the men of your village," Charles said. "The most influential among them. Whoever the others will listen to. They must stop whatever it is they're planning."

"I don't know of any plans, sa'ab."

"Don't play with me. I'll not be thought foolish by a simple servant. They talk of armed revolt. They are not to think of it. Not ever. Every crime, every Indian crime, from this point forward only lends credence to the notion that you're unfit to have a hand in governing your own country. Do you understand?"

"I do not."

"I would believe that from some people, but not you. There is all manner of notions you understand."

"How awful you make that sound," Catherine said. Charles fell silent. "Eligius, we British came here as friends to the Indian. We have so much to teach you. It is a fatherly hand we offer. But right now, my husband's is not the predominant view. You cannot maintain crops, yet we can. You cannot rise above poverty and sickness, yet we can. This is what is said of you. They expect you to answer these charges with work, industriousness, persever-ance. If your people respond with thuggishness and insolence instead of reason, as your father tried to do, what is Charles to say on your behalf?"

"My father." He hated the look on her face. Her sympathy enraged him.

"He was a reasonable fellow," Charles said. "I could tell. A good man. He had my respect."

"My father came to court that day because there was a man who he thought would listen. I know it was you."

"Then I make the same point to you that I made to your father. Act from your better nature."

"So that you will respect me," Eligius said, "when you remember me."

He saw the color rise in the old lion's cheeks, bringing red relief to the weary terrain of his face.

Catherine's hand touched her husband's. "You will make your own way. Whether it is a course that allows you to remain with us is your choice. But I've seen enough of you to know that the hate already visited upon you at so young an age has not bred hate within you. Don't give in to it now. Will you think on this?"

"Yes, memsa'ab."

"You may go," she said softly. "Tell Ewen I have need of him in Holland House."

He did as he was told, with the sounds of their whispers in his ears. They were discussing him. Whether he ought to remain.

He passed the sa'ab's study. The sa'ab's map of Ceylon sat on the desk.

In a few days' time he would return to Matara. Chandrak would come from wherever he and the others were, to see what amount of manhood grew in a week. Maybe there would be a fresh banyan strip dangling against Chandrak's withered side.

He put the map in his room, under his blanket, then sat next to its dismal hump and wept.

IN THE STUDY, Catherine blew on the embers in the hearth. They rose to her efforts, glowing a deep cerise.

"I believe him," she said.

"Do you have any understanding, Catherine? Any appreciation for my position on the Court? What if he lies? How shall it affect Andrew's opinion of me? Of my dependability? My very loyalty to the Crown turns on the unproven word of an Indian boy whose father died on the Court's very ground. Despite your arrogant belief that nothing is beyond your perception, you don't know him."

She came and sat at his feet. When he'd courted her, it was this posture that she'd selected to portray acquiescence with his proposal of marriage. She remembered how it had softened him then and over the years, to have her at his feet. She wondered if he ever recalled days before she wore his ring, when she was still someone who could speak a word and send him back into the world with no love.

"I have known you through many different lives," she said gently. "Well off. Struggling, as we may be now. Understand that I do not inquire nor worry. You are a man above other men, and I am made confident when I but look at you."

She waited. If he'd quieted within himself, she could not tell.

"I have never known you to be concerned with the opinions of others. You determine the right and true course and that is that. What is it about this man, governor though he may be, that unsettles you?"

"I am neither unsettled nor a man who is questioned by his wife. Now tell me, Catherine. What is it in the correspondence with a distant man and the services of an Indian boy that emboldens you? You spend more time considering them than me."

She rose. The simple act turned the air in the study. "I have watched you for far too long, Charles. Recall that I have attended to your duties as a barrister as any clerk. I have seen you argue before judge and jurist and I know when you have the facts at your side. When you redden in the face and growl, you have none. The nature of my correspondence with Sir John has not changed since last you cut me for it. The matter of his science interests me. There is no more to it than that."

"And Eligius?"

Angry though she was, she could not readily answer her husband's question. Why believe an Indian boy? What could she know of him that might be relied upon by a man of letters and laws? Nothing. Eligius was born of bruises and poverty. He stood in two worlds and resided in neither.

He was, too, a boy who had left a shadow, and a boy who having seen a shadow, brought it to her. He had not turned away. Most men would find no meaning in a black stain. They would see no grace in the vestiges left on their hands.

Charles waited for her response. Holland House beckoned. Sir John had written of a new chemical combination. New proportions, a longer time open in the aperture.

Who is Eligius, she thought. I think I know who he is not. He is not a boy who could watch pieces of time fall from me into a cistern of water and set fire to it all.

"Eligius," she said, "is a boy who remains in the mind."

She left her husband for Holland House.

THEY SPOKE OF him through the night. Julia told him this as he lay on his mat. "My mother will have a ladies' lunch and ask for money for you."

"What is it that I'm expected to say, I wonder."

"Show gratitude."

"If your parents really wish to help, more rupees. A doctor for my sister. Walls for my mother's house. I don't know what to do with women's prayers for my welfare."

"This lament is tiresome. You're able, so do for yourself. You seem terribly confident in my father's empathy, but I advise you against it, no matter the past. He can turn. The governor's favor is more important to him. As is my mother's, though he'll never admit it."

She was enjoying this, he thought. But she was right. He needed to relinquish pride. One with nothing but mud and millet had no claim to that luxury. His life and the lives of his sister and mother depended on his ability not to give in to the demons whispering in his ear, that he was worth more than the clothes on his back, that learning their words lifted his price. He had no worth. None of them did.

"I'm sorry," he said.

"I expected more of an argument. Perhaps next time. For now, help me write."

"I don't know how to help you."

"Carry my supplies. Make a fire in the gazebo pit. Talk to me."

"What shall I talk about, young memsa'ab?"

She thought about this. "I should like to hear about where you live. How it looks. And I want you to wear the glass I gave you. Unless you've sold it."

He held up the bauble around his neck. This pleased her.

She took him to Holland House and showed him what she'd been working on. A sheaf of her mother's papers of modest thickness. She'd washed them lightly with boiled water and dried them in the sun that spilled in through the roof. "To lend character," she told him as he carried her things to the gazebo. "Until I can lend character with my own hand."

He made a compost of dry palm fronds in the shallow pit dug at the gazebo's center. It would give off smoke, so he situated Julia's work downwind. "How will you know when you're able to lend character?"

"I'll just know. Or maybe I won't. Who can say?"

"Then why do this? Why not just look at a thing?"

She was quiet for a time. He wondered if he had offended her.

"I don't agree with most of what my mother does," she finally said. "She is not what an English-bred woman is supposed to be. She upstages her husband and chases after her own ends to his exclusion. I fear that this new passion of hers will be our undoing, yet she is tireless. I know there's something of her in me."

Goosebumps rose on her arms. He added a bit of scrap wood to the fire, filling the gazebo with a nutty cloud that reminded him of Diwali.

She rubbed her hands together. "She may yet matter despite it all. What a thing, for a woman to matter, eh?"

"That creature in the cottage. It is for that purpose. To matter."

"The Court was her earliest effort. A poor one. She has not puzzled out how to paint with light."

He thought of the feather's shadow.

"Perhaps she's mad," Julia sighed. "Spending us into poverty and ridicule just to chase God. To punish him, I suppose."

"I don't understand."

"How would you punish the colonials?"

He couldn't conceal his shock. "I shouldn't discuss such a thing."

"Listen to what I'm discussing."

"You can be free with your words."

"To really punish, you don't fight. You don't steal. You show your betters that you can do what they can do."

The fire crackled, sending a hot shower of stars to the gazebo's ceiling. Sparks lingered there before falling to the earth and fading like loose grains of sunset.

"My mother is right about this much," Julia said. "I know what it is to live with someone who has never realized joy. It is a hard thing."

She hadn't written so much as a stroke. Yet she wielded her dry quill against the silver-grained paper, weaving unseeable words.

"It is not me," Eligius said. "She spoke of someone else, perhaps."

"I know." Her quill strokes grew softer and slower. She came to the end. "My father."

She was no ordinary female, any more than her mother. They were both capable of outrageous conduct far outside their station. Yet there was pain at the core of them, even as they dallied with men and with the mechanisms of mysteries like the spider and the written word.

He poked at the fire, rustling up more sparks. Their flight made her smile. "I want to write about them," she said. "They look like stars."

He held up a small pot of ink. "Dip your quill."

"Are you telling me what to do? You are not the right ilk of man."

"Please."

She flicked the quill tip across the top of the black ink, then held it up. It sparkled in the fire.

"Now listen while I tell you what you can see of my world from the door of my hut."

He closed his eyes and waited until his squalid servant quarters were gone and Dimbola was gone, and the men of the Court and the men spitting rage at the Court gates, and the men at the fire and the man who lay with his mother and left his mark in banyan-infused blood, all gone. Only the stars, like embers that stopped rising and remained.

She waited with no complaints. Unusual, he thought, for a Britisher. In time she even wrote, in counterpoint to his voice.

IN THE DAYS following his time in the gazebo with the young memsa'ab, Mary remained at a further distance from everyone. She came when called and fulfilled all of her responsibilities, but her moods varied as wildly as Ceylon's weather. One day she was talkative, the next distant and hostile, the next wounded. Between the two servants only she spoke freely, and only occasionally. Nothing presaged her bouts of openness. They came like cloudbursts.

She betrayed emotion only once. He found her weeping softly in the hall leading to the servants' rooms. Her room was just to the right of his, yet she rarely slept there. She preferred an unadorned hutch next to the kitchen. It was unusual to find her in this part of the house.

"Don't," she said when he asked her what was wrong. Her first words to him in days, and her last for days more.

It was becoming harder to hide Julia's preference for his company. At night, she would gather her writing utensils and wait for him in the gazebo. He wondered if this was at the heart of Mary's melancholy. She had been replaced.

As the week wore on, his thoughts turned to Chandrak and the others, and by Saturday his stomach was knotted so tightly he fell short of breath. The options were dismal. He could go home with nothing but a servant's wages and face the men and their sons, or he could steal and face never returning to Dimbola, where his life consisted of errands to the post ship, to the market, to the roof of Holland House, days in the employ of a man who watched his father fail and die, nights spent sitting like a man, listening to the whisper of a girl's quill across parchment paper while the true beating heart of Dimbola labored in the dim light of the cottage, to best her god.

That Saturday he was working alongside Mary in the

kitchen when Ewen ran by. A bit of light glinted on the boy's cheek. He was crying. His sobs echoed down the corridor.

Mary dropped her knife and crossed herself when Catherine came to the door and demanded that Eligius accompany her. "I must send word."

Her face, Eligius thought. She's trembling with joy.

After laboring over a sheet of her glistening paper, she gave the letter to him and told him to seal it with candle wax. She could not touch it, she explained, and held up her hands to him. Not without staining it.

The marks had not looked like this before. Now, a discernible mendhi of light laced the skin of her palms.

He sealed the letter in the kitchen. It was addressed to Holland. *My good friend: You speak of improving the daguerreotype. Perfecting the salt print. Chemicals and processes. Today I put my hand to it. I held it. I have begun the journey to arresting beauty, forever. Catherine.*

"Post it," she said.

He made the journey to the port and back in six hours. By the time he returned to Dimbola, all he wanted to do was lie down and bring the morning on. Whatever happened on the morrow felt like someone else's cares. He could think only of Gita's cough and his beating scars. Maybe his mother would close his eyes that night with another story of billowing steam clouds and journeys across the sea.

There were footsteps in the hall, closing. Catherine came to the doorway. She held out her hands. The pale areas he'd seen before had smeared. "Look closely," she said. "I want you to. I want someone to. It is a wondrous thing. From now on, your labors will be restricted to Holland House. I have already informed Mary. She will not corrupt your time. I can't do this alone, and at the moment I seem to inspire no one save myself. But a boy such as you can't say no. You don't want to."

After she left he lay upon his mat and let the quiet settle

on him. Soon it was broken by muffled sobbing in the hall. He found Ewen tucked in a corner, his knees pulled up to his chin.

Eligius gave him a torn sheet of linen to wipe his tears. Ewen seized his hand. "Mama says she's going to make me stay still, but I said no. Was it me on her?"

"I don't understand."

"Like Hardy. Mama prayed if he could stay, but he couldn't. Now he's made of paint. Nothing else." He stood, letting the blanket fall from his quivering shoulders. "I'll show you."

Taking Eligius by the hand, Ewen led him to the painting of the angel bearing his own face. "That's Hardy."

"I thought it was of you. I thought you posed for your family friend."

"Hardy looked like me. After Mama asked God to let him stay, but he didn't."

"When did your brother leave?"

"When he was born. Mama said she's not asking God permission to keep us anymore. She's going to do it herself."

Outside, the wind stirred the tops of the palms ringing Dimbola. For a moment the house was alive with the whisperings of Ceylon, then fell quiet again.

"Are you staying?" Ewen asked.

"Tomorrow I go back to my village."

"But then you'll come back?"

Mary appeared at the end of the hall. She paused to watch them.

"I have to go to bed," Ewen said. He let go of Eligius' hand.

"My father left too," Eligius said.

"Did you make him a painting?"

"No."

"Did you get him on your skin?"

He thought of the memsa'ab's hands. "Such things don't happen."

"In there they do."

Ewen ran down the hall to Mary. She took him away.

Eligius waited until the corridors grew quiet before retrieving his diya. He crossed the yard to Holland House and closed the door. Dimbola was still. No one would see.

He lit his diya. Trays filled with shallow pools of water lined the wall. Little slicks of silver floated on their surfaces. A wood-framed square of the grainy paper rested against the spider's legs. Ripples marred its surface.

Whatever made the memsa'ab shake like a child and Ewen fear sitting still, he saw nothing of it here.

He examined the spider. Its legs were wooden poles, squared at the top to fit into a large box. Under the cloak he found a hole with a glass piece pushed into it.

Setting the flickering diya on the chair, he looked through the hole again. The hole changed the shape of the light, turned it, constricted it.

Another wooden frame lay hidden within the spider's box body. He slid it out. Holding the captured paper to the light, he saw vague, corporeal shapes that resembled eyes. A nose. A mouth. They could scarcely be seen, but he could tell they were not drawn, not sketched. The shadows Catherine communed with had touched the feather and stolen its soul. They'd made vapors of the Court lobby. Now they'd taken the barest memory of Ewen's face and pressed it into the fine particles of the paper.

What he'd seen on her hands, he saw now on his own skin. A fine dust of silver sand with inflections of life.

He ran swiftly through the black yard, past the smoking ghosts rising from the snuffed gas lamps and into his room. There he took the sa'ab's map from its hiding place. Carrying it back to the study, he set it down in its spot.

Mary was in the dining room, tidying up. Their eyes met briefly as he left the study empty-handed.

He hurried to his mat and huddled against the wall. Dawn always began at the far corner of this room, under the window. It would be nearly six when the light reached him and revealed his hand for whatever the night made of it. Then he would know whether he, too, had become a portrait. Nothing – not his flesh, not the dark of this house, could be thought of as empty. Not anymore.

The Canals and the Sea

IN THE MORNING, SHE MADE ELIGIUS A PART OF IT.

First, the water. Three full buckets brought from the sea. After the water, the silver nitrate crystals.

Eligius sifted the glistening sand. He listened to the names for these things. The sand, the glass, the beast itself. Camera. The memsa'ab called out the words from Holland's correspondence; each piece took its place.

Reading from Sir John's letter, she instructed Eligius through the process. She showed him how to immerse the paper in sea water, dry it over candles, then brush it on one side with the silver nitrate. All was completed in shadow, which she thought ironic. This man who lectured her from across the sea, hadn't he been the one to warn her against holding shadows for too long?

Lifting the paper to the light, she pronounced it acceptable, then slid it into a wooden frame. "Julia, come sit. It's time."

Julia watched their progress from Holland House's doorway. Her lace dress gathered in the air, then settled around her porcelain legs. The chair was no more than a few steps from her, yet she eyed it as if it were a distant point she'd been ordered to.

"No more of this baseless fear," Catherine told her daughter. "This is science, and a little faith. There is nothing of the devil at work. I will explain each thing I do. Will that finally calm you?"

"This nameless pursuit shouldn't be yours," Julia said. "It

is a man's avocation. If father isn't taking it up, it's not for us to do so."

"If it suits you to bow quietly, then do so. I see what Charles does not. I pray, where Charles considers and reasons. We differ. Perhaps you are more his child than mine. All the more reason for you to sit."

Julia did as she was told, grudgingly. She arranged her dress over her legs and stared vacantly at the wall behind the camera.

"When I'm ready, you will look as I require. Until then, have your sulk. Eligius, we place the paper into its frame, and the frame in turn into the camera. She lifted the cloak for him. "Come look."

He slipped under, entering darkness. Her hand joined him. It opened a small sliding door. "The aperture," she said. "Press your eye to it."

He did, and Julia was instantly in the dark with him. A familiarly arrogant girl with an imperious tilt to her head. It was as if she'd been made a sunlit painting of flesh.

Her eyes misted. Her hands fluttered every few seconds. She could not sit still as her mother told her.

She is afraid of becoming a shadow, he thought.

He took the bauble from around his neck, left the camera's cloak and let the bauble's string coil into her upturned palm. The glass momentarily shot through with veins of sun, passing them onto the skin of her arm in an emulsion of light. Its touch calmed her.

"Smile or don't smile," Catherine told Julia. "But don't move. Hold yourself still until I say otherwise. This will be a while."

"Yes, mother."

"Begin."

For an interminable time, Julia kept herself composed. Her hands folded demurely in her lap with the bauble for company. Its surface dangled bells of light onto her skin that moved with the sun.

While she sat, Catherine read from the letter. She spoke with wonderment of the circuitous path her daughter's image might follow. If all was well and ordained, Julia would rest as a second skin upon the paper.

"Talbot and Daguerre have failed thus far to reproduce the images as anything but faded stains on paper," she read from Holland's account. "They can take a moment – a tree, a cathedral – and oddly invert it. Turn its natural light inside out, as it were. But to truly hold it for all time? Paper to paper, we lose what we hold immediately, and what we are left with is faint, vaporous, dying. No, something is capricious in this process and won't be tamed with mere paper. I've tried it myself. Once I saw my assistant George as black Elgin marble on the treated sheet. But I could not slow the crystals' reactions. Instantly, he was no more."

In the afternoon, she withdrew the plate from the camera while Julia wept frustrated tears. She daubed at the paper with tufts of gauze she dipped gingerly into a small beaker of rust-colored liquid. Boils of silvery air rose from the surface, then burst.

Eligius came to her side. In thirty breaths, they saw it stir.

Waves of silver slowly spread through the paper's fibers to form a cloudy streak. No more than an inch, the patch disgorged mercurial edges in either direction, then became dissolute.

Seizing a second sheet, she pressed the papers together. "Eligius, help me!"

He reluctantly put his hands on the sheets next to hers and pressed as hard as he could. Something like warmth passed into his skin.

"Stop, stop!" she cried, as a blaze raged in her palms. She threw the papers down and upended the bucket. Water twinned with silver and flecks of something else, the fleeting essence of pale skin, splashed over Eligius' hands.

"It's gone," she moaned. "Only the merest moment of her. But you saw."

"It was water catching light," he murmured. "Nothing more."

"You saw her breathe." She crumpled Holland's letter. "Salt prints. Daguerreotypes. It is not enough! I will make these moments draw themselves, and I will not watch them fade. God can strike me down if I don't."

She threw the wooden frame against the wall and stalked out.

"What did you see?" Ewen whispered.

Eligius closed his eyes, and it was there. A hazy patch the hue of milky coffee. The bauble. Next to it, a hint of Julia's hand.

"I see only a mess to be cleaned up," he said, but the boy's eyes spoke of his disbelief.

A small spot of black formed on the web of skin between his thumb and forefinger. He wiped it against his tunic. It remained. In its center was a point of lighter pigment. A curvature he'd learned by heart. He shook his hand until he felt his bones rattle, but the bauble's shape did not leave his skin.

MY DEAR JOHN,

I fear it is no better with me than with you in the matter of the camera. I can neither raise nor hold more than a vestige. I lose hope by the day. I cannot afford to continue throwing heart and soul into paper and silver and iodide. For what? Failures. Shadows. Do I ask too much to beseech you for more of these precious commodities? Yet I do. Please send what you can, and should the Lord in His boundless goodness see fit to raise Charles from his worries over matters of state and health, I will repay you. Our crops fail. Charles' standing and pride fails with them. I remind him of his place on the Court and all its prestiges. Why, just the other day the entire Court was here, and the Governor himself! But he is gripped by worries I cannot reach. I fear for our future, which grows as dark as these terrible windows I fashion from paper. The worst kind of black, John. It takes my hope. Yet I persist. You steam to Ceylon as I write, and what do I have to show you? Nothing. I fear I burden you with my soul's contents. For that,

*I beg your pardon. I wish I could end this cursed need of mine
to see more. I wish I could be content with what I have. Things
would be easier. Sadly, I have never been a contented woman,
but why should I be? Women keep nothing of themselves.
Nothing lasts in the end, eh? Write to me, even if it is harsh. Send
what you can, but if not, send at least your words. It grows
quieter here.*

    Catherine

Eligius returned the letter to its envelope when he heard
footsteps approaching. Catherine came from her husband's
study into the dining room. She held out his rupees and told him
to post her correspondence.

"But he is at sea, memsa'ab."

"I've written the name of his ship. It will find its way,
through ports of call. What matters is that I send these words
somewhere. They cannot remain here."

"Will you try again, memsa'ab?"

He saw her eyes fill before she turned away. "The feather
shadow is still under my mat," he told her. "It came. Maybe we
cannot be held. Only small things."

"Are you still afraid of it?"

He nodded. "But I will bring more casks, if you want me to."

"Have the missionary bring you back by cart if they're too
heavy to carry."

He took the memsa'ab's sad letter. She had written it on
her special paper.

It had only been a week since he was last in the jungle, yet
it felt like seasons had gone by. The sensations he loved – the
dewy lushness under his bare feet, the wind cutting between
leaves and bringing faint hints of spice and rain, the low mewlings
of unseen animals – filled him with a fresh appreciation for his
country.

On the outskirts of Rahatungode, he heard a sound behind
Ceylon's green curtain. It began as a murmur that at first he

thought he was imagining. Only the subtly cocked heads of the field hands at the plantations he passed told him he wasn't alone in hearing it. By the time he reached the village of Devampiya, four hours' walk away from Dimbola, the sound became a rain of screams. Women's lamentations. The only men's voices he heard belonged to colonials.

He dropped to the ground when he spotted the soldiers. They had taken positions before a grove of teak trees ringing Devampiya. Three of them stood over a weeping woman. Her children clung to her as she pled for their compassion. Other soldiers took the last of her meager belongings and tossed them into the street. Two glistening servants hefting sharp-bladed shovels began cracking her home open. Wailing rose. There was still someone inside.

Part of the hut wall crumpled inward. An old woman screamed that they were killing her.

Two children brought Ault from the far side of the village road. "Why are you doing this?" he cried.

"Their land is forfeited," one of the soldiers told him. "It's mandated by the governor's law. Devampiya's men are missing and presumed to have abandoned their village to the tax assessor. Old woman, I won't ask again. You can stay and let the walls bury you for all I care!"

Ault came to her door, pleading in his ragged Tamil. "Please come out. There is nothing more we can do."

From his hiding place between the root coils of a fig tree, Eligius watched the rest of the old woman's home bow to the insistent blades. It was over in minutes. When the soldiers were done and a safe distance away, he went to the missionary.

"What are you doing here?" Ault demanded. "It's dangerous."

Eligius pressed his rupees into Ault's hand. "Give these to my mother. Whatever she needs for tax. I swear I will pay you back. I will work it off. Do not let this happen to her."

"Are you going to join these men, Eligius? The ones from

your village, and this one, and all the others? Will you kill me in my sleep?"

Eligius turned and ran. Dimbola was hours away. Behind him, a village very much like his own fell into memory.

HE POUNDED THE servant's side door until Mary opened it. "You shouldn't be here," she said.

"I know it's late."

"No one is asleep." She stepped aside to let him pass. He found the Colebrooks gathered in the study. Only Ewen was missing, likely in his bed.

Charles sat in his chair. His legs and arms were swaddled in blankets that radiated the last of the hearthstones' heat. His snowy beard rose and fell with his coughing.

"Forgive me," Eligius said. They were all staring at him. "The hour, and your Sunday. But I have been to Devampiya. The governor's law has already started, sa'ab. He is not waiting for you to tell him anything. The village has been destroyed."

"On what basis does a servant accuse the governor of destroying whole villages?" His voice shook.

"Sa'ab. I was there – "

"How dare you accuse an Englishman?"

"Father." Julia looked up at Charles from her seat on a blanketed duvet. "He's trying to help you."

"He is a thief! Is it not true? Have we not heard enough tonight to know that?" He pounded the armrest of his chair. "Was it my friend the governor who came into my study in the dead of night to steal from me? Tell me, boy. Did you find something that would fetch a good price in here? Were you going to buy a gun with it? Would you lead your men through our doors after all we've done for you?"

Mary quietly stepped away from the study door. Eligius hadn't noticed her until just now, and with her silent retreat, he understood. "I took nothing."

Catherine's eyes were on him and he couldn't simply stand there, damned before her.

"Yes, I thought about it. But I didn't. I left it where I found it. Please. I have done nothing wrong."

"What was it to be?"

He pointed to the map of Ceylon.

"Fitting," Charles said.

"My husband, I cannot be quiet." Catherine tucked Charles' blanket around his legs. "If this boy was a thief and a seditionist, the bauble around his neck that your daughter made a gift of would already have been sold for guns or butter."

Julia's face reddened.

"There is a place for forgiveness, husband. The Christian thing to do – "

"Who is master of this house?" Charles' words pulled him up from his chair. "The time has come to resolve this question, which is on the lips of our neighbors and the men of the Court. Who is master of this house?"

"You," Julia said.

"Yes," Catherine said.

"And do you take the word of a servant you don't know over the word of a maid who has served my predecessor, and now us, for years? An English girl?"

"I place you above all," Catherine said.

"Do you, Catherine? Do you place me above your own ambition? Is it me you think of in the guest house? Or am I found further down your list, behind that contraption and the written attentions of Sir John Holland and God knows who else? And all of these efforts are to what end? You make a pathetic figure."

"I cannot bear this." Catherine left the room. In a moment she was crossing the yard toward Holland House.

"Eligius. Look at me." The old man's eyes were rimmed with red. "You must leave us now. I wish it weren't so, but I have done what I can. You reject your father's path, it seems."

"You're wrong," Eligius said.

"Nevertheless."

"His family will starve," Julia said.

"They are a resourceful people."

"If he were to apologize – "

"I cannot." Eligius walked to the door. "I stole nothing. I have given you more than you had a right to. It is you who took from me."

Julia ran after him and caught him in the yard, just below the porch where he had first seen her in the slanting rain. "I'll talk to him," she said breathlessly. "Tomorrow, without my mother to kindle his feelings. He'll see nothing is missing."

"I'm a servant. It shouldn't matter to you."

"Nevertheless." She composed herself. Her head tilted as if she looked down at him from a great height. "A wrong has been done. That is all."

He removed the bauble.

"No," she said.

"Take it or they will take it from me. Then there will be another gun." He held it out and waited.

"I'll send word through the missionary," Julia said. "About your return."

"If you wish."

"What made you decide not to take father's map?"

He stood quietly, wondering the same thing. "Taking it from you," he finally said, "is not something my father would have done. I am a man like my father."

Her hand opened. He let the bauble fall through black space.

SHE STOOD BACK from the cottage doorway so she would not be seen. So she would see no more of this, the drift of her life. Out there, Eligius returned Julia's gifted bauble. He turned and left Dimbola.

Behind her, the Court image fluttered in the breeze leaking in, to become trapped between the walls of Holland House.

She'd said nothing.

Ault would know how to get word to Eligius. In time there would be softening. Charles would relent. This would pass into the dustbin of memory with the other regretted words of a marriage.

The terrible shaking began in her faint-stained hands. In Paris she'd learned of the far flung canals of the heart. How they traversed the breadth of the body like streams in search of the sea. The shaking took her at the shoulders, traversed her, found her heart and washed her away.

She sobbed until her chest burned. She'd said nothing to stop this.

Dimbola was quiet where Eligius had been.

She remained where she was. Movement felt like the will of someone else. Standing there, halfway in, halfway out, she thought that this was the first time she'd found refuge in the cottage, yet it was something outside that remained with her.

Thirty Breaths

FROM THE SAFETY OF THE BANYANS, ELIGIUS WATCHED
Gita play in front of their hut. Her hands stretched hopelessly
at a macaw preening in the low boughs. Over a year old and still
no words. Chronic illness had slowed her, the way it did so many
of Matara's babies.

At twilight the cooking scents made him giddy with hunger,
yet he still couldn't bring himself to leave the safety of the trees.
If he did, he would have to tell his mother he'd failed even at being
a servant.

Sudarma came out. She folded some chapati in a banana
leaf and walked into the jungle not thirty yards from him. Gita
nuzzled her neck, breathing her mother's skin in sleep.

In the fading light, the purpling swell under Sudarma's
left eye shone like blood. Her lip was split raggedly. Sounds made
her flinch. The jungle was no longer a house she knew.

He waited for her to open a safe distance, then followed.
Immediately, he knew where her path would lead.

Teal and jackfruit formed a canopy above his head, crowd-
ing out the faint stars. The air grew crisp. He kept well back
from his mother as the trees overtook the horizon. At its highest
point, the beach at Port Colombo resembled a sea of fine dust.
The last of the fishermen perched above the gentle tides on stilts,
their reflections shaded to shadow by the waning light.
Austere, blazingly white government buildings and Dutch mer-
chant houses lined the coastline inland to the Galle Face.

They passed the first of three caves where long dead priests had painted his people's history in raw colors. Buddhist frescoes told of the hell awaiting those who strayed from the path.

Soon the route gave way to a sharp turn alongside a plunging waterfall that irrigated cultivated terraces of rice. It was still the greenest, mossiest place he'd ever seen.

He stopped near a pillar of the elephant temple. His mother kissed her fingertips gingerly and touched a plaque as if it were Gita's cheek. Flat, of brushed copper, it had been hammered by artisans with the likeness of Ganesha, elephant-faced lord of obstacles and beginnings.

Sudarma went up a short flight of stone steps into the temple's broken sanctuary. In a moment he heard Chandrak. "There isn't enough for all of us." Drunk.

Gita started to cry.

He clenched his fists impotently, listening to the sound of his mother's beating. After some minutes, the others – he heard many – stopped their approving grunts. His mother emerged on the stairs. She held Gita in her arms and was careful not to fall. Distant monkeys howled at her passing.

When she was clear, he climbed the stairs.

A dozen men lay on woven mats, licking their fingers. Teeth-gouged fruit littered the temple's stone floor, next to a small pyre of broken bottles. The smell of spilled lihuli permeated the air.

He recognized two of the men as once-friends of his father. Lalajith, a fisherman who sold in the market until his drinking overtook him. Then, even his son wouldn't share nets. Varini, who pulled a hansom for the colonials in Tangalla. They were insufficient for the world. Not strong enough to provide for their families or resist the soldiers.

Reaching down, he plucked a large, flat shard of glass from the pile. Gray as a storm sky, resilient in his hands, it would make for a distraction when the sun reappeared and he could resume his redirection of the light. He wondered where he could keep it. He wondered where he lived, now.

Chandrak stared at him.

"I bring nothing," Eligius told him.

"And yet you're here."

He sat on the opposite side of the dying fire. "I can gather more wood."

"We keep it small. So we can't be seen."

"What happens when it dies?"

Chandrak hoisted a bottle.

"No," Eligius said.

"Be a man tonight. Tonight, a son joins me." He raised his fist and shook it. There was still some blood on his knuckles, drying in the fire's heat. "We'll make room for you. All is forgiven." He offered his bottle again.

Eligius picked it up and drank. Bitter liquid scoured his throat. Another man, thrown away.

Chandrak's head nodded loosely. "Be quick with the wood, Eligius."

Eligius got up. The sound of rustling paper in his tunic was like thunder through the trees, yet when he glanced over at them, the men hadn't stirred. Their rubbery bodies faded towards sleep.

Under the copper shield, where the elephants waited for their cousins the clouds to lift them, he searched his tunic for the memsa'ab's letter. He found it, but found no clouds of steam rising from his mother's prophesy to carry him away.

The liquor raced up into his gullet. In a thicket of orchids, it left him.

"WAKE UP, BOY. We've need of you."

Varini shoved him again. Eligius rose groggily to his feet. His body felt encased in stone.

Chandrak was gone, as were the others.

Varini motioned for him to follow. In the half-light of dawn, Eligius saw another boy waiting for them near the treeline. As he drew closer, he saw that it was Hari. His once-neighbor had grown gaunt and hard since Diwali, when he'd pronounced Gretel's death in English to Eligius' approval.

"Where are we going?" Hari asked. His lips were thin and bloodless with hunger.

"Be quiet, the both of you. There are colonials across the clearing."

Varini led them around the crescent perimeter of a field carpeted with woven vines and the far-flung root coils of the surrounding trees. Eligius studied the furthest wall of the jungle for signs of the Britishers, but saw only Chandrak, who waved them over. They entered the trees, careful to keep low.

"Walk into the clearing," Chandrak told them. "Both of you."

"Varini said there are colonials," Eligius protested. "They'll see us! We're trespassing."

"There's only one. Let him see you."

"For what reason?"

"He is useless," Lalajith said. "Hari will be obedient."

"Give me a moment with him."

Chandrak turned Eligius away from the other men standing among the trees. "Do you love Ceylon?"

"Yes," Eligius said uncertainly.

"Do you understand now, they will not do as your father hoped? They will not allow us a voice in our own lives. You left their world and came back to ours. Do you see that I am all you have?"

His bitter breath lit Eligius' eyes. It pushed rivers through his body and made him long for the lion's mouth. Up so high above the neem growing out of the mountainside, nothing could reach him.

"We've no other way to live, Eligius."

"I don't want to hurt anyone."

Chandrak pushed Eligius and Hari to the tree line. "Do not stand up until you're halfway."

They fell to their knees and began to crawl. Glancing back, Eligius saw faces peering between the leafy curtain. The sun broke through the pickets of tree trunks and glinted brilliantly from the silver blades of machetes.

He froze.

"What are you doing?" Hari hissed. "We're not halfway."

"I can't do this." He slowly stood into the young light and waited for Chandrak to emerge in a hobbled-leg rage. But Chandrak remained hidden with the others.

The husk-dry sound of breaking branches spun Eligius around. A man entered the clearing from the opposite end of the field, his uniform like blood across the lush growth.

Hari whimpered against the ground. When he gazed up at Eligius, his eyes were terrible eclipsing moons.

"Soldier," Eligius mouthed.

"You there!" the soldier cried.

Hari leapt to his feet and ran. Eligius couldn't move. The soldier leveled his rifle and all Eligius could see was the black cave at the end of the barrel. There would be no warning when the ruby light rose and gray smoke belched, and he would seep sticky glistening ponds into the dirt like his father before him.

A shot rang out and he sprinted without realizing he'd moved. Something hot and humming flew past his head. A tree trunk ahead of him burst open in a split flower of bark and green wood.

Chandrak knocked him down the moment he pierced the trees. He clasped Eligius' throat and pressed him against the jungle floor as Hari flew past, tears streaking his face. The veins in Hari's neck were as thick as tack lines. His lips peeled back as if by the force of winds.

The other men converged on the soldier as he ran into the trees. The jungle sprang to life in a downpour of hammering hands and tumbling bodies.

A rifle emerged from the mass. It was closely followed by the soldier's boots, his coat and brass buckles.

Chandrak released his grip. Air forced its way into Eligius' lungs.

The soldier lay splayed-legged on the ground, pinned by a thicket of bodies. Stripped to his underclothes, he whimpered and begged in English. He was young and slightly built. His face was slick with sweat and fear.

The soldier's eyes found Eligius, and hated him. "Listen to me," he pleaded. "Please, you may have what you want. Please, just listen."

Chandrak brought Eligius to the weeping soldier's side. The men holding him down tightened their grip. Forcing Eligius to his knees, Chandrak took out a knife and put it into Eligius' hands. He wrapped his own hands around its hilt and pressed it against the soldier's chest. Its gleaming tooth sent tremors through the soldier. His torso pitched wildly, but there were too many against him.

"I won't," Eligius cried.

Madness filled Chandrak's face. "They left a stain on us. Wash it away."

Chandrak was scared. Eligius could see beneath the leathered face and the foundry-pocked flesh; he saw the face of the man at Court, crying for home.

Chandrak pressed down on Eligius' hands. Eligius tried to hold the blade away from the soldier's chest, but Chandrak's grip crushed his fingers into the knife handle.

Pain flared through Eligius' wrists, into his arms and shoulders as Chandrak leaned hard against him. The blade's tip sliced shallowly into the soldier's skin. A small trickle seeped to the soldier's shirt. He screamed. Someone's hand covered his mouth, sealing his pleas inside.

Hari came to Chandrak's side.

"Help me," Eligius pleaded as the men gathered around them.

Hari added his hands to Chandrak's. Tears fell from his chin. "I'm afraid." He closed his eyes.

Eligius screamed as something fibrous in the reaches of his back snapped. He tore his hands away, jerking the knife sideways. The thin gash he left in the soldier's chest beaded with blood. The soldier's head shook faster and faster.

Eligius leapt to his feet and bolted past Chandrak's outstretched arms, past the others and into the trees before any of them could react. He heard the violent passage of men rising in angry pursuit of him. Hari's cries mingled with those of the young soldier. English words of prayer erupted into the sky like rousted birds. Then the sputtering sound of someone drowning. Then only Hari, but by then Eligius was too far to be sure of anything.

Soon the sounds behind him fell away. When the night found him, he was still running on legs he no longer felt.

AT DEVAMPIYA, HE stopped. When it was light enough to see the abandoned village and its broken huts, he gathered wood apples. Cracking their hard shells, he scooped out their sour custard with his fingers. He took coconuts for their sweet water and gourds to make a bitter stew, the way his mother did. In the trees he found a hung line of seer fish. They were dry and only a little rotten. His stomach would reject much of it, but so be it.

The jungle was a living map, alive with destinations. He could go to the port and operate the cooling punkah fans for the colonials. He could become a water carrier, a messenger, a door opener. He could cut grass, make bricks, sweep children's rooms clear of scorpions. He could build his own hut, plant cotton and become a village unto himself. Or he could sneak back into Dimbola and steal to his heart's content. Maybe he would find other men and throw the Colebrooks' home open to them. What would it require, to ascend in the eyes of his own? A blade, he guessed, plunged into the soft skin of colonials whose names and voices and wants he had come to know.

Around him, the light folded. He waited to see if the shadows of the trees might become permanent on the jungle floor or on his skin. But they kept shifting into each other until the sharp demarcations of the leaves and the broken hut walls melted away. There were no feathers in the world outside the memsa'ab's camera. Nothing was held, in the dark or the light.

The young soldier's cries would not leave him.

He reached into his tunic. The memsa'ab's correspondence to Holland still lay against his skin, where he'd folded it for safekeeping. Her precious, starry paper from across the sea, wasted on such a sad letter.

He let it slip from his fingers, and his glass with it.

HE AWOKE IN a beam of morning sun. His skin felt agreeably warm. The glass shard broke the light into pillars that touched everything within his bleary sight.

Rising stiffly, he squinted as the light's reflection on the glass burst brilliantly before him. He put his hand over his eyes, letting bubbles of color fill and fade back into the dusk of his palm.

The memsa'ab's letter lay on the ground, under the glass. Bits of leaves and dew drops were trapped between them like insects in amber. He lifted the glass to brush them off, but something of them remained. The letter was dotted with discolorations in the shape and location of the leaves. They were on the glass as well, in the same configuration.

He held the glass into the sun. Faint as dissipating mist, their images spattered the shard's surface, unmistakable in shape, down to the perforations and hushed tracings of veins.

Something stirred his mind. He wiped some dew from fallen leaves and slickened the memsa'ab's paper. Finding a larger leaf, he laid it atop the paper and pressed it into the light.

The last of the bauble was rapidly departing his skin. Days in the jungle had all but scoured it from his hand.

The bauble had been in Julia's hand, that day in Holland House. It made a halo of sun on her skin. Nothing else of her survived the journey through the camera to the memsa'ab's paper, nothing but its image.

There. A dream of the leaf began. Faint tracings of veins,

threading from the silver salt to the glass. As he breathed, they darkened ever so slowly. The light moved with the sun's rise and he moved with it, keeping the paper and glass bathed. Over countless minutes the leaf filled in. He withdrew it from the sun. It held, like the feather. Like Julia, but only that part of her touched by the bauble's bent, concentrated light.

He left Devampiya's ruins behind.

MARY OPENED THE front door. He raced past her without a word. She gave chase but he moved as if devils sped after him.

Catherine was in the study, composing at a small table set up by Charles' chair. Charles' color had not improved. He stared vacantly out the window.

"Madam, I'm sorry."

Catherine and Charles looked up at Mary's voice. Eligius stood in the doorway, heaving with the effort to take breaths. His hair and face were slickened with sweat. Catherine despised the thought rising from the tumult in her. *He looks as if he's just been born.*

Eligius raised the glass. She saw the image imprinted there. A stain bearing the unmistakable marks. The veins were as frail as thread. The leaves bore scalloped edges. The faint permeable light of it told her that he had somehow brought it forth from life.

Charles and Mary, their stares of indignation; the both of them could join hands and stroll to hell. Look at it.

"I need a hammer," Eligius said.

"Mary," Catherine said, "get him a hammer."

"What? I will not –"

"Now."

In the yard, Eligius found the ladder and ascended to Holland House's roof. His entry had roused Julia and Ewen. While Catherine set up the camera, they gathered at the foot of the structure to watch him pull his crude wooden patches loose and toss them to the ground. The shadowy interior of Holland House filled with sunlight. When the strongest light found the chair, he went inside, where he took out the window panes with a gentle tap of the hammer.

"How?" Catherine held up the leaf.

"The light. The light was on Julia's arm. It was the only part of her that came. And the feather sat atop your paper in the sun before I patched the roof. If we concentrate more light on the work, it will stay longer. I know it. We'll use glass to make the light stronger."

He wielded the hammer to fashion rough, cracked squares from the window panes. Catherine brought silver salt. Somewhere, she thought, Sir John is smiling at the woman who longed to possess shadows, who now finds the missing light.

"Wait," she said. "In one of the letters I received, Sir John enclosed cotton. He spoke of life and death."

She gave him her key to the locked room.

"All of your most precious things are in there," he said.

"Go. Bring his letter to me. I think there may be a way to hold these images still."

He ran. His heart ran ahead of him. In her room, he found Sir John's letter, the guncotton and a tin. Life and death, Sir John had written, in eternal stalemate.

In Holland House Catherine opened the tin of collodion and dipped one of Julia's quills into it. A foul, heady stench filled the air. "Sir John said it had the power to hold the guncotton still. Why not this?"

She brushed collodion onto the glass. Tilting it this way and that, she directed the crawling tide across the surface until it was coated with a second skin that bent the colors from the light.

Eligius slipped it inside the camera.

"Mother."

Julia sat in the chair, wrapped in a brocade shawl. Her head tilted up, a girl of great privilege and station.

He arranged the glass around her. Sunlight sparkled from one pane to the next, bathing her in gold.

"Is it right?" Eligius asked. He held up the cloak for Catherine.

"Let us see." Slipping under, she captured Julia through the lens. The light made baubles of her daughter's eyes.

Julia let her shawl slip from her shoulders. Her lips parted. Her gaze wandered from the eye of the camera to Eligius.

Great swaths of daylight passed as they waited; so many breaths passed before she pulled the plate from the camera and bathed it, and prayed that they would make the glass live this time.

It came in tides of shape and shadow. Julia's folded hands, her arms, the soft lace of her dress, her thin neck and her hair cascading over her shoulders, unfastened to catch the wind. Her face came and stayed, longer and more vividly than ever before.

"Bring your father," Catherine said. "Hurry."

Julia ran for the house and returned with Charles.

"Watch me," Catherine said to her husband. "This once."

She bathed the plate with water while Eligius held it. The collodion writhed beneath her fingers. Her flesh buzzed with chemical.

Later, Eligius thought, I may see her on me.

Charles drew close to it. His hand flickered, then came back to rest atop the golden buttons of his overcoat. Catherine leaned to be near him. Together they gazed at the dripping frame, the remains of their eldest child washing away. Everything around them stilled; the cold world he lived in, and the world that she knew, made of lost children and the lights that illuminated the way back to them.

She examined their faces. Eligius, Charles, Julia. They know. For them, for me, this will remain.

In that held moment, Eligius saw what it was that bound these two strangers together for all their remaining days. He'd seen betrothal, and obligation, and the silent suffering of wives following their husbands from fallen huts to dirt roads. But he'd never before seen how small, how easily missed, how impregnable love could be until the memsa'ab had added her solutions to his light, and burned it into glass.

Soon she was lost to her work. She studied the light of it and let the world fall. She saw only what came after Julia's arrested moment. It glinted through the coated glass and the liquid fog that was her child's face. There was a beauty in its leaving.

Eligius approached Charles and spoke quietly. "There is a man, Chandrak. He is from my village. He was the other man shot on that day, when my father died."

"I remember. What of him?"

"He is the one stealing. He and others. Men follow him. They're trying to get guns. He wanted me to steal from you."

"This doesn't excuse what you did. I've no trust in you."

"He killed a soldier."

Julia stared at him. Charles took his face in his hands. Tremors passed from the old lion's fingers into the hollows of Eligius' cheeks.

Tears fell from Eligius' eyes. He told Charles of the clearing. "He was little more than a boy and he's dead because of me."

"And you swear to me, this is the truth? You had no hand in this?"

"I ran away. I ran to you."

"I believe him." Catherine stood beside Eligius. "He puts himself at terrible risk, coming to you."

"Will you testify to this?" Charles demanded.

"Yes."

"For the present," Charles said, "I will keep you here under my protection while this matter is looked into. The governor will need to be informed. No doubt he'll send soldiers after this man, and then to the gallows with him. But Eligius, I pity you if I learn other than what you've told me. You have no country, boy."

"You're right," Catherine said. "And now you will listen to me, husband. He came to you for the same reason his father did.

Do something to be worthy of it. Give him another reason to remember you."

She took the glass plate outside and held it up to the sky. As its collodion skin peeled away in drops of silver rain, she wept. The last tattered flecks of Julia fell away to the ground.

No matter, she thought, that the picture washes away. We will hold it eventually. One day it will be nothing of consequence, to be stilled.

2.

You have been transported from your houses in Leadenhall Street to the dominion of the richest Empire in the world, and left as if by dream in that amazing pitch of exultation and riches. Rejoice, and hold fast to our course.

Pamphleteer, to directors and stockholders of the East India Company, on their hold over India, 1836

I had the opportunity to see each step in the operation of the process. The plate, used for the purpose of stealing my likeness, the polished surface afterwards exposed to the action of vapor until golden in hue. The plate was, in my presence, placed in a small box and thereafter in a solution of unknown origin; by this action was my visage to be produced. Yet when the plate was removed, I was invisible. The cry went out: Failure!

Affidavit of Lord Dalhouse, on a visit to a photographer's premises, June 1837 (Public Record Office, ref. number C31/585 box 2)

If only you could have seen it. No longer do I chase shadows as you have counseled against. My house is full of fumes and frames, cut glass and in the cottage house, the blessings of an industrious young Indian man. Where there were holes in the roof, there are now windows and black curtains, and pulleys and levers. Quite the luminist, that one. He can assert at least a bit of control over Ceylon's capricious light.

I fail no more. In truth I cannot say where my son Hardy resides now, nor what has become of my belief in such things as Heaven. But I will never again accept the loss of a child to the distant regions of memory. I know too much now."

Letter from Catherine Colebrook to Sir John Holland December 19, 1837

Servitudes

"WHERE IS ELIGIUS, MARY?"

At the sound of her mistress' voice, Mary came to the dining room with a fresh cup of tea. "Outside with the master."

"Charles is outside? How could you let him outside in his condition?"

"He insisted after mistress Julia spoke with him. On Eligius' behalf, madam."

She finished her letter to Sir John.

Send me nothing more, dearest friend and mentor. Soon it will be my turn to send something your way. Something wondrous.

She sealed the letter and brought it with her for Eligius to post. She found him at the gate, holding a large palm frond over Charles and a bent Indian woman standing with Ault. Behind them, stretching past the road and into the trees, were men, women, children, their clothes and faces dusty from walking the dry paths that bound their lives to the colonials' estates.

"These people come from three villages," Charles said. "Their tale is a tragic one."

"Please," Eligius said. "It's been too long that you are outside, sa'ab."

"There is only one old woman present, boy, and she is over there."

Eligius exchanged looks with Catherine.

"Stephen," Charles said, "what do you say about their accounts?"

"I have seen what they're speaking of. Their huts are being razed and their land seized under order of the governor. Since that poor devil's body was found, there have been abuses, Charles. Beatings at the hands of the soldiers. They cite the doctrine of lapse. Does this have any meaning to you?"

"Let these people know that they have my full attention. Eligius, I wish to be in my study with papers and quills. Now, please."

"Let me help you," Catherine said.

"No. The boy will do it."

Eligius led Charles to the house. He helped the old man into the chair at his writing desk and said that he would locate some paper and quills.

"I'm not yet prepared to say that I fully believe you," Charles said. "Though it would seem your story is corroborated."

"I thank you for listening, sa'ab."

He left, and returned with the paper and quills. He asked Charles what would be done with them.

"Certainly I will do what I can, but I am limited in these matters." His hand rested on the map of Ceylon. "In the Cape of Good Hope, I was given this. I was an old man with no prospects. Convalescing then and ever after, I suppose. I have never been well. This map was the terrain where my redemption was to be found. I thought I would come, make my mark on this country. Give her laws that she might care for herself. No small matter, I thought I would make a coffee fortune and return to London a valued civil servant untouched by his time away. But Ceylon has come to be a part of me in ways I never expected. I love it in the senseless manner that compels my wife in her own pursuits. To love something that eludes me is a terrible enough thing. To see it on the verge of catastrophe, to be too old and too indebted to do anything? I fear what will become of my soul if I leave it like this."

"Then don't leave it, sa'ab"

" You're young yet. You cannot be expected to understand. What I begin now may end all that I care for. Yet my silence will certainly end all that I ever believed I was. It is a sorry state that I find myself."

He patted the map. "I sent this away once, with a prayer that it and my wife would return to me. Know this, Eligius. There is no worse thing you could have considered taking from me."

AFTER CHARLES' MEETINGS with the villagers became public knowledge, an even more pronounced scarcity of company took hold in Dimbola. When Eligius walked the grounds at night he heard the lilt of colonial voices carrying over from festive parties the Colebrooks were not asked to attend.

The Britishers are not so different, he thought. They had their own castes.

As Sir John Holland's arrival neared, Catherine planned a feast. Eligius delivered invitations to colonial households in Port Colombo. He erected a tent in front of the cottage house. Tables and place settings were readied. Catherine prepared a menu calling for lamb and pheasant, a whole roast pig, seer fish, pastries and a sheet of marzipan for the children, wine and beer. She gave him the task of placing the order at the market and told him what to say to the butchers and bakers who would surely resist when they heard which family the food was meant for. "Have them speak to the governor of Ceylon," she told him, "if they doubt my word."

"Shall Mary accompany me?"

"Mary ministers to my husband. Sir John's arrival is ours to prepare for."

He understood. Mary was her master's maid now. Openly disdainful of Catherine even on his first day in the rain five months before, Mary now perceived Catherine as aligned with the Indian kutha.

An invisible line bisected the house. The dining room was

neutral ground, the study and kitchen hostile, the trees, the sky and Holland House, theirs.

If it had to be this way, he thought, at least their territory was worth having.

He saw the other servants at the market. Without Mary to intimidate them with her haughtiness, they surrounded him and peppered him with questions about the feast, this man Holland, about his memsa'ab's storied incursions to realms she had no business dallying with.

"Will there be another of her horrid plays?" asked one red-haired girl, her face a riot of blotches. She struck a vainglorious pose.

He laughed in spite of himself. "She has been working on something, though it isn't a play. I'm as disappointed as you."

The girls laughed and offered him a sip of rum from a battered metal flask they passed between themselves. He declined.

"How you must suffer at her beck and call," another said. She twisted her black braids with a hand shorn of two fingers.

"Who?" the redhead interjected. "Mary or the mistress?"

"Pick your poison's, what I say."

He handed his list to the butcher who had rebuffed Mary on his first trip to the market. "Two days from now," he told the man. "The memsa'ab said the governor's representative had spoken to you."

"He has. Something about her displaying his life's work, and her own."

"I've heard of this."

An elder maid came forward. Her hands clasped in front of her, she moved with the quiet humility of the pious. She was in her forties, it seemed, with deep creases under her eyes and around her mouth, as if pebbles had broken the surface of her skin and rippled outward. "She spoke with my master about it. Inappropriate of her, I thought, but when has she been a decorous woman? She said she had found a way to put a frame around God's hand. Her words."

The servants confided with each other in hushed tones.
The list trembled in the butcher's hands. "Blasphemous."
"A lie," the elder maid said.

"I watched her do it," Eligius said. "It was something I cannot describe. I cannot imagine it was anything to make your god upset. It is because of him that she tries. It is prayer. Now what of this list?"

His eyes darting from face to face, the butcher set the paper down on his cutting table in a dry place. "Tomorrow. This will be all across the market by then. Me, selling good meat for prayers." He shook his head.

Eligius made his way to the baker's modest clay oven, where fumes of browning bread made the low sky shimmer. The elder maid followed him. "Your mistress invited my master to come see her triumph."

"When the day comes, you should accompany him. I will make you some tea and you can watch. It is like a dream to see a face come out of nothing. I do not understand it."

Her brow furrowed. "Perhaps. But is it wrong?"

"I am a heathen, I think you would say. But her daughter Julia is a Christian, and she was the memsa'ab's first."

"I wish I could see. Then my mind might rest on this."

She stepped aside to let him pass. "You know they all speak of you, too. The Indian who chose us over his own."

"I do not wish to be spoken of."

He finished his errands, bid farewell to the maids and walked from the market. Away from the colors and braying voices, Queen Street teemed with colonial families shadowed by sun-baked Tamil and Malay, waiting for carts to pass with pallets destined for the John Company. Medicines, cured meats, vegetables, wood and unpolished stone, flowers and exotic birds, the blood and bone of their country departed in wagons and carts on the way to sea. The poor kept watch over the ground, waiting for a bit of waste. When the carts were gone, they scurried onto the cracked dirt to pick up the horses' defecation with the flat side of rubber leaves. Setting it out to dry, they would sell it later for fuel to their fellow villagers in their own approximations of the colonials' marketplace.

Further down the road, children played in clouds of dust raised by the carts while their mothers worked. One small cough, speckled with wetness despite the dry season, rose above the din of their voices.

Eligius saw Sudarma leave her pile in the road and go to Gita. Behind her, the other women jostled for the abandoned manure. Sudarma raised Gita up and turned her so she might cough her lungs clear.

In each discrete movement he saw where the light was, where he might direct it, what of his mother and Gita might find the way to glass, what of them would be lost.

The sight of them made him shiver. It was like the careless finding of a raw wound, the way Sudarma looked up from Gita to see her son so far from her.

CHARLES WAS ON the verge of collapse, yet over the days he pressed on with his writing. His papers were filled with elegant lines. Some drowned in small seas of ink. Others he scratched into oblivion.

Eligius wanted to ask where the answer to his people's problems might be found in those pages. But an illness of distrust still permeated the study, its epicenter the map Charles kept close to his work.

He approached Mary in the scullery one evening while she was pouring goat's milk through a cloth to strain it for cheese. "Do you think the Colebrooks would let my mother come work for them?"

Mary sighed wearily, then kept pouring.

"She would have to bring my sister Gita. But she's a baby and would be no trouble. My mother could clean and wash. She would do as you asked."

Mary held the cloth above a plate. She scraped it with a flat knife. Crumblings of clotted milk fell away.

"I fear the sa'ab won't be able to stop what is happening. I don't want my family to starve."

Mary let the cloth fall to the floor, then kicked it towards him. "What's a servant's place?"

He picked the cloth up.

"How'd it get there?" she asked.

"It was my fault," he said.

"I always knew you were a sly one. I knew it the moment I laid eyes on you in the rain, listening to every word the mistress said. You're watchful and you're quiet. Why, I'll wager when you kill them in their beds, they won't even wake."

"I would never –"

"What does a maid do, kutha?"

He seethed. Her words were strips of banyan across his back. "Cooks. Cleans. Tends to the children. Brings dishes and takes them away. Waits to see when the sa'ab's tobacco is low. Bargains. Never tells them they don't have enough money to buy what others have. Makes a little go farther. Never says they smell or spilled. Goes quietly about it all."

"Sly one, is what you are. Should your mother starve, it would only be one less of you."

"Your god should damn you."

"You're quiet and you listen, but you can be provoked. My God will certainly damn me, but for nothing I say to a filthy beggar who pulled the wool over a foolish family's eyes. No, I'll pay for letting a blasphemous woman fritter away what remains of her husband's self-respect. And now she has you to help her. A murderer, I'll wager. Tell me, if she burns the rest of her own home down to raise her dead child, who will you steal from then? Who will you cut open?"

"You think you know me. But I know you. You're white like them, but low like me. You think they forget what you are because you put their children to bed. You may lift Ewen when he reaches for you, but that doesn't make you one of them. You're just something to be ridden. And now there's me."

Her eyes gleamed with wetness and anger. She would make a good painting of light, he thought.

Scraping the milk fat into a mold, she spread it with the knife until it was smooth, then placed it in a shaded corner, out of the coming high heat of the day. She stepped by him without a word.

In the morning, she was gone.

Pillars of Smoke

EWEN CRIED AS IF FOR A DEATH. JULIA SAID NOTHING; it was only a maid. Charles rose and hobbled into his study, closing the door behind him. An English girl had chosen leaving over remaining. No doubt she would find placement in another colonial household. Certainly she lacked means to return home. But what would she say of them?

What could she say that had not already been said, Catherine thought. The fashionable notion of a servant among the Directors' wives was to let only their successful performance of tasks be noticed. The rest fell outside the sphere of appropriate women. Maids such as Mary belonged to the background of dinners, of children's bedtimes and nursemaid needs. The event itself belonged to the proper women, the details to those with dirt under their nails and stooped postures.

Between her and Mary there had been antagonism of a puzzling sort. The girl resented all she'd seen at Dimbola. Now, this. A fête for the man she most wanted to shine before, and no one to help.

It was Friday. She came to Eligius in a panic.

"I know someone who will work hard," he said. "But I must speak to the sa'ab. To the governor as well."

He cleaned the house, went to market and reminded the butcher to be prompt. After, he stopped at the missionary's pitiable pastoral and asked that word be sent to his mother in Matara.

"You can't go there alone," the missionary told him. "Not now. If any of your own learn you'll be there, I fear for you."

"I will be safe," he said, and said no more.

The next day, he left Dimbola for his village. At the lion's mouth, he saw two pillars of smoke. Both were days away. One was white. As it rose above the furthest horizon of the ocean, the wind sifted it into gauze. Holland's ship, perhaps.

The other bloomed in the east, over the land. The green carpet of jungle was broken by a reef of smoke from the fire that raged below it.

He wondered what fed it, to make it grow darker as it rose.

ALL OF MATARA waited by the road as Ault slowed the cart to let Eligius disembark. "I'll see to your mother," Ault said. He walked down the road to Eligius' old hut.

Eligius let the villagers gather near him. Their rage coalesced into something communal. It didn't take long for the man he sought to come.

Chandrak walked towards the cart, a smile gathering at his lips. His rib cage filled with labored air. As the villagers stood nearby, watching intently, he coughed pink foam into his cupped palm. Starvation laced his torso. "So you've come to make servants of us all. Who can blame you for leaving? We're dying. But everyone talks about you. The boy who carved such a lofty place for himself among the colonials that the governor pays him visits. Not even his father could speak to him now."

"It is not that way."

"I'll let Swaran know that I saw you. I'll tell him the best of you died along with him."

"Eligius!"

Ault stood at Sudarma's hut, beckoning her to come. She emerged with Gita and climbed aboard the cart, her head bowed.

"I have to go," Eligius said. He took up the reins. "Let my mother and Gita leave with me. If you care about them at all, you will do what's best for them. Don't try to stop us."

"I remember you at the Overstone fields. You were weak even then. When you left for the colonials, I knew you'd never come back. I feared you wouldn't find manhood, but never did I think you would turn your back like this. Remember, your back isn't white, kutha."

He drew close. "As for Sudarma, she makes her own choices and she has chosen you. I am a man. I don't need a woman's protection. In the days to come, it would be better if I don't see you again. But I will find you. Then will you have the courage to end things between us?"

"I already have," Eligius said.

Women brought bread tied in cloth and water for Chakran. Children drew petals at his feet with sticks. A good luck prayer. The women glared at Eligius before returning to their cooking pots. Paltry curries dusted the air but conjured nothing of his days playing in the village streets.

It was a strange thing, to wish that his childhood in this place could somehow be hurled under the cart's turning wheels and crushed.

"Who was that man?" Ault asked as they rolled away from the villagers. "Didn't he accompany you on the day you first came to me?"

"He's no one."

Ault gave his donkey a pat on the neck. "What news from your master Charles, then? What can he make of this business with Governor Wynfield's doctrine?"

"I don't know."

He guided the cart and its cargo – his silent mother and a sleeping Gita – past fallen roofs of battered thrush, past fragments and families in awe that only one stricken woman and her baby had a destination.

Ahead was a stand of intertwined neem. Eligius guided the old animal onto a path around it, towards the clearing on the other side.

Ault chattered on. "I hear their maid has left them, in her

first year no less. And this camera. Catherine's sent word of it to the vicar, the lords of the court, all the great men, it seems. I wonder what her husband thinks of it." He shook his head. "That such things should come to pass. Progress, I suppose."

Gita began to sob in her sleep. "She doesn't know the feel of me," Sudarma said. "These clothes are not what she usually touches." She pulled at her servant's smock with a sour expression.

More neighbors gathered across the road behind them. The women brought empty baskets.

"Your bruises are almost healed," Eligius said.

"Tell Gita about the clouds and the elephants. She'll stop crying like you used to. Remember? You don't believe such things anymore."

"I'm older, amma."

She shook her head. As if he was wrong.

There was no smoke over the trees anymore. The colonials were protective of their holdings and quick to suffocate such things.

"You'll keep me informed of Charles' progress," Ault said. "Whether it's a bill to be presented to Court or word of the next town to be levied. I wish to know."

Eligius flicked the reins, startling the weary donkey into a faster trot.

"I'll miss Matara very much indeed," Ault said. "There were good people here. I'll remember it fondly." He put his hands over a careworn Bible. "Your father taught you to read there, outside your home. You never wanted to stay inside, he said, even in the rain. Always so restless!"

"Must we talk about what was?" Eligius said. "It's of no use to anyone now."

"You've never held your tongue with me, like I've seen you do with others. Curious."

Eligius turned to watch the villagers cross the road towards their hut. Children were faster; their mothers sent them first.

"Perhaps you're right to be bitter," Ault said. "Sometimes

it seems like there's no kindness left anywhere. Hard men like Wynfield take what they want. Even in my line, it's no different. As the Galle Face goes up, fewer of my countrymen need me. I'm left to the side with all of you. Another weak man crying out for fairness."

The rest of their hut came free in shreds of fabric, some tins of tea, cooking pots, the altar. His mother's wedding sari dragged the hard ground behind the woman carrying it away. Tiny hands grabbed at its beads, tearing them loose to roll in the dust.

Half of Matara's dwellings had fallen to Wynfield's soldiers. Like the craggy tops of sunken mountains, their points emerged from the dry ground.

"People pass your kind by without so much as a glance." Ault patted Eligius' knee. "You should be thankful."

They reached the clearing and the contingent of soldiers waiting there. One broke ranks. He guided his horse, a sleek-skinned animal, to the cart.

"Did you see the man speaking to me?" Eligius asked. "The crippled one."

"I saw him."

"He is the one."

The soldiers thundered past, through the trees and into Matara's ruins. The villagers screamed. The sound of their flight fell under the percussive wash of the soldiers.

"You succeed in surprising me," Ault said.

The sounds he expected came from the cart. A prayer of mourning. He gathered all of it – his mother's voice, Matara's fall – and put it into the empty cask where his heart had been.

EWEN MET THEIR cart at Dimbola's gate. He held an apron out to Sudarma. "Mother says to see that the baby's quiet. She asked me to sit in the chair. Will you stay with me while I sit?"

"Yes." Eligius could feel his mother's eyes on him.

"I have to sit still."

"I understand. I will be there."

"Good." He ran off towards the gazebo.

Sudarma handed Gita to him, then fastened the apron around her waist. "Show me where to draw water. And the pantry."

"Mother, you understand why I had to do this. Don't you?"

"Am I to market as well?"

"Yes."

"Tell me what else." Her gaze fell on a brightly tressed peacock strutting across the yard. She pointed Gita's attention to it.

"You've no right to be angry," Eligius said. "What else should I have done? Wait for the soldiers to bury you with your own walls? Wait for Chandrak to kill me?"

"I hear the colonials' homes have fine linen on their floors, as soft as sheep's wool."

"I've told you. We move the rug with the sun to keep it from fading. We beat the dust from it."

"This will fall to me."

She walked ahead of him towards the house. He stopped her before she could enter the front door. "Enter in the back. So you are not seen unless called."

He despised her quiet gait. It was as if a feeble woman had donned a sari fashioned from his mother's skin.

He took her inside and showed her everything he'd ever seen Mary do. It surprised him how versed he'd become in the Colebrooks' expectations. There was the rug, the gas lamps and hearth fires, the brandy and tobacco and the time to bear them into the study on a tray, with a blanket for the sa'ab's swollen legs. He instructed her not to regard the sa'ab too closely. The old man was vain to the blood roses blooming along his shins.

He showed her what to clear, and when, and with what utensil. He brought her to the well and the pantry, where she set to work on a dinner of lamb belly and boiled root vegetables. He showed her how to bake bread, though he didn't know what Mary used to make it swell the way it did.

Through it all, she said nothing. She served dinner and took the plates away. When he passed through with fresh water for the night's laundering, he found the Colebrooks staring at their plates while his mother ministered to them as if she'd always been there. Charles leaned a little when she departed them, to see where she went.

"I put Gita in my room and gave her a plume to play with," Eligius told her at the end of her first evening. "She's been quiet."

"I will have her back now."

"I want to show you something before you retire."

"It's been enough for one day."

"Let me show you what I've done. Surely you've heard talk of the camera."

"I don't know of such things."

"Isn't that reason enough to come see?"

"I don't want to."

Hefting Gita in his arms, he walked to the servant's door. She followed, only pausing to consider the paintings before continuing out to the yard, and to the door of Holland House. "The roof was as open as ours," he said. "I put glass in the holes. I showed the memsa'ab where to find the sun in here. I made curtains and a lever." He pulled on a dangling cord, opening the curtains across the ceiling to reveal stars pressed against the glass.

He turned to show her the camera. "I thought it was a beast, but it's wondrous."

She was already through the cottage door. Gita sat high in her arms, watching him as they returned to the main house.

He fought the urge to chase after them. The notion struck him as distasteful. Things were different now.

Julia sat in the gazebo, regarding Sudarma and Gita as they passed. "I require ink," she called to him. "And some paper, and a way to hold them still in this wind."

"I will get them."

"See to your mother first. Then come out, Eligius. Bring something for me to write about, up close. Holland House will be the backdrop, but I need something of my own to gaze upon. Something right here."

He went inside the main house. The night was deepening around him. The smoldering gas lamps in the house pierced only as far as the edge of the porch.

He took his mother to Mary's quarters, then brought her the maid's thin, stiff linen to fit over her straw mat. It was in all respects a marked improvement over their hut's meager shelter, yet Sudarma looked around with a bitter, disapproving expression. She placed the sheet atop her bed and sat upon it. Gita crawled through the dirt on the floor, flecking her hair with it.

"Do you require anything else?" he asked.

"You are called. The mistress outside."

"In the morning, I'll come wake you. I'll show you where everything is to make breakfast. The food for the feast will arrive at dawn, and you'll start cooking immediately. Some of it is being roasted by the butcher in a pit. There will be much to see to. I'll help you as best I can."

"I know you will. I know all you've done is for us." She was a storm of discontent. "I don't want to die here. I don't know these walls. Their stares are worse than I ever thought. I would never have sent you if I'd known what it was like to be looked at this way. Better the fields. I want to see my home."

"And him? You were lonely. It wasn't like it was with appa."

She was silent.

"He took a life and life has to be made whole. It's done. Make a home of it here, mother. As I did. As I was asked to do. Our village is gone, don't you know that? We are in their house now, and we have to make of these small corners something like a life. That's all. Nothing else." She nodded.

Later, he thought, he might reflect on her in this moment. It was just a little nod of her head. A simple enough thing. But after a lifetime supporting unbearable burdens, the words that finally sank her to her knees were his.

"If you go to your window," he said, "you and Gita can see me. I'm not far away." His eyes wandered. "May I take that?"

"Go." She went to the window.

He took the battered diya and ran outside gratefully. There was wind, and the trees to give it voice.

That evening, his mother sat at her new room's window, facing the side of the yard and the jungle beyond. Her body was cut from candlelight. He couldn't see her features but felt certain she was watching him.

Julia wrote of Holland House as being much more proximate to the gazebo than it was in fact. When she began to shape the diya with her words, he told her it sounded so real that he wanted to pick it up from her paper and see the two of them reflected in its dimpled brass hide. She smiled.

It was a while before he glanced at the house again. By then it was late, and his mother was gone from the window.

BEFORE DAWN, HE stoked a fire in the oven and surrounded it with porous stones as Mary had done, to radiate heat to the ends of the oven's crevices. It would stay piping for hours, and keep the meat and breads warm without burning.

He slipped through the still house. The brisk air pulled his skin into a million tingling little knots. Outside, he surveyed the grounds, envisioning the throngs that would descend on Dimbola in anticipation of Sir John Holland's arrival. By then he would have staked torchiers along the path they would walk, to be lit when the humidity drew the insects.

The smells of roasted pig, charred lamb and game hen filled the air long before the butcher's cart sidled into view. Together they unloaded the cart and stacked the meats in the ovens. "I'll wager you've never seen such food in this house," the butcher said. "Nor will you again, unless your mistress charms her way to another suitor."

"Suitor?"

"It's what's being said, boy. She cares little for her husband's reputation or else she wouldn't race the devil to outdo it. You wouldn't know such things, but she's a shame in polite society. Bringing her conquest over the ocean, no less."

"The man who comes is a teacher and friend. He comes for his own work. She has said."

"What would a servant know? My customers are her betters. I put my faith in them. Ah, I see I've troubled you."

"It is no business of mine."

"Do you know that my best customer now employs the Colebrooks' girl, Mary? She asked me to send word to you. They are in need of a boy for their horses."

A servant who only performed one task? he thought.

"Come to the market." The butcher stepped up to his cart and took up the reins. "Ask for Seward. That's me. I'll get you to a paying house."

"What does it matter to Mary, what happens to me?"

"I can tell you for a fact it doesn't. But they'll put an extra shilling in her pocket for locating a boy. And she'll take care of me in turn." He grinned. "I'll be looking for you."

Eligius returned to the house. His mother was in the kitchen, staring at the ovens. "Baste them regularly," he told her.

"Our master and mistress were arguing." She kept a hand on Gita, who crawled over the cutting block. "The master is upset at the cost of all this."

"He didn't pay. It's of no matter to us. It's for you to cook this as if it were always here."

"How you've learned."

"Yes. I've picked up quite a bit. I've much to do this morning. I'll check back on you in a while. Make sure all the tables are set with linen and silver. You remember. I showed you."

"Yes."

"Take your sari off, mother. We are not in Matara."

Outside, he climbed to the top of Holland House, the better to see the ship bearing his memsa'ab's mystery man, Wynfield's son and their possessions. By the time of their expected arrival, and taking into account the journey from the port to Dimbola, there would be precious little time left to show Holland her work.

He scanned the sea and found the ship easily. A second ship trailed it. Its shadow cut open the waves like a maid's mending shears.

He turned to yell at the house, then paused. Catherine was seated on the porch, awaiting all her guests. There was Ewen, as usual chasing peacocks, but every now and again he slowed a little, his attention wandering away from childish pursuits. There was Sudarma, polishing the last of the plates in the sun. Gita sat at her feet, fascinated with Ewen's games. And there was Julia, paper and quills at her side, turning the bracelets adorning her wrists like a self-conscious bride feeling the foreign weight of her ring.

He climbed down and adjusted the curtain over the roof window before walking to the porch. "Two ships in the harbor, memsa'ab. They're close."

"Hurry, then. Guests will be arriving shortly."

"I will. I'll return soon." He glanced at his mother.

"I will see that she does all that is required," Catherine said.

He nodded and left the porch. He heard his memsa'ab's voice, louder than usual. "How odd our little family has become. Yet we persevere, eh?"

The Windowed World

QUEEN AND CHATHAM STREETS WERE EMPTY. COILS OF
voices led him to the St. John Company and its dock. It seemed
all of colonial Ceylon had come to greet the ships. Over the heads
of the murmuring crowd, great conicals rose like volcanoes
stolen from his mother's mythic bedtime stories, to be machine-
stamped in British metal.

The crowd was oddly cheered by the sight of the vessels.
Every hint of activity aboard sent a thrill through them, especially the men; they cheered as if at a cricket match.

The vicar of the Galle Face sat aboard his carriage near the
lip of the dock. The carriage door was open to allow the public
their glimpse of this reposed creature in white flowing robes. Two
boys were in the carriage as well, sitting awkwardly at the
vicar's feet. Dressed in lucent pearl robes of their own, the boys
pulled at the ruffled collars mercilessly binding their necks.

Gangplanks rolled down from the great ships' bellies. The
first men showed themselves above the deck railings, and
Eligius understood why all these people had come to holler and
preen.

One after another, the soldiers stepped down the planks
of both ships, rifles atop their shoulders, bayonets fixed, their
uniforms vivid against the dull gray hulls. They made their way
through the crowd to cries of "give them hell all!" and strewn
orchids in their path. The grim set of their jaws did nothing to
detract from their youth. More boys.

Eligius stood atop his cart. The rest of the soldiers disembarked, the crowd thinned, and on the first ship, a series of crates emerged from the hold in the hands of unsteady porters. An elderly man with an unkempt silver shock of hair that shuddered in the shore breeze moved to the gangplank on distrusting, seaworn legs. His arm was held by a younger man with curly tresses arranged perfectly on the padded shoulders of his brown jacket. The younger man gazed across the dock with pursed lips. He spat into a kerchief, which he let fall to the ground.

Eligius tied his cart horse to a sapling and made his way to the dock. "Holland sa'ab? I am sent by Colebrook memsa'ab to meet you."

The older man smiled. Close, he was as old as Charles, but thinner. His eyes blazed with intelligence.

It was Wynfield's boy who spoke. "Our things," George said dismissively. "We will ride with the vicar. I trust that you know your way back."

Eligius waved to the porters, who trundled down the gangplank onto the dock. He led them to his cart, where they made a small mountain of trunks and crates. While he tied the crates down, the vicar welcomed both men with a proffered hand and a nod towards the road. They all turned and looked at him.

The vicar's altar boys stepped out of the carriage. They listened as the vicar spoke, then walked towards his cart while behind them, Holland and Wynfield stepped into the Galle Face carriage. "There's no room for us," one of the boys told Eligius. "We ride with you."

They climbed atop his cart. The bigger boy took up the reins and whippered them ineffectually. Eligius stepped up. The vicar's boy relinquished the reins and under Eligius' knowing hand, the horse trundled forward.

He guided his overburdened cart alongside the vicar's grand carriage. Inside, the men raised snifters to their lips.

The journey bled everything out: the air of any comfort, the sky of any cover, the boys of any semblance of civility.

Despite his demonstrable understanding of their language, they spoke of the soldiers and what they had in store for Ceylon's troublemakers. "Back to the dirt that made them," said the bigger boy. "Vicar prayed it from the pulpit and here they are, come to push the kuthas into the sea."

The small one was younger by a good five years. He asked the boy to say it, say how the soldiers would proceed. "Will they march one by one or two by two? Will they march straight through the forest to the drums? Will they make a route of it?"

"They'll march straight down the heathens' throats. Then the fires will go out and it'll be a different cry goes up."

"I hear the Indians don't use guns."

"The sepoys can't abide that there's tallow in the cartridges, how's that for you?"

Eligius tried to block them out. His mind grasped for the first thing he could hold that wouldn't break, and it found Julia in Holland House, her hair lit by candles.

Guests were arriving as he pulled his cart to Dimbola's gate. The women gathered under the tarp while their men stood smoking in groups. The vicar's boys half-fell to the ground. Their rowdy energy knew no bounds. Behind them, the vicar's carriage pulled to a stop. Others followed aboard finely constructed vehicles piloted by top-hatted men dressed for another land and climate, who climbed down and held the hands of dainty, cautious women as they stepped out.

Governor Wynfield put his arm around his son's shoulders. Lady Wynfield rose from her table and kissed him tenderly.

"Keep that crate out of the sun!" the young Wynfield said. "The canvases will be ruined."

"I am well aware of the light's effects," Eligius said.

He carried a crate into Holland House. Setting it down, he found that a corner of the lid had been split open. Carefully, he lifted it up enough to peer inside. There he saw a painting of dense blackness. It was woven with swirls of luminous, random shapes made all the more vivid by the void around them.

He opened the lid further, revealing more of the designs, until he understood what he was looking at.

Outside, the young Wynfield stood among a group of colonial women. "Tell us of London, George," one of the older dowagers said between sips of tea. "I suspect our new contrivances are years in the routine for you."

"You forget," George said, "I too have been away these many years now, with Sir John. I pine for civility, though perhaps not as much as you."

"But what must our old home think of us?" the woman said. As Eligius passed on his way to retrieve another crate, he saw her hands tremble. "Our unrest. These thugs."

"Thuggees," a younger woman, pretty in pale orchid lace, corrected her. "They attack defenseless women on the street and take what they want!"

"I myself was offered a civil service post, like my father." George snapped his fingers at Sudarma. She went to retrieve a cup. "But the call of art was too strong. My blood boils at what I heard on the journey here. We docked at Calcutta at my father's direction, to pick up the garrison. Those soldiers spoke of terrible injustices these people have perpetrated on us, and after all we've done. We build rails for them, and now? We use them to ferry our children from their violence and sickness."

"Would that we could ferry ourselves from boredom and ennui," the younger woman said. "Well, I for one have been awaiting your arrival. It's high time I was portrayed by a legitimate English-bred artist, not these street painters. I insist you schedule me immediately."

Eligius finished carrying the crates into Holland House while the colonial wives accosted George for his painter's hand. Each had a thought as to how she should be depicted. George offered flattering words and promises of great beauty as his parents looked on approvingly.

In another hour, he had unpacked his cart and put everything in the cottage. By then all the guests had arrived; more than Dimbola had ever seen. The vicar occupied a seat of honor next to Sir John at a front table.

And then Catherine emerged from the house, and everyone paused to look at her. Sir John stepped past George as if he were a low branch in his path. He held out his hands and Catherine came. She let him embrace her.

They exchanged soft words and as they began to walk together, Catherine felt the want within herself. She longed to give herself over to the sort of benign gaiety she saw in other women. Seeing Sir John again, with her now, she possessed only her struggles. So much had gone past since she'd pressed her letter into his hands and hoped that in the unseeable future, he would be within her sphere, speaking to her of science and loss. Now he was here, come halfway around the span of the world, and all she could think of was what she had lived, with no one to speak to. The qualities of the rain in the cottage. Its sound against the glass Eligius had installed. The smell of the jungle at dusk, strong despite the raw flame in her nostrils from the chemicals. Lustrous light in the emulsions she'd learned to apply from his letters. How his letters were prayer for her now.

She felt Charles' eyes, Julia's, the wives. She stared at the ground and listened to the padding feet moving towards her. Eligius.

Odd, she thought. To know the sounds of this boy more readily than anyone else's.

"It's almost time," Eligius said. "I have a suggestion."

She excused herself and followed him to the cottage, where he'd set up the camera and prepared solutions of collodion and water to bathe the plate. He fit the frame and operated the pulleys that swathed the roof glass in muslin, trapping the sun in the front of the room.

Last, he showed her the painting in the crate and told her of his thoughts. "If we can steal a moment out of the air," he told her, "can we also build one of our own?"

"Painters make a life of such stagecraft. An interesting thought. Can you direct the light?"

"I know I can."

"Then let us give Sir John an eyeful."

She left him to his work on the roof, gauging the sun. It pleased him to see the vigor in her step as she returned to her guests.

"Have you been prying into my belongings?"

He hadn't even heard anyone approaching the cottage. George Wynfield stood in the doorway below. Julia was with him.

"The crate has been pried open," George said. "The wood has been split. I saw for myself its condition before we left the ship."

Eligius climbed down. "I looked at the painting. I am at fault and I apologize. I've seen your paintings in the house, and I get lost when I look. I just wanted to see more."

He hoped that flattery would cool any anger and spare the memsa'ab from further gossip. It was enough that colonial Ceylon considered her ill-fitting.

George touched his finger to a cold smile. "Are you what they call ... what was that phrase I heard in Calcutta, marvelously evocative ... untouchable?"

"No."

"What does it mean? That no one would have anything to do with you, isn't that it? Doesn't that make you one?"

"There are some who would have something to do with me, sa'ab."

"I would suggest that you think very carefully on how you address me. Perhaps Madame Colebrook tolerates your insolence in the name of cheap labor, but I have no need. A word from me and you will be begging in the street, or in prison."

"I beg only your forgiveness."

Julia's presence behind him boiled the blood in his stomach to steam.

"Is something wrong?" Sir John and Catherine came to

the doorway. Behind them, Eligius saw the elder Wynfield holding court. Among them were some directors he'd seen with Charles. They were listening to the governor speak and nodding gravely.

"It seems that this servant couldn't wait for a look at my work," George said. "Strange that he appears to be the only servant in this household. One would expect him to be too busy for prying, Lady Colebrook."

"I offer my own apologies for my servant," Catherine said. "I'm sure he meant no harm."

"No, I suppose he didn't. But that's hardly the point, is it? I shall mention this to my father."

"I'm sure there's no need," Sir John said. "Certainly there's no harm that I can see, and no one of consequence has seen it. I think we can put it to rest, George."

"I defer as always to your tolerance. Tell me, boy, did you even understand what you saw?"

"It's a map, sa'ab."

"How could you possibly know that?" George's anger rose.

"Perhaps his betters told him," Sir John said. "Young man, come here."

Eligius approached the crate. "You've seen maps before?" Sir John asked.

"Yes."

"But how could you see this as a map? Do you not see mere points of light?"

"Only up close. But if I make my sight wide, I see shapes."

"Make your sight wide?"

"I learned to do it when I was little. There's a place where I go to see the sky, and I can see small or wide. One star or all."

"I would like to see this place."

"I will take you, sa'ab. From there, maybe you will see a map."

Sir John laughed, a warm chime that made Eligius smile. "From there, I will see the untied end of the tapestry I have been weaving for many years. Science brings me from one end of the earth to the other so that I can map the whole of the heavens.

George here is painting my map according to my notations. He takes excellent direction."

"Thank you," George said quietly.

"And now I hear I'm to see yet another advance in science, isn't that right, Catherine? What of this portraiture of yours? Tell me you've found a way forward, out of the mire."

George lifted the camera cloak and peered beneath it. "I should hardly equate portraits with what our host dabbles in, this fad of phantoms on glass."

"Nor would I equate it," Catherine said, "with your paintings or anything else. It is but an inquiry. Certainly nothing to seize the mind, as with your remarkable journey."

"Memsa'ab, the sun is just right."

"Gentlemen, I beg you to excuse us. Please enjoy the feast, and I'll rejoin you shortly."

George let the camera cloak drop. "Julia, shall we leave your mother to her contraption and spend some time reacquainting ourselves?"

"I need her," Catherine said. "I ask for your patience."

"Of course. Sir John, I shall have to settle for your quite familiar face."

"Might I stay?" Sir John asked Catherine. "I'd like to see the process."

"Indulge me just this one time, so that I might startle your eyes. After that, you may both grind these images down with analysis."

"Then I shall set a seat aside for you, if your husband won't mind."

"I'll find you."

"Bring the servant with you," Sir John said. "I would like to hear more about the southern skies from someone who lives beneath them."

After they left to rejoin the feast, Eligius drew the curtain closed.

"I'm only glad father isn't here," Julia said. "It's enough that he draws into himself at the thought of hard earned money paying your posts to another man. Must you be so obvious on his property?"

Catherine busied herself with the camera lens. "I'll not hear of this. Not now. I have been waiting a long time to show Sir John what I can do with the science he helped bring into the world." She opened the aperture. "Do you think I simply want to seduce him? Is that as far as you can see? Outside there is an arrogant boy, and if you think no more of yourself than what men think of you, he will own you too. Now sit still and follow my instructions."

Julia turned away. She raised a hand to her pale eyes to shield them from the sun.

Eligius put the bauble in her hand. Points of light danced across the wall. He turned it until one jewel came to her fingertips.

"There," Catherine said. "Yes, Julia." She opened the camera shutter.

He let out his breath as Julia's face burned into glass. In time, he tipped a clay pot and washed the glass plate. Catherine retreated with it to a shaded corner. She cradled it in her arms. In a moment, she lifted her head. "Go. I can see it."

Eligius ran from the cottage. He saw Gita sitting on the grass near the edge of the Colebrooks' land, watching the other children make their mad dashes around her. It amazed him that she didn't cry at the chaos. Already, she had seen so much.

He found Sir John at Charles' table. "The memsa'ab asks that you come now."

"I can see excitement in your eyes," Sir John said. Behind them, George and his father also rose. Eligius thought of protesting, but held his tongue.

"My boy," Sir John said. "Your hand."

His palms and the tips of his fingers were black, save the pinprick of light glinting from the spread flesh between his thumb and forefinger. "Sometimes, sa'ab, her portraits live on more than glass."

He brought Sir John to the cottage door. Catherine held the plate up like a mirror to Sir John. "My God," he whispered. "Catherine, tell me how."

Watching the astonishment rain across this wizened old man's face, she thought that most lives, if lived long enough, came to make rational sense. Once per year happenings that filled a letter, matters of no consequence that moved each minute to the next; these made good sense. She believed this. Her life made no sense at all, or else she would not feel what she felt. She would not feel that this was worth losing everything for, to arrest a scientific heart. Such a life could not make sense to anyone.

She told him of the cotton and collodion, the amber for her arrested paintings of light and time. "Still, they escape."

"But the glass. Such a thing hasn't occurred before. I will write a paper on this. We shall pierce the mystery."

He drew closer, touching the plate's wooden shell. Julia's image had risen so much more. Turned away from the camera, she sat before utter darkness. The bauble's refracted light rained white jewels on the curtain behind her. They scattered meaninglessly around her, all save one – the one he directed to rest just above her outstretched hand. That one was enough to make a bedtime story of her. The girl who cradled a star.

"Before it is lost," Catherine told Sir John, "do me the honor of giving it a name."

"Why does one bother putting a name to something that won't last?" Governor Wynfield stood in the doorway with his son. Behind them, guests gravitated to the cottage, drawn by the proclaimed interest of their most distinguished guest. "Paintings deserve names," he said. "I can't say the same for this. We should hardly remember it beyond now."

"There are many things that come to us that don't stay," Catherine said. "You and I differ on their worthiness of memory."

"For myself," Sir John said, "I won't forget the moment this young woman came into the world a second time."

Julia's face was becoming dissolute. "It will be lost in moments," Catherine said resignedly. "I cannot fix the image long."

"Nor can Reijlander or Talbott, your peers in Europe."

"Peers," George snorted.

"Bring it to the door," Sir John said. "Quickly now."

Catherine did as he asked. With Julia at her side, she held the fading image out for her guests to see. Sir John joined her. "A marriage of the mortal and the divine!" he announced.

The guests passed the plate. The men took first glance and raised questions of chemicals and time frames. They were analytical and practical, their comments limited to materials and labor.

"Other than time," Governor Wynfield said loudly, "what is gained by this over a painting? It is vague and offers no more to the eye than can be seen by the average man. There is nothing divine here."

"Nevertheless, we must find a way to fix it," Sir John said. "Your post enables you to import from London at will, does it not?"

"It does."

"I'll prepare a list of chemicals. Might I expedite receipt?"

The Governor's eyes narrowed. "I trust you won't be abandoning your project with my son for this. Not after so much time and money has been invested."

"There will be due time for both."

Sir John carried the frame into the yard. Their processional wound between the tables, and with each step they gained a following of guests. "Hurry," Sir John said, "for those of you who wish to see. This beauty, so like a woman, is fickle!"

"Tell me," Lady Wynfield asked Catherine when the image came to her for viewing. "How would you portray me? Or any of my friends? Would you have us grasping at stars? Would we stand interminably in your hut?"

"I would simply capture you. What the glass reveals of you

is up to the beholder. I would dare say, we might all see something quite different in you."

"Really, madam. Do you hope to open a portraiture? Hang a shingle, as it were?"

"Why not? Why not a new manner of portrait, and why not by my hand? While we ponder, I ask, why not more than portraiture?"

"I believe a painter's eye and a gifted brush will always speak to the soul." Lady Wynfield tapped the glass plate with a reckless fingernail. All of Julia that remained was her shining iris.

A woman emerged from the guests to touch the frame. She was in her twilight, Catherine thought, but there had been a beauty once. "My husband arranged for me to pose for a painter in Florence. I cannot argue that his work was lovely. But should I not see it daily where it now hangs, I would not remember it at all because its details are not mine. I'm festooned with flowers I did not grow, in a room with a window view I'd never seen before. He made a dutiful, obedient wife of me. I understand that is what every woman should be. But there was another me. If your contraption finds her, I'll happily sit in front of it. And if it finds me beautiful, so much the better."

"Really, Jane," Lady Wynfield said. "My son is quite capable of rendering you in any manner you see fit to be immortalized."

"It is difficult to understand, I suppose."

"For me, it would be a café window in Paris."

The women stirred at Catherine's voice. Outsider. Flouter of their lives.

"On the eve of my trip abroad, my mother spoke to me. She said, 'A good mother should tell you to study, to regard art, to learn to speak of literature and verse.' But she didn't. Rather, she told me to learn to drink sherry and watch the world pass from the panes of cafes. She said I would feel wicked and unbridled and unique. I would watch the women walking alongside important men, tethered by the hands to their children. Women looking neither this way nor that. She told me I was young and arrogant, and that surely I would be certain that they never sat where I sat at the moment of their passing. They never saw what I saw. But one day I would understand why such women could not bring themselves to look around. For fear that they might see the likes of me in the window, and in me the girl they once imagined themselves to be.'

"I thought it sad to hear my mother say such things. I was fifteen. I was terrified that before I or my sisters ever came to the world, before she met my father, there had been another woman who lived in the full bloom of expectation for an altogether different life. She could not take refuge from that memory, even fifteen, twenty years later."

"You speak eloquently of yourself," Lady Wynfield said.

"If I don't, madam, I am confident no one else will. I bear no slight to your son's esteemed talents. But there is in every moment something to startle the eye and the heart. There must be. A painting seeks to make a summary of those moments. This that I do, it is the moment. I point the camera and I wait, and I trust that I might see it. I shall endeavor to improve the process. When I do, may I portray you and make a gift of it, Jane?"

"You've had a moment to call your own," Lady Wynfield said. "That moment, like your piece of glass, has ended." She walked to her son's table. Her friends followed.

Let it all come down, Catherine thought. She'd placed herself among the wives however briefly and moved in the appropriately deferential manner. She'd been loyal to a man, and to a sensible marriage built on respect and civility, and love, after a fashion. These were not matters to be lightly set aside because of the tyranny of her desire to lay open time. Yet listening to the chatter of these women only underscored how far away she now was, from the girl who journaled in a café at the heart of the world.

Some lives, she thought, were destined to make no sense.

Sir John patted her shoulder, breaking her reverie.

"There will be critics at every turn. You cannot take a step in this world without hearing from them. All the more so for a woman. I've no doubt of your ability, Catherine, but I would be remiss if I didn't tell you that I worry about the propriety of what you do."

"There are those who question the propriety of mapping the heavens, John. You've heard the whispers. As if fixing the location of the stars negates their existence. How do you answer them? Or do you answer at all?"

"Truly, Catherine, I am coming about to this opinion. You should have been born a man."

She took the frame from Eligius' hands. Another baby born to the world, who failed to puzzle out the trick of staying. "Think of all I would have missed," she said, staring at the empty glass.

The End of the Sky

THE FOLLOWING EVENING, ELIGIUS FINISHED LINING
Holland House's walls with thirty of Sir John's maps. They
spanned the length of the cottage and formed a continuous tapestry of the sky and its boundless constellations. At his direction,
Eligius left room for what would come. A map of the southern
hemisphere's canopy.

After, the Colebrooks gathered on the grass. Catherine
recited verses from Tennyson's *Ulysses* while Charles and
Sir John smoked and listened from opposite sides of the gazebo.

Eligius lay on the grass with Gita. She lifted her head
and met his hand with her own. He was enjoying his sister's alertness. Food and a roof agreed with her.

Sudarma gathered up the remains of the feast's cakes,
crushed them with a bit of anise and chutney, and shaped them
into delicate squares. She served them with tea and brandy,
then returned to the kitchen and filled the quiet evening with the
sound of clattering earthenware and splashing well water.

Everyone paused in their conversation to listen. So familiar,
so mundane, yet they huddled around the din of normalcy as if
it were the first fire of winter.

Matara came to Eligius' mind. Its own sounds were lost
now. One day a child might view its ruins and hear a story
of what the crumpled walls once held. A place of magic, where
girls' hands sprouted mendhi veins to mark them married, and
men swam with lights at Diwali.

"I wish to offer a prayer," Catherine said. "For our guest's safe passage to us." She bowed her head, as did Julia and Sir John. Ewen fidgeted at his father's feet, but Charles did not chastise him. He gazed over the grounds.

Eligius bowed his head as well. Catherine had a quiet, calming prayer voice. The words made him think of the great hall of colored glass and stone figures. It had been a long time since she'd gone to the church. Not since its desecration. But she was no less religious. He saw her pause each day before the house's many crosses.

He was grateful his mother was not outside to see him.

"All that I have prayed for," Catherine intoned, "has come to be. My children thrive. My husband pursues his great work. My esteemed guest has arrived safely. I ask nothing for myself."

I cannot pray to you, she thought. *What you did cannot be undone. And if my prayers to this golem of wood and glass are answered, then it shall hold my heart. I wonder if you'll notice the absence of one heart.*

"We stand on the cusp of a new year," she said, "and I am grateful for what has been."

Sudarma poured brandy for her, Charles and Sir John, who was unfolding one of George's sketches. "It's all right. Young Wynfield isn't here, and it's my work, after all."

Eligius surrounded the drawing with candles. The light found hidden hues, blue orchid in the stars and misty gray in the night sky. Despite himself, he had to admit George's adeptness.

"See here." Sir John gestured to the drawing's edge with one of Julia's quills. "The last of the visible nebulae from Cape Town, as seen from Table Mountain. That's where Catherine and I met."

"1836," Catherine said. "I daresay I was at low ebb."

"All of us who left England for other lands can be thought of as such. You, Charles, you were there, were you not?"

"Briefly. For all the good it did."

Catherine patted her husband's leg. "Charles had complications from malarial fever. It was terrible that year. Yet he risked all to come here. My dearest still suffers from it."

"It astonishes me, Charles, how you overcame illness to sit on the John Company Board. And you, Catherine. How far you've come from that terrible day, when I saw you holding sadness itself in your hands."

"In truth, I'm surprised you ever agreed to favor me with inclusion in your work. Why did you? Am I merely a muse?"

"Catherine, my enquiries are nothing more than theorizing. There is no blood in them. Questions to be answered in my corner of the ellipse, on the journey to the next question and the next. But then I saw you that day… "

His voice trailed off.

She knew where it had lost its way.

"I shan't forget the child's face, you see. You have tied him to this work. I've not experienced such a thing before. Not even in the starmap. I came to the end of the visible sky in Alexandria, now to the hemispheric expanse above Ceylon, and yet I think of the boy."

Julia held her father's hand tightly.

Eligius could see the old lion's sad anger emerge. He could see as well Catherine and Sir John, lost in the memory of a child Charles never glimpsed.

"You came to the end of the sky?" he asked, hoping to shift the moment to a simple Indian who needed British guidance. "How is it possible to know?"

"I mapped all that I could and marked where I left off by the Arc of Meridian. I spent the next six years establishing an observatory to sharpen the sight we mortals can train on that great house."

He brought Julia's quill to a cluster of stars that resembled a crouched child. "Every night I made sketches of what I saw around that constellation. Over these many months, I hope to finish."

"Will you pinpoint the cities of the moon?" Charles asked.

"Hasn't Sir John suffered enough of that nonsense?" Catherine said curtly. "Please don't display your ill temper for our guest."

"Cities on the moon?" Julia asked.

"A hoax," Sir John said resignedly. "Courtesy of an American journalist. He published a series of newspaper articles, all attributed to me, detailing life on the moon. The scamp went so far as suggesting my father had discovered it and bequeathed to me the continuation of his work. That truly was the insult. The rest was simply a child's prank as far as I'm concerned. Yet I still hear of it. Those who seek introduction to me place it in their letters. 'I'm familiar with your observation of our moon brethren.' Imagine."

"Did your father show you which star to start with?"

Sir John turned to regard Eligius. "A servant who asks such questions. It is truly a blessing to see our intellectual curiosity rubbing off on these people. Charles, it is a validation of all you came here to do."

"I suppose," Charles said quietly.

"Eligius, my father Sir William built his house of stars for a king."

Into the night Eligius listened to Sir John's living map: his father's astronomy for King George, his own first survey of the skies above England and France, his career at Cambridge and election to the Royal Society, his tally of a thousand nebulae in Orion, his bearing witness to the return of a flying star the colonials called Halley's, and his meeting Catherine in the Cape, where cholera and malaria thinned Britishers like drought thinned his people.

"Since then we have sought to perfect this process from our respective points on the globe," Catherine said. "There are others. Reijlander has ideas."

"And now, I have a question of our curious young Ceylonese." Sir John relit his pipe. "Where did you learn to shape the light?

Catherine told me how you helped construct that marvelous image of beauty."

"When I was very young, I would take glass from the men of my village and play with the sun. I taught myself to make the lights dance in the trees and burn the eyes of the village boys as they played. I helped my father read."

"Glass is precious," Sir John said, "especially to poor people. Was your father an artisan? Did he work on the church I saw at the port?"

Catherine caught Sir John's eyes. She shook her head.

No matter, Eligius thought. I wear your daughter on my skin and keep your shadow under me as I sleep. What trouble could it cause, to talk of difficult things in a place such as this? "My father served this house as I now do. But in my village, many men drink. They smash the bottles when they're done. What was broken, I learned from."

"I'm sorry, my boy."

"Don't pity him." Charles gripped the arms of his chair, sending creaking shudders through the woven wood. "My father drank. He made a fool of himself and made cowards of my mother and sisters. Drink diminishes the man, but only if he allows it."

He shook his daughter's hand from his. She looked at him, stricken. "I don't feel well," he said. "I want to go inside. Eligius, see to it."

"I will help you," Catherine said.

"Eligius."

Eligius took him to his study and put the ratted blanket over his legs. "A cigar and my writing implements, boy. I have work to do."

"Perhaps you should rest. It's late."

"Someone must do this and I don't see anyone to help. Do you?"

He was angry. It was better to give him what he asked for.

When he finished ministering to Charles, he went outside.

Gita was asleep next to Ewen on the grass. He picked her up and put her to bed, and only then did the quiet of the house strike him. His mother's tell-tale sounds had fallen to nothing.

The kitchen was dark. His mother's quarters were empty, but the window was open. He heard branches and leaves being swept aside. She was in the jungle, moving fast.

He followed her trail through the accumulated growth of centuries, a thick stitching of shrubs, vines and branches that reassembled themselves in his wake. Beyond a copse of bread-fruit he saw the boxed roof of a familiar plantation and realized that his mother's path paralleled the one he took back to Matara. But this one was covered, a secret to British eyes.

He saw his mother ahead, moving towards a small clearing amongst the trees. She didn't walk like a woman visiting her once-home. She seemed to punish the land beneath her; the food in her arms made soft colliding sounds, like a sari over grass. She came to a stop at the clearing edge, plates in hand. Waiting.

He whispered her name. She waved him off without looking at him. "You shouldn't be here," she said.

He could hear the sounds of approaching – dry limbs cracking, murmuring voices – and wanted to run. He would leave her where she stood, because she had chosen to be here over the safety he had delivered to her.

No, his father would say. Stay and receive what comes. You are not a man who leaves. There is no name for such a man.

He left the cover of the trees. "Amma, we have to go back before they accuse you of stealing food."

Hari and two other boys appeared. They crossed the clearing to take the food from her plate. He watched them, feeling sick with the sight of them. They were emaciated and in the plain expansion of their protruding ribs, he could see that they would do anything to eat, to get what they did not have. They would kill.

Hari lay his banyan limb on the ground. "The men in the fields and the Britishers' houses all talk of the fine things you've learned. Then they sing in mourning for Chandrak. They do this every day since the soldiers hung him on your word."

Hari's face was no longer that of the boy struggling with the colonials' words. His haunted expression was no different than that of Chandrak by the fire, bottle in hand.

"Bring the machine to us," Hari said. "It has parts of glass and wood. It sounds very rare and valuable. It will fetch a high price."

"No."

Other feral boys emerged at the far side of the clearing. Sudarma moved toward them. Eligius held her back by the arm.

"Remember how afraid you were in the field, with the soldier?" Hari asked. "You cried. You ran. Now you're more afraid to be a man and stand against these people. Forget what you think we will do to you. Do you understand what they do? How they take our land and push us all into the sea?"

"The only beatings I have ever taken," Eligius said, "are from a man like you will become. I will not steal. Chandrak was a murderer. So are you."

Hari's club came down with enough force to drive both Eligius and Sudarma to the ground. She absorbed the brunt. Her palms split open where Hari had brought the club to bear on his intended target, the top of Eligius' head.

"You shame us all!" Hari screamed. "You are worth nothing!"

He raised the club again. Eligius closed his eyes.

"Don't."

Catherine and Julia stood at the edge of the razor grass, with Sir John. Sir John's pistol was level, its hammer cocked. The barrel pointed at Hari.

"Careful, old man," Hari said warily.

"I am old, true enough. But I assure you, the gun is quite new."

"Leave this place!" Catherine stepped in front of her daughter. "I will call the authorities!"

"You be assured, we will be back." Hari slipped into the far trees. "Dimbola will not be safe. There are so many of us and so few of you."

Julia came to Eligius' side. "I heard you call in the jungle."

"Is my mother all right?"

"Her hands need attention," Sir John said. "We must get her back."

"They wanted me to steal the camera. I told him no –"

"I heard you." Catherine took his hand. She and Julia helped him rise. "Every word."

Her eyes glowed softly in the starlight. Something about the long road that light traveled, from the southern skies to her, to him, made him terribly sad. He fell sobbing into her arms. Julia's hand alighted on his back and remained.

Sudarma walked ahead, with Sir John. At the sound of her son's cries, her shoulders fell a little, but she never turned.

GOVERNOR WYNFIELD CAME at midweek with the sergeant of the newly-installed Port Colombo garrison. They took statements from Sir John, Julia and Catherine about the men. No one mentioned Sudarma.

The sergeant came to Eligius last. "You, boy. Do you have anything to add?"

"They threatened to come here. I believe they could. They're angry."

"I suppose you wish to plead the case of these boys," Wynfield said.

"There will be no pleading from me."

After they left, it fell to him to beg forgiveness for his mother's judgment. Sudarma had stolen, he implored Catherine, but out of fear and obligation to feed starving faces she'd known from birth, not a desire to add herself to Ceylon's growing restlessness.

"I hold your word in my hand," she finally said, "that you will be responsible for her. The next transgression and I will have no choice but to say goodbye to you both. And you know how I loathe goodbyes."

After the jungle, Eligius' life at Dimbola took on new configurations. While his mother cooked, he ate in the dining room, listening to Catherine and Sir John regale each other with tales of Paris, of gaily dressed people strolling boulevards alive with perfume and music, of boats as intimate as a wedding vow floating through a city constructed of light. Nights were speckled with candles and torches and hissing gas lamps. By day its buildings made gossip of the sun, passing it from window to brass balcony to the street, each adding to the light a bit of itself: hues, density, a stroke from the palette of shadows that only a city of cobblestone and metallurgy could possess.

"That's where you must find yourself," Sir John told Julia one night. "If you truly intend on writing, that is. There you'll see artists simply daub their brushes in the air and put the light on canvas and paper."

"Now, Sir John," Catherine said, "answer this question. Why do you encourage Julia to cross the ocean to write, which surely men do, yet you express misgivings for my pursuit?"

"She walks in others' well-trod footprints, Catherine. You could be first. There is a difference to men."

"Yet you help me."

"I'm not one to let social convention stand in the way of learning. I intend to publish our progress, and have a name for it. Photography. We shall see if we can't arrest beauty, as you so eloquently put it."

"Do you think I do this only to make beautiful portraits, John?"

"I've offended you."

"No. You've underestimated me. I may have no voyages to my name save that which brought me here. But I know things no man can know. In this world, the babies we women raise are yours, the ones we bury, ours. Our losses to bear, and we're expected to bear them quietly and properly, with only our memories to see us through. I am your equal, and Charles', and any man in this one way. Men grow ill in the name of their work, just as I surely will in mine."

Sudarma returned with a plate full of food. "The sa'ab still hasn't eaten."

"What is he doing?" Julia asked.

"Writing."

Julia cast an imploring look at her mother. "Chase these portraits if you must, but if you wish to arrest something of value, arrest him before he is no longer here."

A tear threatened her eye, but she tilted her head in the defiant gesture that Catherine knew well.

She rose and went to the study. After she was safely away, Julia turned on Sir John. "My mother's correspondence with you set tongues wagging. He's disconsolate. She, distracted. It falls to me to state these matters openly."

"I assure you, I have an abiding respect for your father and no desire to romance Catherine."

"Would that you could convince the gossips of Ceylon otherwise."

"Young lady, it occurs to me that it's your tongue that's taken up this issue most forcefully. I've heard nothing from any-one save you, and that includes Charles himself."

"Only the women speak up in this house, sir. My father prefers to write. How quaintly quiet."

Sir John slapped the table and laughed heartily. "Is every woman in this house dead set on having her say? Eligius, be grateful your mother moves through her tasks with the good sense to be silent."

Sudarma passed through the dining room, her bandaged hands hanging limply. Eligius watched where she went. "A woman's words are only valuable to babies in my world, sa'ab."

"Now you've seen another world," Julia said. "What do you prefer, I wonder."

There was only the smallest hint of play in her voice. "In

my world," he told her, "I would never hear words like these. I would never see what I've seen. Amma, are you finished for the night?"

When she didn't respond, he left for the hall of paintings and his mother's room. Sudarma stood at the window, staring out at the trees swaying in the dark while Gita cried. "She won't stop. I've nothing to give her."

He lit his battered diya. The flame fluttered in the mirrors of Gita's eyes. Softly, he began to hum to her. It was an old song, nameless so far as he knew. He pressed the tune into her ear, and soon its sound washed her mewling under.

"I used to sing that to you," Sudarma said. "To calm your fears."

"I remember."

"There was a time when I worried about all the things you feared. Now I hear you sing it to her. I wonder what Gita fears."

"No matter. Do you have all you need?"

"Yes."

"I have no choice but to do this, mother. You shouldn't have taken from them. It puts us at risk."

"They don't know where else to go. They would never hurt me, Eligius."

"No. Only me."

He closed her door and locked it. Outside, he slid a rusty bar through two slots, sealing her window. She gazed at him through the glass, unmoving. Held.

He walked away before she could fade.

Topographies

OVER THE COURSE OF FEBRUARY AND MARCH, CATHERINE and Sir John experimented with various chemical combinations. They used guncotton to bathe the plates in silver salt. They lacquered skins of collodion onto them and potassium mixed with oil of lavender to lend flexibility. They conversed in drams and durations. Light and shadow became their accomplices. Around a meal or in sleep, there was always a part of them not present; they were pacing the floor of Holland House before Sir John's star maps, lost to all save the glass and the chemical sea from which their obsession might rise, and remain.

Sir John taught her and Eligius how to grind and polish glass for lenses. They reconfigured the camera's plate holder with a spring-loaded trap of imported rosewood. For the collodion and silver salt, Eligius constructed vertical baths so the plates might be coated evenly. On his own he experimented with mirrors and angles. By spring he'd created his own topography of the light's possibilities in Holland House.

It was time to try again.

The morning she chose was cloudy, so Eligius lit candles and placed them in constellations around Holland House. Imagining how they would throw their light once the curtains were closed over the windows and across the ceiling glass, he brought in mirrors. In the corner of the room he fashioned a tiny warren of dark gingham, with an opening at the top to let the heat escape.

She expressed awe at his ability to visualize the light's path. Even he was a little mystified by it. It had always been a part of him, a good part he hoped would never fade. If anything, working with her had honed his abilities even further. He felt important in his role. She could not conjure her images without him, and told him so.

The Wynfields arrived at mid-morning, interrupting their preparations. Their carriage pulled to the gate just ahead of a long column of British soldiers on the march. The soldiers continued on, pausing to bow their heads at the disembarking family.

Eligius met them. "I wish to see Charles immediately," the governor said.

"I'll ask him to come out."

"Is he so unwell that he cannot take the breeze these days?"

"We are hoping he gets better, sa'ab."

Wynfield brushed past. "And what of your mistress?" He pointed to Holland House.

"Get my wife some tea. I will see myself to your sahib."

George exited the carriage last. He opened the gates and strode onto the grounds as if he owned them.

Eligius escorted the Wynfields to the main house. The governor headed for the study, closing the door behind him.

"My tea," Lady Wynfield said.

He knew Catherine and Sir John were setting up the camera and would have need of him. Circumstances would not wait for long.

"I will make it." Sudarma stood in the hall. "He has work for the memsa'ab. I will see to any need you have."

Grateful, Eligius ran out to the yard. Julia and George were in the gazebo. George was speaking to her sternly. She sat with her head bowed as George wagged a disapproving finger at her.

Her writing implements were near; perhaps, Eligius thought, George was critiquing her. But Julia wasn't answering back. Her passivity disquieted him.

Catherine and Sir John were positioning the camera when

he entered Holland House. "Tell her it's time," Catherine said. "This cannot wait."

"She's coming," Sir John said. "Young Wynfield is escorting her."

"How chivalrous," she said dryly.

Julia crossed the yard as if she'd just awakened from a broken sleep. George linked his arm in hers. "You should be proud of your lovely daughter," he said. "She is to be my next portrait. I've put off all other commissions for her."

"If you wish," Catherine said.

"In point of fact, the theme of this portrait is love." He took Julia's hand and kissed it. "We begin immediately. I shall insist on a dress suited to the theme. Julia, see to it."

"Yes."

"Till tomorrow, then."

Julia took her seat. Hot blush decanted her cheeks.

Catherine peered through the camera lens. Julia sat at its center, yet scarcely occupied the frame.

Eligius moved candles closer to her until a pale shadow rippled the door behind her. "Did he hurt you?" he whispered as he arranged the candles in a circle.

"What would a servant do about such a thing?" Julia's eyes found something within the years-old shadow on the wall; the memory of a portrait.

He lit the last of the candles. Catherine selected a glass plate. Under her watchful gaze, he held it steady as she lacquered collodion onto the glass and slid it into place.

Smoke from the candles made ripples in the air. Inside the camera, a process moved like the carrying sea. She could almost hear the rustling of Eligius' light as it burned this silent, remembering girl into a sculpture.

Julia was looking away. It was too late to change her.

"Willful child," Sir John muttered.

Under the cloak, Catherine let go. She lost the touch of the wooden box. The partition of glass at her eye ceased its separation and became simply her sight.

She studied her daughter's frank beauty. The turn of her head. The casual clasp of hands in her lap. The serenity on her face; no longer did the muscles of her mouth or the aperture of her eye speak of youth in perpetual search of adolescent outrage at perceived slights. When had she become a woman? When had so much of the child departed?

There was in Julia's repose something terrible and powerful. Only death was as still as this.

This thing I do, she thought. May it tie a bit of light to we who come into the world already on the path to departing it. Just a bit of light, so we can be seen a little while after we're gone.

"Now," she said.

They coated the glass with sodium hyposulfite, then bathed it. She felt the burning sink through her skin, running into her blood like groundwater.

Positioning the plate inside the warren, she lit more candles and put a mirror next to the light, intensifying it. Julia's image came in a thin cumulus. Haze from the smoking candles came with her, wrapping her glassed face in a gray fog. Her eyes glistened with silver and steel.

Her image did not leave. The boy next to her could have breathed and breathed. The glass held her.

"My lord," Sir John muttered. "Catherine, my lord. Look at it. The first."

"Let me see." Julia came no closer than the edge of the candle circle. She held out her hand for the portrait.

"The first triumph is of you," Sir John said.

"How odd, that it should happen to be this moment and no other. There is a tyranny of happenstance to it."

She knelt and blew the candles out, then slipped over them carelessly. A few tumbled in the wake of her dress, spilling droplets of wax that swiftly hardened on the floor. "You are to be congratulated, mother. Perhaps later, I can see it again in a different light."

She returned to the gazebo. There, George motioned for her writing pad. He sat across from her, studying her and making swift strokes across the paper with a quill.

"Such indulgence," Sir John said. "Really, Catherine. Your eldest gives free reign to her every emotional whim."

He considered the image. "This cloud, Eligius, is this from the smoke? An interesting effect and not at all unpleasant. Catherine, you can re-create this at will. Now, what to call it? Catherine, are you listening?"

Hardy, so still at her side. The light in the bungalow at the moment he came and did not breathe. The ride to the Maclears'. The lichen blooms along the sea path. All of it had slipped between her fingers long ago. All of it, now too far away to bring back.

What she'd prayed for, she held. The stilled moment told her that prayer meant nothing.

This was something else. Prayers were dead words elevated to divinity by finite men. But this.

I brought forth the holy. I made light stop.

Outside in the gazebo, George stood over Julia. She kept her gaze to the ground. The distance and the somber gauze of threatened rain veiled her. To those in Holland House who saw her, she was as marble-gray as her photograph.

SUDARMA ASKED TO be locked in early that night, after the last dish was cleared and fruit set aside to ripen for the morning meal. Gita was crying again, only this time Eligius could not find the diya to calm her. Ewen had taken it for a plaything, he concluded. A servant had little right to object.

Julia remained in the gazebo after the Wynfields departed. The wind took up loose sheets from her writing pad and made scattering leaves of them.

After seeing to his mother, he gathered the papers.

George had sketched intersecting ovals and circles, different studies of the same subject: her.

Her face was all that he had detailed. Her mouth. Her cast-off eyes.

"I want to be alone," she said when he presented the gathered papers to her.

He held up his hands. "See the black skin. Can you see yourself? I think it will last a long time."

She didn't answer. He waited. He counted breaths and hoped something would surface in her eyes. "I'll leave you to your thoughts," he finally said.

When he'd almost reached the main house, she called to him. "Name my photograph. Before my mother does. It should be yours to name. It was your light."

He said that he would, then left her for his bed. Reaching under his mat, he withdrew the feather paper. Daylight would come soon. Until then he would try to think of a name for her stillness. Maybe he would conjure one that fit. Then his heart would murmur like the innards of the camera, and all would remain.

NEWS OF JULIA'S photograph gripped Ceylon that spring. It eclipsed the whispers of a rising tide among the native populace, of thuggee bands, theft, fires set against shops and even plantations. Seeking something to distract them, the Britishers found in Julia's image an ember of divinity with which to warm themselves.

By midsummer, every husband of importance had contacted Catherine. Whether for their wives or themselves, they sought her out for what she provided. Irrefutable proof of one privileged moment in their lives, to hold back what threatened to overtake them. They even braved the monsoon season to show up on Dimbola's doorstep, yearning for immortality.

Jane Pike came first. She spoke of her disappointment in the Florence portraitist, and her secret self. "I wanted to sing in the great opera houses. In my dreams, the sound of my voice broke hearts."

Catherine positioned the camera further back in Holland House and dressed one wall in curtains. Eligius strew orchids on the floor and put a stand to the left of a small coal line. Mrs. Pike followed instruction assiduously. She held her arms out just so and cast her eyes to the sky. She opened her mouth around the words to her favorite aria. While positioning her, Catherine told Ewen to pretend he was in the audience at a great hall. "Think of something to keep you still," she said.

Whatever Ewen thought of brought tears to his eyes. Mrs. Pike's silently sung note became the second triumphant photograph.

Ewen appeared in many of the portraits she took that summer. Acolyte, student, muse, even a servant, which made Eligius laugh. Julia had only been in one, before George sought more of her time.

Some of the women paid for their portraits. She kept many of them for her own uses; Eligius helped her make extra prints from the glass of those she especially liked. She was less drawn to the fanciful, the princesses and the triumphant figures from the Bible so many of the women asked for. She favored sadness in its many forms and saw it in places Eligius did not. Mrs. Pike's singer, doomed to be heard only in the theater of her mind. Mrs. Greer's Juliet, dying next to her one true love.

Her favorite, and Eligius', was Mrs. Martin. Her Gretel lay atop a tule sea, waiting for God's hand to take her down.

She and Eligius developed a wordless alchemy amidst the poisons, glass and light. They knew their roles from the moment a patron entered Dimbola. The provision of tea and an improving quality of biscuits fell to him; elicitation of old dreams and some tears fell to her. The moment water met glass, light met paper, the moment to be taken, the position of the last folded cloth, the lens and the light; all this they shared.

They each, in their own way, thought of Julia as summer

gave way to fall. She was gone for long hours. At night she was too sealed within herself to appear in the gazebo. She would catch herself with her hand up near her hair, or at her lips, and she would shiver the posture away as if it was a spider nesting on her skin.

There were other moments like that. Charles had yet to emerge from his study, not truly. At dinner he ate morsels in silence. Most nights he needed help with even the simplest movement. His absence became a guest in the house.

One midnight-dark afternoon, she found Ewen standing at the front door, intent on the shears of rain sweeping the visible world away. She asked what it had been that made him cry, that day in Holland House with Mrs. Pike.

"Father is always sick." He spied Eligius in the hall. "The soldiers killed your father. Soon none of us will have fathers."

He walked away, nodding as if considering the worthiness of what he'd said.

She watched her son return his childish attention to the great outside world. Perhaps he was beginning to understand. Melancholy images resonated in him. Love, dreams. These were things always in the next moment, always ahead. Sadness, though, was a loyal thing. It waited.

MRS. PIKE RETURNED at summers's end. By then, the rains had lessened. Autumn took hold of Ceylon and made a twilight world of it. "The photograph has had such a profound effect on me," Mrs. Pike confessed, "that I am compelled to beg of you. Share them."

She brought forth a small velvet sack. In it were more rupees than Eligius had seen in one place before, and a slip of paper.

Catherine turned the paper over in her hand. "This is an address in London."

"My brother manages a gallery there. I would be pleased to send him some of your portraits."

"I'm honored, but I am not a worthy enough artist."

"Let others be the judge of that. All I know is that I cannot stop thinking of the photograph. Each time I look at it, I find something I didn't notice before."

Catherine spoke to Sir John of the invitation. He favored the idea. "Make a collection of these portraits, Catherine. An album. Important men, perhaps, that will make the appropriate impression in London or Paris. If others see how posterity favors them, there will be a line of society members from the door to the gate. You've already done a world of good distracting your neighbors from Ceylon's troubles. That is no mere trifle."

Seeing her room aglow late into the night, Eligius brewed some tea and brought it to her. He set the cup and saucer down on her desk, next to Julia's photograph and a glass with a dry film of brandy. "Will you send Julia's to London?" he asked.

"No. Not that one."

He was glad.

"Have you noticed this before?" She gestured to a bright glow in Julia's left eye. A reflection of a candle, imprecise and pale as milk.

"I see it, memsa'ab."

"It was chance that I caught it. The life in her eyes. I've nothing to do with it. Why do I chase this? I can only fail."

Brandy and a photo had reduced her to a child. The chemical fumes had burned her cheeks and made a butcher's table of her hands but she could not stop nor imagine stopping, not at Julia or Mrs. Murphy or Mrs. Pike, or at an album of Ceylon's most important people.

"When my father died," Eligius told her, "I saw myself in his eyes, and the soldiers behind me. I will never see it again. It left with him. I don't know what you hope for. But I can tell you that while I don't remember any particular leaf, I know the one we made will remain. Maybe that is enough."

"Stay with me a while."

They looked at the images they'd created. They spoke of

Sir John's ideas for grinding new breeds of glass lenses. Eligius promised her. "I will make such a lens one day that will make portrait sitters of the stars."

She promised him. "We will burn dreams onto glass. We will carve memory in light."

"Perhaps we say the same thing. These promises."

"Perhaps we are saying that we will always be together, doing this. Or perhaps we are just hopeless romantics, you and I."

He smiled at the notion, and pored over the images while time let them be. Finally he glanced up and saw that she'd fallen asleep with her head resting atop her arm, and the images displayed before her.

He left her. His thoughts drifted on a sea of doubts and questions. He wondered if she would dream at all. If she would spend the night making maps of the light in her loved ones' eyes. The topography of the way from here to there.

A Map of Ceylon

IN THE MORNING, SHE ASKED CHARLES FOR HIS PER-
mission to be photographed. "No false settings. No candled
clouds. Just you, my husband."

She reached over his desk to take a sliver of mango from
his plate. He hadn't touched any of the breakfast Sudarma
had prepared. Coffee, tea when Sudarma brought it from market,
some biscuits Sir John had secreted in his luggage, brandy and
an evening smoke – this was what he had been subsisting on for
weeks.

That and his work, she thought as she sat in the study with
him. An edifice of paper grew six inches from his desk.

"You worry so," Charles told her. "You think me on the brink."

"It's not that."

"Catherine, your devotion to this pursuit is trivial. There is
too much happening in Ceylon right now. Oh, I've wounded you."

"It is no matter. You've not been yourself. I scarcely see you."

"So this portrait shall serve in my place, then."

"You're terribly skilled with words, Charles. I just wish they
were mine you heard, when I tell you I want to do this for you.
Instead, you seem to listen for what you can cut yourself on."

"Eligius, open that cabinet. The one with the key in the lock."

Charles gave Eligius his papers and told him to place them
inside the cabinet. Eligius locked them in and brought Charles
the key, which the old man secreted in the pocket of his woolen
coat.

"I've not been myself." Charles patted the pocket absently. "Not for as long as I can remember. Catherine, would you remain with me if I lost everything? If I were forced to take charity?"

"I've never pried into your affairs, but I'm not blind. I know illness limits your abilities on the Court. We have less than others, but we get by. That's always been enough. Now please, tell me what is wrong. Is it the Court? Wynfield? Charles, is it me?"

He touched her, nothing but a cracked, age-spotted hand on her cheek. Yet the simple gesture stunned her. She'd never known Charles to reach for anyone.

"Soon," he said, "I will sit with you and speak of things that have been on my mind for a long time. I fear that moment, Catherine. I fear a great many things, it seems, and that causes me to be a difficult man. I know this. It causes me to act in ways I never thought I would."

"I love you." She took his hand and kept it. "There's nothing you can say to part us. Don't you know that?"

He blinked back tears. "The thing you do with Eligius. Those photographs, as Sir John dubs them."

"Yes, my husband. It is an amazing thing."

"I should not be held. It would be better if I faded, like the first ones."

CHARLES REFUSED DINNER and spent the evening poring over a detailed map of southern Ceylon. Eligius brought his food back to the kitchen, hoping the old man would take it later.

Sudarma came from the well with a bucket of fresh water to rinse potatoes from the plates. "At market, everyone is speaking your name. That you said a word and Chandrak died. That you raised a gun against your own. Against children."

She set her bucket down. "In the fields, the men believe you a traitor. Did you know this?"

"What would they have me do? Should I kill a soldier?"

"You had a chance to do something."

"When did you become this person, amma? Once, it was

enough to send me off to work for them, to feed you and Gita. This I have done. Now you'd have me kill them in their sleep. These people are not like the others. They suffer too."

"Every night I pray that you wash these people from your eyes. That woman has captured you in that contraption of hers. Why can't you see this?"

"Perhaps if I drank and beat you, you'd think more of me."

Her hands went to her cheeks. She began to murmur prayers.

"And as for that light box, one day I will show you what it does. You will see there is something of me in every glass portrait that will never die. I will always be. Not even my father could say such a thing."

He left her there, whispering to the walls.

THE MAP ON Charles' study desk was more detailed than the old lion's beloved, spare rendering of Ceylon. This one marked the villages that had fallen across the region's south and midsection, from the Arabian eastward.

Eligius saw a circle around Matara.

Sir John pointed to the village of Puttalam. "Charles, do you see how far you'll have to travel? There's unrest spreading through the very provinces you'll pass."

"And for what?" Ault rocked nervously in his chair. He'd come at Charles' request. "What can you say that could possibly change things? They have no control over these mobs, nor do you. The populace has been looking for a reason to get angry."

Charles shook his head. "The populace is looking for justice. They don't want a rebellion any more than we. These are the actions of a few, but they are spreading out of anyone's control. If I can gather the remaining provincial leaders, we can restore calm. Stephen, you need not make this journey. I will ask the governor for some soldiers. But I must at least try to do something."

"Look at me, Charles."

Catherine searched his eyes. Blankness, as if finally there was nothing left to think about. The man who wrote her a letter of remembrance and prayer for return, the man who needed nothing save to matter, wasn't there.

"I know what this is." She took his hand and held it as if it might break. "Forget the court. You've given them more than any man could. Please forgive what I tell you now. It does no good to battle anymore. You've never been fully well, and God alone knows how many years we've left. Spend this time in the study, in thought. Pursue what you can have."

"What good will I ever have been to anyone if I do nothing?"

"I don't want to see you lose your life over this. Whether your health or the countryside, you're not fit to withstand it. I'm sorry, but I must say it. You're not the same man. You're ill."

"It's done. Make your peace with it, Catherine."

"I will not. What becomes of us if something should happen to you?"

Charles' eyes fluttered. They became pale windows. He gestured for the plantation shutters to be closed against the rising sun. "I've failed in everything I've done," he said while Eligius closed them. "I've failed to protect the dignity of my family. Or else you would not turn to seeking money from your own endeavors. You would not turn to another man."

"There is no one else!" Catherine stood and stalked away to the other side of the study. "Sir John is a colleague!"

"I know what I am," Charles said, "and what I am not. I care nothing for stars and wisps on glass. I don't know how. I only care for the land, for its people, for my children's future, and my wife's station. May God help me, but right now, I care most of all for the boundless conquest of all these things by dishonest men. I may be sick, dying even. But if this is all I have to carry away with me, it will be a miserable parting."

He rose unsteadily. "I'll tell the children. Eligius, I have a task for you."

At Charles' request, Eligius rounded up Justice Newhope,

the rotund barrister; and the youngest director, the dour Kenneth Crowell. He brought them back to Dimbola, where Charles took the papers from his cabinet and gave them over to his fellows. They read in silence. Crowell began to pace feverishly, while New-hope simply folded his paper and stood quietly, head bowed.

"Please say something, my dearest friends."

"How does it come to this?" Newhope asked.

"Let us take a walk, gentlemen."

Charles asked for his heavy woolen coat. Eligius brought it and slipped it about his shoulders. "I should like to speak to you of morals," Charles told his guests. "Just what was it that brought us far from home with the hope of spreading our particular brand of civilization? Perhaps we can reclaim some-thing of that youthful optimism in our twilight."

He smiled at Eligius as he allowed himself to be buttoned into his overcoat. In it, he appeared small and lost.

He's shrunk, Eligius thought as he helped Charles to the door. Even in the past week, he's grown smaller.

At the front door, Charles asked Eligius to leave them. "I can still walk my lands," he said.

"Very well, sa'ab. Call if you need me and I will come."

"I know."

He seemed to be waiting for Eligius to do something. Then he broke away. "My friends. Let us discuss how we should be remembered."

CHARLES HAD SET something in motion. That much Eligius knew, and it was momentous enough to send Crowell and Newhope home in silence. They engaged in none of the disparag-ing banter he'd grown used to when among other Britishers, who seemed most alive when in pursuit of one of their own. On the journey to their homes, he longed for more of their words. Then he might know what was happening, how many villages had fallen and would yet fall before it was over. But he was a servant, and servants were above all else quiet. No one spoke of the Court or Charles' papers, and it was not his place to ask.

He returned to Dimbola to find Catherine in Holland House with Sir John, sipping tepid tea and bemoaning the imperfections in her photographic plates. White lines had mysteriously appeared across some of the prints. Some turned a pale shade of green, as if they were squares of bread spoiling in the larder. Hairs, cracks in the plates from overuse, dirt, all imperceptible, yet all had become vines and boulders to her now.

He'd noticed these imperfections before but made no mention of them. They were a part of the world she'd created and seemed to him to have as much place within the frame of the print as her subject. Yet her upset caused him to consider how to guard against them. He began to devise a box with a lid that could seal tight, with a window through which light might pour, but imperfections might be kept out. It was almost enough to turn his attention away from the despair gripping the Colebrooks.

At the end of the week, Catherine told Eligius to hitch the horse. "I want some time in church," she said. "Ewen and I."

"And Julia, memsa'ab?"

"She is very tired. Let her sleep."

Lately, she had only seen Julia in the morning and at night, and only for glimpses. Once that week, she came upon her daughter in the scullery, thieving some cheese. Julia's eyes were puffy and red. Her native vitality had left her. She was too weary to raise her head in defiance of anything.

Before leaving, she asked Eligius to bring an extra pillow for the carriage's hard edge. "We'll have a guest with us on our return. The missionary Ault."

Eligius' heart sank. This was to be the day Charles left, with Ault as his guide.

"Does it help?" he asked. "Church?"

How to explain something that I've merely always known, she wondered as Eligius searched her face for signs of strength. She'd come into the world in 1815, Charles in 1795. Twenty years her senior. The man she wed in a civil ceremony bore witness to different times. He had a foot in another century.

Perhaps not this way, she thought, nor precisely this place, but isn't this departure merely the truth that has always been here with us, arriving at last?

"I suppose it prepares me," she said.

He brought them to the Galle Face and remained outside with the other servants. The air stirred lightly in the manes of the steaming horses. The church had been largely finished. Only one scaffolding remained where stonemasons tapped nephilim from quarry rock. Its restored windows glittered with the sunlit sea.

Tying the horse to a thicket, he wandered past the open door of the church. Spotting the memsa'ab was easy enough. She was the only colonial to wear native dress rather than a lace-festooned hat or a head pin of feathers.

Ewen sat next to her. He was growing fast. Only last summer, his head couldn't be seen above the back of the pew bench. Now the bench came to his slight shoulders.

He is still a frail boy, Eligius thought, and Ceylon is so much harder now.

Wynfield's servant stood across the crescent lane where the carriages pulled up to the church doors to disembark their passengers. He spotted Eligius and looked away, taking hasty interest in his carriage horse's bridle. He didn't look up again until his master and mistress had climbed into their compartment following services. Before closing the carriage door, the servant gestured. Wynfield looked in Eligius' direction, expressionless, then slipped inside with his wife. George wasn't with them.

Catherine and Ewen emerged with Ault. The ride back was quiet. His passengers were lost to their thoughts. In two hours, they arrived at Dimbola. He climbed down and opened the gate. Ewen ran into the yard, suddenly a boy again. Ault held out his hand for Catherine, but she remained seated. "If you must take him," she said coldly, "watch over him. He is not in God's hands. He is in yours."

"I will. Please know this is not my idea. Charles was quite insistent. Truth be told, I'm not entirely clear what's to be accomplished."

Eligius walked to the porch, where Charles sat amidst a small collection of boxes. His maps, Eligius thought.

"Place them carefully in the carriage," Charles said, "so these roads don't jar everything. No one knows the pitfalls of these roads as do you."

"I will take care in packing them."

"Your memsahib is coming. Listen to me. Watch over them while I am away."

"I will."

"You have everything that is precious to me. Do you understand?"

"Yes. But you won't be gone long, sa'ab."

Charles hooked his arm through Eligius' and walked to his wife. "I've said my goodbyes to Sir John, and to Julia, such as it was. Perhaps you will have some words with her, Catherine, so I might return to a less sullen girl. To be the object of so many suitors, including an esteemed artist, is no cause for ill humor."

"I will try, but she is at a delicate time."

"When is a woman not at a delicate time?"

He kissed his wife's cheek and walked past her. At the carriage he let his weight fall on Eligius' shoulders as he took each step. Eligius bore it easily, and Charles's ascent was smooth.

"Do you have your maps, sa'ab? Your pipes and tobacco?"

"I have all I need."

"Be well," Catherine told her husband, "and be home soon."

"A few days' time is all."

"All the same. Ceylon is not as safe as when we were young."

"Ceylon was never safe, and I was never young."

Ault climbed onto the carriage and flicked the lead line.

The old horse stuttered forward. In moments, only a dissipating curtain of fine dust remained of them.

Eligius took Ewen through the front door and bade his mother to put a fire under a kettle of broth. Sudarma asked if Catherine would be dining as well; there might not be enough, though she thought she might stretch it with some roots and a bit of fish.

He left the boy and walked to the front door. Catherine and Sir John sat in the gazebo, staring at the road.

"Only for Ewen," he told his mother in the kitchen.

He went to his room, for what he didn't know. There was much to do, yet nothing came to mind.

A package rested on his sleeping mat, wrapped in simple butcher paper. Watch over it until I return, written in Charles' unmistakable patrician hand. Before going to sleep that night, he opened it and set Charles' beloved map of Ceylon against the wall, where his diya had once been.

3.

On the failure of Parliament's second attempt to reform abuses in the East India Company's governance of India, nothing was done or attempted to prevent the operation of the interests of delinquent servants of the Company in the General Court, by which they might even come to be their own judges, and in effect to become the masters in that body which ought to govern them.

9th report of the Select Committee of the House of Commons, 1837

Such a thing, this cobbling of muses and minerals! One may pose a model, arrange deftly her shawl and taper fingers, call her by an appellation of the seasons, yet she is not so. The blurring of what is real and what is artfully imagined is inappropriate. This conjuring is at once an imposter, and too truthful.

"A Critique: Photography in London"
The Times of London, June 1838

It honors me to submit to your exhibition a series of photographs which I hope will please and perchance move you to see in their presentation what it is that made me create them. Think of them what you will, but know of what they are composed: chemicals, light, and within each subject, a secret.

*Letter from Catherine Colebrook to Walter Scott Hughes, Curator
London Gallery of Portraiture, September 6, 1838*

God's Language

CATHERINE WALKED THE GROUNDS. SHE SAT ALONE AT the dining table. She closed herself up in his study and turned the mothwing pages of his legal tomes. She fashioned each gesture, each touch, in her mind before bringing it into the world. *I shall pick up his book. I shall sit at the foot of his chair. I shall walk to the gate and regard the curvature of the lane and the base of the trees he wanted us to see.*

She did not mean them to conjure love, or Charles' safe return. These were places they'd been together, that she had not spent enough time knowing. He would be in each place had he not left.

God, she decided, would favor her and bring him back. He would not let so much space in one woman's life fall silent.

DIMBOLA BORE THE first days of Charles' absence the way Charles bore everything else. Stoically, within itself, confined to far corners.

Julia only opened her door once, to ask Sudarma for a clean dress. Sir John, for his part, was taking his morning walk, a time he loudly proclaimed as his alone.

Eligius found Ewen pacing the length of the yard between the gazebo and Holland House. They walked to the barn together. Ewen gathered some straw and fell back in it, wriggling into the crackling nest he'd made but taking no satisfaction from it. His scowl remained fixed. "I don't like how quiet every-one is. It's too sad."

"They miss your father."

"They should pretend he's in the study."

"Your mother is afraid for him."

"I know." He was impatient. "But Julia told me that it was like this before. When Hardy died."

"When I first met you, you couldn't say the word for death. You said he left."

"I did? Oh, I remember now."

"There's nothing your mother can do. However much noise she might make."

"She thinks that box will stop everything."

"It does. But only for a moment."

From the barn, they went to the well outside the gate. Ewen helped tie the knot around the bucket handle, then climbed up on the stone lip to watch it descend into the water below.

"The first day after my father's death," Eligius said, "I told myself that he'd only gone away for an hour. By that night, he hadn't come back. During that time, it was this kind of quiet, where everyone moves as if they might break."

"What did you do?"

"I listened."

Hand over hand, he drew the bucket up. Cool water spilled. Soon it would spill into basins, cooking pots, over windows and faces, and if the memsa'ab could be coaxed, the glass twin of a Ceylon society matron or one of its great men. "I listened and I learned that it had a sound all its own. Like a distant ringing. I could hear it over the wind and the sea. Soon I learned to live with it. After a while I couldn't hear it anymore. I just heard the sound of me, not thinking about him."

He set the bucket down. Ewen was staring at the ground. "Listen to me, Ewen. I'm just a servant in your house, but I'm also a boy without a father to keep watch over him. I think you will know more years without your father than with him."

The boy nodded.

"Then don't wait too long to become a man. Being a boy with no father does no good."

Ewen was sullen after that, yet still followed him to Holland House. While he took up the box he'd been fashioning, Ewen paced along the wall where Catherine had hung her photographs among Sir John's star maps. She was up to a dozen, which she reorganized every couple of days, trying to approximate the ideal constellation for her album. Always, Julia's photo held the center.

Soon Eligius lost himself in his work – the aperture of the box, the corroded hinges he'd bartered for at a bazaar that opened like bronzed butterflies. The day dissolved around him. When he looked up again, suddenly aware that the box's pale wood had fused with the twilight seeping into Holland House, Ewen was curled up against the album wall, asleep.

He touched the boy's shoulder to stir him. Groggy, Ewen put his arms out to be lifted. It was as if the act woke him; he withdrew his arms and stood, alone. Passing Eligius, he walked back to the main house.

Eligius finished his work. He left three trays filled with well water, set the canister of sodium hyposulfite alongside, and checked to make sure there were candles and lamps with oil, should the memsa'ab decide to escape the quiet of Dimbola and her husband's empty study.

After dinner, he brought the box from Holland House. "Help me test it," he asked Ewen.

They took a piece of Catherine's paper and slipped it inside. "I want to see if enough light can enter," Eligius said. "I need something small."

Ewen searched through the dining room. He held up a spoon. "Perhaps," Eligius said, "we could use my diya. You remember the oil lamp I had."

"I haven't seen it in the longest time. Where is it? I'll bring it."

"Perhaps the spoon after all." There was nothing to be

gained in accusing the boy. If he took the diya, it was now his; such was the way of things for a servant.

They placed the spoon inside atop the paper and surrounded the box with candles.

"An experiment!" Sir John walked into the dining room. He peered into the box, careful to keep his unruly mane clear of the candles. "Eligius, I have a task for you. I would like you to lead a small expedition. It's only just dark, and we've hours of evening yet. I'd very much like to see this lion's mouth of yours. Let us see who will accompany us."

Catherine begged off. "I intend to bring my Bible into the study. I shall read a bit of old wanderers until Charles' safe return."

She forbade Ewen from going. The disappointed boy stormed off to his room, taking the newly-anointed paper and its indelible spoon shadow with him.

Before leaving, Eligius knocked at Julia's door. She opened it a crack. "We're going to the lion's mouth," he told her. "Sir John will begin mapping the southern skies tonight. He will bring his telescope. He says the stars will seem as close as flowers in the garden."

"George has requested me to remain at Dimbola while he is painting me."

"Many times I have seen your father or mother instruct you. This is the first time I've seen you obey."

"You bait me."

"I simply observe."

Her bony shoulders slumped. She seemed weary even of the effort it took to remain standing. It worried him.

"The things he tells me," she said. "I cannot stand to sit for him."

"Then stop."

"I don't have the luxury of stopping. Only he does."

"Has he made a servant of you?"

She pushed her door closed. "Listen," he said, to the

patterns of splitting wood. "For when you write, this is what can be seen from the lion's mouth. There is a rock overhang that looks like the open mouth of a stalking lion. The moss in its mouth swings when the wind comes. Below, a valley. In the valley, a neem tree by a stream that fills when it rains. The sharpest eye cannot tell where we broke the ground open under that tree and buried my father. But I can. To not come is to miss ... what is the way to say it ... the world of it."

"Your world."

The sound of the latch washed over him. "Wait for me," she said.

THE WALK TO the lion's mouth was a blur of leaves and distant sky lights. Eligius hefted the heavy tube Sir John gave him to carry. It had legs like the memsa'ab's camera, but smaller. The tube was almost as long as he was tall.

The footing was difficult for a pale English girl unaccustomed to the jungle. He offered Julia a hand but she waved him off, hiked up her gauzy dress and clambered further ahead on the rocky path. Below them, buried in a sea of mist and darkness, lay the valley of the departed, miles of dense vegetation, villages and to the west, Port Colombo and the sea.

"Let her be, Eligius."

Sir John toted his sketches and calculations in a worn leather valise. Eligius could hear the old colonial's breath in his chest. This walk was taxing enough to young legs. He suggested they stop, but Sir John refused. "Let me tell you of my exploits to take your mind off of your labors. Have you ever heard of mathematics?"

"No."

"God's language is numbers. With them, I can bridge the veils of oceans and sky. Did you know that together with Sir Robert Nysmith, I calculated the duration of the seas? He set sail with a dozen cryptographs and as many cartologies as his ship could carry. We calculated the time of the tides to within a fort-night, give or take..."

Eligius didn't ask what the colonial's words meant. They came in a flood and he set his pace by their strange cadence. Sir John's enthusiasm for his own work was something joyous and foreign. He'd only known men who pitied their lives.

"Point in the direction of this lion's mouth for me."

"You can't see it in the dark, sa'ab."

"No matter. I like to fix on the horizon line and stare it down until it is revealed. A habit born of too many voyages, I suspect."

He had a kind smile, Eligius thought. Good teeth for a colonial, free of the rot and yellow cake so many of them suffered. It occurred to him that he knew nothing of Sir John's private life. Was he married? Were there children or grandchildren waiting for him in this London he'd heard so much about? Was this yet another man who thought nothing of wandering far from his family?

"There." He pointed Sir John in the right direction. The moon bobbed just above his finger.

In half an hour they arrived. Julia made her way between the lanyards of moss. She brushed them with her fingers and watched him. Behind her, clouds floated in from the sea. He walked to the lip and saw the neem trees below fill with pale moonlit rivers. The world we knew is gone, appa.

"When I was a boy," he told her, "my mother would take me to the sea on Diwali. We brought little lamps with oil, and we would light them and set them out on the water. She would point to the sky and say 'look up, remember your diya? That's where they go to live and they never go out. Your light is always there for you to see.'"

They stood in silence, listening to the wind murmur in the valley. He hoped a childish hope that his father could see him up here, speaking to a girl who'd never beheld the landscapes of absence that made up his world.

"It's beautiful," she said. "You spoke truly of it."

"You're not writing."

"Better to just look. Someone told me that once."

"He sounds very wise."

She leaned into him, bumping his shoulder, and it was so easy to forget who they were. It was dangerous to put faith in such things. They didn't last. They weren't real.

"Come," she said. "Let us see what mischief Sir John has in store."

They helped spread the legs of the stand, upon which they fixed the heavy brass and wood tube. Sir John tinkered with the knobs studding its smooth hide, then cranked its length to almost triple.

"It's like the camera," Eligius said. "It has a glass eye."

"The lens on this is cut in a particular, exacting way, to bring far things close. Here. Look for yourself."

Sir John tilted the telescope up to the dark skies. Eligius stepped behind it and peered through the lens. He felt exposed, having grown used to the blanketing dark of the camera shroud. "They're right with me!"

Millions of pinprick lights on the sky's curtain swelled in the eye of the telescope. He thought of Julia's photo, of the pool in her eye. The stars looked like that up close.

For hours they captured what they saw, each in their language. Julia made renderings of words. Sir John surveyed the stars and drew intersecting lines, then dotted their surface with approximations of the sky's lights. Some he named, odd-shaped words that felt exotic in Eligius' mouth.

While they worked, Eligius pointed the lens to every corner of Ceylon's sky. He studied the telescope glass, letting his fingers trace its curves and puzzling out how such a lens might be made for the camera. "To reach up there," he explained when Sir John asked what use such a lens might have for Catherine's contraption.

"Your intellect is an awful grace." Sir John bent over his sketches, which covered a dozen pages of minute observation.

"Why do you do this?"

"Do what, boy? The map?"

"Yes. What good is it to make a map of a place no one can reach? A map of lamps?"

"A question from the unwashed masses! But I will tell you. While I speak, I want you to look at those lamps of yours. Every well-determined star, from the moment I register its place in the veil, becomes to the astronomer, the geographer, the naviga-tor, a point of departure which can never deceive or fail him. Imagine! A light that can guide you all the rest of your journey. Those lamps are the same in all places in the world. Do you see?"

"I think so. But aren't you afraid someone will make up stories about the stars like they did with the moon?"

"And there lies my cursed head."

He wasn't smiling, this man who seemed to have found something like tranquility in his lifetime. "They all laugh at the time I spend on the paths of heaven. It's my madness, I sup-pose. The lights of the farthest cities are the only ones I've ever cared to see."

He wrote on his paper. Tearing off a corner, he handed it to Eligius. "This is where you are, in relation to the lamps above us. This is your place on the map."

Eligius studied the markings. Six degrees and thirty five minutes north latitude, eighty degrees east longitude. A secret language that could guide him the rest of the way through the world. Something to look at, should he ever get lost.

GEORGE ARRIVED AT Dimbola the next evening bearing more portraits of English society for Holland House's walls. "I am most appreciative of the courtesies you have afforded me," he told Catherine in the dining room. "I wish for Ceylon to glimpse my portrait of Julia before I ship it to London, where it will hang at the Royal Academy. Prominently, I am told."

"I cannot hide my curiosity," Sir John said.

"It is an exquisite rendering of her, I assure you."

"I daresay. It is the venue, however, that sparks my curiosity. Why here, as opposed to your father's estate?"

"Because the topic is love, sir, and it is here that love is found. That is Julia's own sentiment as told to me on the occasion of my requesting her presence before my canvas. 'If you will paint me, let it be only here. Let it be of love.' Beautiful words, then and now. I treasure them. Tell me, Julia, did I do justice to your request?"

"I see in it what I hoped to see, yes."

"I'm glad you are satisfied."

A party was planned, a menu drawn up, and the day was selected for the unveiling of Julia's portrait a week hence. Sudarma listened and nodded at the recitation of her duties.

George sought to kiss Julia's cheek. She turned from him and went into her father's study. "When does Charles return?" George called after her.

Julia closed the door with no answer. Catherine spoke up. "I expect my husband in the next day."

"Manner dictates that I obtain his permission. I presume Julia informed you of my intentions."

"There was no need. From your arrival with Sir John, your intentions towards my daughter have been plain."

Eligius heard the study door creak. He turned to see Julia's fingers clasping the wood.

"Where will you settle?" Sir John asked George. "Will you remain in Ceylon?"

"I have commissions in London. My status as a portraitist rises and with due respect to Sir John, I am tired of travel. I do not wish to be his stenographer any longer. Nor do I covet a seat at the John Company, though it is mine for the asking. Its machinations fill me with loathing, never more so than these days. No, I have prospects sufficient to provide a privileged life for your daughter. No doubt you would expect nothing less than a man determined to make his own mark on the world."

"Indeed," Catherine said. "I'm sure you'll understand, I

wish to hear from my daughter and my husband on the matter of your proposal."

"Of course. This is no arranged marriage. We are not heathens." He slipped a pocket watch from his coat, examined it, then tucked it away. "Please tell Charles when he returns not to do anything to jeopardize our union. I carry that message from my father directly."

Catherine pushed her tea toward Sudarma, who took the cup to the kitchen. "Your father's friendship is a blessing to us and we are grateful. But a blessing does not produce an entitlement, young man. Julia is not yours by right."

"I think there's something you should know. Julia, we must speak of it."

Julia pushed the study door open enough to be heard. "It is sufficient that I wish to be married. Nothing else matters."

"Love," Catherine said. "Love matters above all. If you cannot say it, do not do this. Do not tie yourself to a man you don't love. What sort of life will this be?"

"There are worse things, mother. Better a man who makes himself known, whatever may be said of him. Do you know about father? A sick and indebted man." She glanced at Eligius, then dropped her eyes. "He is Andrew's servant, nothing more."

"I'm afraid it's so, Catherine." George slipped on his coat. "The John long ago dismissed your husband with a paltry pension. Ceylon needs youth and strength, and Charles possesses none. He is indebted to many. He's borrowed beyond his means and yours, I'm afraid. My father allows him some dignity, I suppose, and a place in colonial society. He has the gift of gab, my father always said."

"Does he provide a service?"

Her question perplexed them. She was not mercantile, nor hard in matters of commerce. It was simply what she'd always known, come round for her at last. Her good, stoic, intellectual, distant man, whose eyes lit at the equations of law and governance and at no other time, was just another life that had come to her for want of the ability to survive.

"He must," George allowed, "or else my father should have no use for him."

"Then what matter his health," Catherine said, "or his debts. What matter what he does or can no longer do. He has persisted. That is living, young man."

"I wish to make myself plain, out of affection for Julia and you. Charles has been stripped of his directorship. But matters are worse than this. I fear, Catherine, there will be no garrisons sent to assist him in this jaunt of his. My father doesn't believe soldiers ought to be spared for someone who willingly places himself in danger so these people might think him a friend. It behooves him to find his way home quickly, for the sake of his safety and what remains of your station."

"Your father once called Charles friend. How does my husband deserve this?"

"He shouldn't be doing it, Catherine! His duty is to the Court and my father, not these people! If every man with a regret or a sight in his eyes that he cannot abide abandoned his responsibilities, who would be left?"

"The sights in my eyes are the only thing I care for," she said.

Julia sobbed quietly. "If that be the case, it's evident your husband is not among those sights. That's why he roams the countryside, looking for purpose. How selfish you are, mother."

In a silent moment, the room emptied. Julia closed herself back in her father's study. George departed, as did Catherine. She watched the young man leave Dimbola while late afternoon shadows lay at her feet.

Passing Eligius and Sir John, she went into the corridor where Hardy, winged and wrong, rested on his nail. She removed the painting and set it down on the floor. The nail had been driven shallowly; little strength was needed to pull it out of the wall. A bit of powdered limestone fell after it.

She set the nail's point to the painting. Flecks of black oil flew at her attack, revealing a blight of pale beneath.

Selfish, she thought. The sights in my eyes exclude all around me.

Her face cinched up with anguish. She used the chemical-blackened heel of her hand to wipe her cheek clean.

"Memsa'ab?"

Eligius sat on the floor next to her. "There will be time for tears and anger later. But I think the young Wynfield is right. Your husband is alone out there. Memsa'ab, I know the land. I know what can happen."

For a moment he thought he'd gone too far. But it haunted him, that the old lion could die with no one. That the gazebo could be empty, now and always.

The light of the gas lamps found a place in his eyes. She saw it quiver, as if threatening to explode. Then it stilled.

"Find him," she said. "Bring my husband home."

The Lion's Mouth

HE DRESSED JUST BEFORE MIDNIGHT. OUTSIDE THE SKY shed much of its black skin and bruised over with color. Some dark patches remained where smoke rose over fires that had erupted deep in the night. They had never been this close.

The old lion was out there somewhere. Hari and the others were too. Maybe they'd stolen enough to afford a gun. Maybe they'd even fired it by now, and someone had fallen.

He went to the scullery. His mother was washing the tablecloths in a simmering pot. Later, she was to go to market to place a large order in the Colebrooks' name for George Wynfield's portrait feast. Two such orders over the months, he thought, and both paid for in full. Perhaps it would be enough to repair what little remained of the Colebrooks' reputation.

Sudarma poured him tea. It had been steeping for hours by the bitter, soapy taste. "Memsa'ab told me you were going," she said.

"There's fighting, amma. I've seen smoke all night."

"Stay to the trees. Don't be seen. They know who works for the colonials."

"Amma –" His voice broke. Shame and fear set off terrible equations in his head. "I'm scared to go."

"Then don't." She cut the colonials' bread into soft triangles.

Despite the time spent with it, he still hadn't become accustomed to its sour taste. Full of air, and how quickly it turned.

He longed for a bit of chapati bread baked over stones. He missed Matara.

She handed the bread to him. "Take extra." There was hope and pitiable loyalty in her eyes. *In case you see them and they're hungry.*

"I was wrong to bring you here," he said. "I'm sorry for how you've become. You don't even pray anymore."

A gentle crack rose in the air. Far away, long-traveled, like the wind through the valley. How much distance did the gunshot have to journey, he wondered, to find us here?

"Go," Sudarma said. "I've much to do."

The room began to turn. Sickening black spots appeared in his vision. His stomach boiled an acrid bath into his throat. He vomited tea into a bucket of wash. A pair of pants with pockets. His. Once, she'd told him that she'd cleaned those pants with river water and out of the pocket came the steam of ships that he was fated to take to the wider world.

He wiped his mouth with a trembling hand as the dulled sound of gunshots continued in the distance. Sudarma lifted her head from the boiling cloth and gazed at the pantry wall until the last of the guns fell silent. Then she returned to her work.

JUSTICE NEWHOPE CAME to his door only after Catherine stood at the window and shouted that she wouldn't leave until she'd heard from him. Even then, the burly barrister only opened it a crack. "You're a fool to be out alone! What do you want?"

"I must know what my husband said to you before he left. When you and Crowell came. Please, he's been gone almost four days."

"Gone all this time? He told us only that he was traveling to Puttalam, to meet with village leaders. That's half the time at most."

"He should have returned by now."

"Listen to me, Catherine. You don't want to know the things he told us."

"I know about his debts. How he is beholden to Andrew."

"That's the least of it. This whole settlement will be asked to leave before long, until the soldiers can put down the fighting. Return to Dimbola and pack. Charles will have to fend for himself."

"I cannot. He's not well."

"Nor are any of us."

"I am not a woman in need of protection. You know what I ask. Will he return?"

For a moment, Newhope looked at her as a father, with kindness and sadness. "This land has brought us great misery. Charles knows it, yet he loves it despite all. I think he will die here. I think he wishes for that. Me, I hate this place. There is no hope here anymore."

She turned away as Newhope closed his door. "You heard?"

"Yes, memsa'ab." Eligius stepped from the shadows. She'd told him to remain out of sight, lest this terrified colonial see him as a threat.

"I can't ask you to go any further on our behalf," she said. "It's dangerous, and you're as hated as we."

"I cannot just return, not without at least reaching Puttalam and Devampiya. They are far. I must try."

"I'll come with you."

"Julia and Ewen need you. If something happened..."

No country for the motherless. Charles, how things have come round to find me.

"Memsa'ab, did you ask him if your husband wants to die?"

She took him away from Newhope's premises, back to the road. Dimbola lay in the opposite direction from Puttalam.

"I asked a question that I believe I know the answer to. Spend a day on this, Eligius. No more. Or else I will find the way to you."

"You would do that rather than say goodbye. How you loathe goodbyes."

He smiled.

She opened her arms and he came to her. They parted without a word. Eligius began his walk to the remains of villages, Catherine to what remained of home.

SEASONS OF RAIN and drought had alternated in a terrible maypole since his last glimpse of the East India Court. All the light had been scrubbed from its exterior. Paint peeled from the eaves just below the lip of the roof, revealing dirty gray stone as pockmarked as the day it was broken free and beaten into walls.

Soldiers milled about near the locked gate. A contingent of thirty stood in a phalanx just on the other side of the iron bars, monitoring the Indian men who occupied the road and the cleared field beyond. Eligius saw twice as many soldiers talking in groups, rifles within easy reach.

He crossed the field. A thicket of Tamil men watched the Court and its surrounding buildings. Some turned to see who made the dry sticks break. They nodded at him and returned to their vigil. No one spoke to him or to each other. Whatever had been planned, it was done.

It filled him with dread, watching them wait.

In five hours, he encountered only one village still intact. The sounds of guns broke the stillness every few miles. Through the day they came faster, lingered longer. Not far off. Soon, he'd find them.

At a plantation near a clear stream, he knelt to drink. Warm water broke the dust in his throat. He splashed it over his face and neck, then surveyed the grounds. The estate was prosperous and well-kept. He could see the family on the porch. A young woman in a dress as yellow as saffron, with a hat pulled down to shade her. Her three children played on the grass while an older woman sat in a chair swinging gently from two chains.

The late afternoon light was thinning. There was no one around to ask whether they'd seen Colebrook and the missionary. He wasn't sure how far he'd come and didn't recognize any of the landmarks around him.

A handful of Indian men toiled in the field abutting the house. They picked fat cotton from the coil of green that reached to their ankles.

He was surprised to see anyone still working for colonials. "My brothers," he asked, catching the attention of the closest men. Two of them looked to be his age, but worn to poles by their labors. "Are these fields the colonials'?"

"Everything is theirs." An older man raised his hand to shield his tearing good eye; his left was as cloudy as egg white. "We only get what's dead."

"It used to be our land," one of the boys said.

"Part of it," his peer commented. "Our village was over there." He pointed to the trees. "It was sold to them."

"I'm looking for two of the colonials," Eligius interrupted. "An old man and a missionary. They would have traveled two, maybe three days ago. Maybe they came to your village."

The one eyed man spat on the ground. The younger ones took their cue from him and turned away. "I saw them," the man said. He glanced over his shoulder at the house. The colonials were far away and attending to themselves. "They passed through Devampiya a day and night ago."

"Heading south?"

The man shook his head. "North."

Moving away from Dimbola. Towards the smoke and the guns.

"I was still living in Puttalam even though it lay in ruins," the man said. "It was still my home. When I saw them, the older one was ill, and the missionary made him rest in the shade for a long time. Then he helped him up. The old one was upset that there was no one important to speak to. They had a cart. The old one lay down in the back, where servants would ride – "

A cry went up in the fields as a monstrous plume of smoke rose above the trees. It engulfed the sky over the plantation. The colonial children screamed. Their father came to the porch with his rifle.

So close, Eligius thought. No more than half a mile.

In the fields, one man dropped his hoe. He walked to the road. Two more fieldworkers followed. They marched past the colonials' property line in a parade of rags and coffee skin.

The colonial put a protective arm around his wife. His children and the old woman went into the house.

"Son," the one-eyed man said, "forget the colonials. They'll get what they deserve. Find a weapon or a place to wait, but don't be found doing nothing."

Eligius nodded.

"I spoke to the old one. I brought him some water. Do you know he was the only colonial to ever speak to me like a man?"

"What did he say?"

"That he was sorry for many things. For Swaran Shourie."

Another plume rose. Eligius heard more screams.

"Offer a prayer over the old one." The man dropped his bag of cotton and began to walk. "When you bury him. And one for me. I've no family left to mourn me."

Eligius waited for more of the field workers to leave, then joined them. They passed the house gate, the mob of them, singing old songs he first heard as a child playing on the beach where the fishermen made beautiful melodies that compelled the waves to return day after day.

Now all the colonials were inside the house. He could see movement at their front windows. The children, watching without comprehension.

He thought of plumes of smoke rising over Dimbola.

When the workers turned into the gate, axes and hoes held high, he ran in the opposite direction. Soon the sounds of shots were too faint to hear.

He ran into the night, and the next morning, through a ribbon of sounds and smells, voices and fighting and burning. He slept only a while, and only when he reached the lion's mouth, as the first bruise-violet light could be seen over the mountains. Once, he woke in the night to what sounded like sobbing coming from the valley below. The wind was blowing, he thought, and the dead were whispering their secrets to the appa of the neem tree. He'd tried to will the sound away, then got up and started walking until he couldn't hear anything but the jungle stirring.

It took him until midmorning to find something to eat in the pantry of an abandoned house. How strange, he thought, to see these walls broken like those of the villages. A week since it burned. Maybe less.

A garrison of weary soldiers shuffled by on the road outside. He hid until they passed, then went to find the colonials' well. Drawing up the bucket, he soaked his torn feet and wondered where else to look. Nowhere, everywhere. The sa'ab could have simply gone, never to return out of shame. Maybe he'd already passed Dimbola in the dark. A last look before he fell to the land he loved but increasingly did not know.

If he failed to find the sa'ab, he thought he might do the same.

He left the house and shadowed the garrison until midday. In a field swaying with razor grass, he parted company with the soldiers. They continued up the road.

Pulling up clumps of blades, he cut a patch into the field big enough to sit down in and not be seen. He promised himself that he'd only rest a while. His feet were cracked and bloody. His back ached; he could only bend forward a fraction before daggers pressed against his spine. What would it matter, he thought, if he never returned to Dimbola? What would be missing? A servant. A water bearer, a carpenter. A mover of light. Catherine would make her way with photographs of her betters, depicting their once-hoped for selves. Sir John would map stars. That he would be precise about it would only matter to him. Julia would marry and raise children with Wynfield. She would become a lady under a wide hat that kept her well hidden.

Perhaps she would lose one of her babies, like her mother. She would mourn the stranger that came to her new world broken, then go on.

I would never see what her idea of love was. I would never make portrait sitters of the stars.

A sound grew on the road. Carriage wheels churning up rocks and dirt, and the jagged wheeze of a horse driven too hard.

He peered over the tops of the grass blades. The carriage emerged on the far side of the field. It pulled off the road and the driver hopped down to help a woman out. She moved in a wobbling, unwieldy way. Her distended belly pulled her forward like a cast anchor. She knelt to the dirt. The sounds of sickness filled the air.

Behind her, another woman stepped out unaided. A maid or midwife, Eligius thought, followed by two small children. The downed woman barked at them but the distance made cotton of her words. She held out a demanding hand but still her children slipped into the grass, two blurs of curls melding with the green.

He started to smile, until the high sun glanced off of something brilliant and shiny in the trees across the road from the family. Metal.

He was up and running before those trees parted, before the men spilled onto the road. Like beetles pouring from a split rice sack they scrambled up and over the carriage and its driver. Eligius saw him slip under a rolling wave of blades. The carriage tipped over with their weight. Its horse crumpled as its lead line hung it sideways.

An awful stew of cracking wood, pitiful whinnies and an abrupt cry reached his ears. He scanned the field, terrified. The world spun in a smear of green and flashes of gold hundreds of yards away. The children. They were screaming for their mother. Soon the sounds of last life and the breaking carriage would quiet. They would be heard.

He ran for them as the winds swept the stiff blades against his bare legs, gashing him relentlessly. The children clutched at each other and cried when he reached them. Kneeling next to them, he told them to hush in a harsh tone. They obeyed, eyes wide.

He lay them flat, his palms against their cheeks. Holding them down, he craned his neck. There were men at the carriage, pulling it apart and carrying it off. There were others gathered at the tree line.

He took one child under each arm and rose cautiously. His neck and back burned. Carrying them like parcels from the butcher, he set them down behind a thick coil of neem roots. The children were so small. They slipped into the gaps. The boy held his sister's hand.

"Don't move," he told them. "Don't make a sound."

The boy's eyes flickered with primitive recognition. His hand left his sister's and covered her eyes.

Eligius' heart broke. *They think they're about to die from me.*

A sound made him spin around. Far in the field, one of the men raised his blade into the sun and brought it down, scattering grass into the air and with it, a tumbling sheaf of the maid's frock.

"Hold your sister tight," Eligius ordered the boy. "Don't let her see."

The boy's lip trembled. Tears sprang from him.

"I'm going to cover you both so you won't be spotted. Only I will know where you are. Don't move until I come for you. Do you understand?"

The boy nodded. His little chest filled and fell.

Eligius covered them both with leaves until only a bit of their golden curls protruded like treasure. He found a heavy rock and ran, leaving his mind behind with the children. He ran as if in a silent void, with only the rock in his hand and bubbles of light descending from his vision to dazzle the green swaying grass.

The man never heard him. He was in mid-swing, his machete soaring up in a curtain of red drops and a fluttering flag of lace wrapped stubbornly around the blade, and he never heard Eligius descend on him with the rock. The stone struck bone and didn't stop. The man fell limply.

The maid lay on her back. Her face was turned to one side, demure. She was covered with blood, dirt, and grass. The skin of her cheek lay open and imbrued The man's indiscriminate swings had left that side of her unrecognizable. She was breathing shallowly, expelling ribbons of red foam.

He'd once gone hunting with his father and other men. One was skilled with a slingshot and brought down a bird before it had a chance to escape. Breast split, it waited. He could remember the look in its eyes as their shadows fell over it. How it trembled as his father picked it up and twisted its head until its neck snapped.

The maid looked at him like that. There was nothing to be done to stop her leaving.

He left the dying woman and crept through the grass to the remains of the carriage. They'd torn apart the horse in the same manner. Bits of both lay in broken mounds.

He knew the men could see the road. Were he to take the children that way, they would be spotted.

"Leave me alone!"

He got onto his haunches. Between the men's ranks, he saw the young woman screaming. The remains of her dress hung from her arms. Her breasts and womanhood were bare. Her hands lay protectively across her pregnant belly. The man closest to her set his blade down and went to her, forcing her to her knees. He wore a tunic. A servant once, maybe a day and a lifetime before.

A shot rang out. One of the men who'd stepped forward for a closer look fell. More shots cascaded like rain, and more of the men fell. A small cadre of soldiers ran towards the quickly scattering men, firing flame. The men slipped between trees and were gone. The soldiers followed them.

As quickly as it began, the road fell silent. The sounds of fighting grew muffled behind the canopy of jungle.

He ran to the woman. "Come with me quickly. I have your children safe."

The woman rose but didn't walk.

"Hurry. They could come back."

They reached the trees and for a moment he thought the children were gone. Then one twig rolled from its perch atop a soft rise and a finger wriggled through. He uncovered the children and bid the woman to lie down with them.

"My servant," the woman said. "My driver."

"Stay here. You need clothes."

She embraced her babies against her breasts. They burrowed into her as if seeking a way back.

He returned to the field. The maid was still. "I'm sorry," he whispered. Gently, he pulled her frock from her shoulders and down her torso. It was stained with blood but whole. At least the young mother would be covered.

The dress snagged under the maid's body. He pulled harder, not wishing to touch the ruin of her. His efforts caused her head to loll lazily over, revealing a smooth, clean cheek.

He took a step back as the world spun away from him. A voice rose in his head, bitter from a life of work that never received its adequate due. What does a servant do? *You carry on and you don't see what's plainly there. Kutha.*

He pulled Mary's dress free and brought it to the young mother. While she slipped it over her head, dislodging her children only for the instant it took to let the dress fall across her nudity, he asked her where her home was. Near the port, she responded.

"Near Dimbola," he told her. "Near the Colebrooks."

"You're their servant. The one who helps Catherine with her portraits."

He helped her climb out of the clump of tree roots. They walked through the grass to the road. "She served us well," the woman said when they cleared the field. Her children clung to her maid's dress. The little girl pressed herself against the fabric, leaving a swipe of red on her forehead.

The spot where Mary lay could no longer be discerned from the expanse of grass.

He crossed the road and found a machete. "We stay in the jungle. It's not safe to be seen."

"We should wait for the soldiers to come back," the woman said.

"There are more of us than them, memsa'ab. We're alone. Can you walk?"

She nodded.

"We have far to go. If your children tire, we will carry them."

"Mary told me of you. She said you were good."

"She said nothing of the kind."

The children stood in the shade of a tree canopy, waiting for someone to do something. Were he to leave their mother and take them by the hand, he felt certain they would go willingly. Such was their state of shock.

"Why are you doing this?" the woman asked. "We're nothing to you."

A strong wind blew up around them. One of the dead men lay not far from them. His clothes rippled in the unceasing air.

The noise roused the woman. "My name is Margaret. My baby cannot be born here. My husband won't hear of it."

"It's not long off by the look of you."

"Don't speak to me that way." She was breathing too fast. Shock overtook her. "Help me," she pleaded. "That my children should see me like this." She held Mary's bloody garment away from her skin.

They hewed tightly to the trees as they walked. The children began to cry and he sang Gita's lullaby. In a while it was all he could hear.

Outside Chilaw they found an estate that appeared intact. Margaret broke clear of him and her children and tottered as far as the estate's lush field of coffee before Eligius grabbed her. He clasped his hand over her mouth and pulled her behind the weathered timber of the estate's fence line. "I have been traveling for a day and a night," he whispered, "and I have learned to listen."

She stopped struggling as the sounds of breaking glass reached them. A band of men emerged from the house, their arms full of tapestries, silver, anything that could be pulled from the house and from each other.

Eligius dragged her back behind a stand of areca without being seen. There, in front of her children, he slapped her hard enough to draw tears. "If you leave again, I will let you. I will take your children. They will be raised by someone with more sense."

She hung her head and cried, but did not try to seek help from her kind again. There was none to be found. All the colonials were gone, from Negombo to Weligama.

Under his urging, the children managed to coax another hour from their swollen feet before crumpling to the ground and sobbing. "I know a place where we can rest," he told them. "It's a magical place I know you'll like."

The boy shook his head; what little pride he'd found in protecting his sister had wilted in the face of his maid's death and a day of trudging through terrifying landscapes. But the little girl stood up and brushed leaves from her dress, a yellow frock he suspected she wore to high tea. She looked like a sunflower after a storm. "What kind of magic?" she asked warily.

"The kind that will get you home."

He brought them to the elephant temple on the last drop-lets of their endurance. The boy curled up against the top step and fell into a troubled sleep. His limbs jerked violently, warding off phantoms.

Margaret sat next to him and stroked his hair. Eligius constructed a hasty lean-to, shading her from the sun and the wind. She would not look at him.

Exhaustion lapped at him. He found the gold plaque and

sat beneath it, the machete lying across his thighs. A radiating warmth drizzled his scalp and neck; reflected light from the plaque, bent upon him. The sensation filled him with dread at returning to Dimbola with no word of Charles. What words could he use, to say such a thing?

The trees across from the temple rustled. He saw the glint of a rifle, its barrel aimed at him. "I'll kill you." English. A young Britisher emerged. His weapon quivered wildly. Blonde stubble dotted his young chin. Sixteen, if that. So like the soldier that day. All the ones who fought the colonials' battles, did they all have to be boys?

Eligius let the machete fall to the ground. "I'm not one of them. I'm traveling with a young memsa'ab and her children. We are making our way back to Port Colombo."

"Lies. How have you survived out here with children and a woman?"

"I know this land."

The boy's rifle lowered. He sniffled. "Tell me it's true."

"It is."

"I'm lost. I was running with my family –"

"The governor and most of the Court live in Colombo. I expect your family is there."

"Show me the woman and children. I want to see them for myself."

He led the boy up the first steps. In the center of the temple, Margaret dozed with her son. The girl was making a leafy lean-to, a tiny version of her mother's. She smiled when she saw Eligius.

Eligius woke Margaret. "We have a guest. He will be walking with us."

"Where are you from?" she asked the boy.

"My family's in Tangalla."

"Not here. From home."

"Isle of Wight, ma'am."

Eligius left them to speak of England. He knelt next to the girl. "What's your name?"

She spread her leaves carefully. "Alexandra."

"Alexandra, I promised you magic."

He took her to the temple wall and let her run her hands along its carvings. "They're cousins to the clouds," he said.

She pursed her lips. "They don't look like clouds."

"Nor do you and your brother look alike."

"Elephants don't fly."

"That's why sometimes you see clouds near the ground. They're visiting."

"That's nice of them."

"Say goodbye to the elephants. We have to go."

"I'm very tired."

"I'll carry you."

He lifted her onto his shoulders. Margaret stirred her son and the boy, who'd fallen asleep with his rifle in his arms. Eligius gave the boy his machete. The jungle wasn't as thick from here, he explained, and were they to come upon any soldiers this close to port, he did not wish to be seen with a weapon.

"Another hour," he told Alexandra. "Hold on to me."

She bounced atop him. She let her head fall back and stared up through the trees. Her hair tickled his neck. "I saw you make the man fall down," she said. "In the grass, with Mary."

"Yes."

"Is the man in heaven now?"

"I don't know such things, Alexandra."

"Mama says that none of you get to go. And Mary gets to go, and I don't want the man to go and keep hitting her."

He felt one of her hands leave him. When he looked, she was tracing the sky with a dirty finger. Looking for elephants, he thought.

"Don't fall," she told him.

A VERY DIFFERENT pall of smoke hung over Port Colombo's harbor. Steam, from an immense ship bearing the East India Company's branding. The port's dock was crowded with well-to-do families, their belongings stacked like a child's blocks near a crane and pulley. From the size of the ship and the quantity of the colonials' lives on display – their furnishings, clothes, even bales of their last good crop – these families were sailing to England. Standing with their children clutched in their protective arms, they grew gray and dissolute as the ship belched clouds that the wind bent to the ground.

He led his band of stragglers to the post at the foot of a warehouse. There he found soldiers seated at a tiny table, carefully enscripting names on a tablet that reminded him of Julia's beloved pad. He could not speak for himself when the armed men's suspicious gazes landed on his bloody clothes. "He saved us," Margaret said before doubling over. The baby was close. She trailed tears down her leg.

They asked him where he served. They told him that the families in Ceylon's southern province remained in their homes. For how long, they could not guess. "So much depends on the behavior of your lot," one of them said.

He parted ways with Margaret and her children, leaving them in the Galle Face with a priest and a nurse. The boy was walking from pew to pew, searching the faces of the families. In the first row, the nurse lay Margaret down and began to erect a makeshift curtain of burlap. Soon there would be another life.

He wondered if that one would stay long.

Alexandra amused herself at the church door by tossing a pebble against the wood. For her, he pulled blades of fragrant lemongrass and arrayed them in a blessing near her.

He only turned once on his way to Dimbola, to see the port. By then he was up high; his trail had climbed along a sloping hill. The doorway to the great church was empty, but he did not despair. There was a small shape with a golden crown of hair standing on the docks. She was waving goodbye to the clouds leaving the ship's stack for their long journey up to the sky.

THE WORDS CAME easier now, like a second childbirth after a wrenching first. My husband is dead.

It was surely true. The widow season was upon her. Everywhere was proof of it. Charles' absence. Eligius' absence. Dimbola's encircling quiet.

The waiting life came at her relentlessly. What to say to Julia and Ewen – to Julia, were there words to repay the debt her daughter had assessed? – how to live alone, how to stay in Ceylon. How to leave. How to hold on to what she'd done.

For now, a light needed tying to a departing man.

She was in the bedroom, arranging the first of Charles' possessions, when the knocking came.

DIMBOLA WAS QUIET. The porch and gazebo were empty. No one waited for him or for Charles.

Of course they aren't. They think us both dead.

He knocked at the door. For a moment, dread encased him. What if they're on board that ship? What if I am alone?

Then Sir John let him in with a tousle of his hair, a fatherly gesture that Eligius needed more than he realized. "I could not find him."

Sir John put a hushing hand up. "No one could expect so much from you. Rest now. I'll tell her."

"It is for me to do."

"She's in her room. No one has come to be portrayed. She despairs of her art even in the midst of all this chaos."

"Aren't you afraid of what's happening? What of your map? You'll be forced to leave before you've finished."

Sir John tapped his pipe against the dining room table, dislodging a small coalstone of ash. "I don't believe the stars are going anywhere, even if we do. I'll pick up a different corner of the sky and come round again. It's as I told you. They're the same forever, in all places. They're the only constants I know."

Eligius found the memsa'ab's bedroom door open. She'd rearranged things in ways he couldn't understand. Curtains had been pulled from other rooms and arrayed behind the bed in velvet folds. Palm fronds leaned against the wall. Their tips had begun to curl. Some thick tomes from the study sat on the nightstand next to the headboard. One he recognized as the sa'ab's indispensable volume of English law, the one he turned to while creating the paper stack he'd locked away in his cabinet.

Catherine stood from her vanity when she saw him. "You've returned safe. I am so very glad."

"I couldn't find him, memsa'ab."

She'd placed the camera against the far wall. Its eye fixed on the bed.

"There is more. Mary. I saw her die. I could not help her."

Catherine straightened one of the palm fronds.

"Is there to be a portrait, memsa'ab?"

She pulled the bedcovers back. "Come here, Eligius. Lie down for me."

He didn't want to. A colonial's bed, and all his grime and blood! But her voice barely lived and her eyes were windows onto the sorrow inside her. He did as she asked.

She pulled the covers up to his chin, then stepped back. Tilting her head, she examined him from every angle. The worst came when she instructed him to close his eyes and hold his breath. Then he understood the portrait she wanted to make.

He thought of Mary laying in the field, her face and hair blending with the leaves and dirt, becoming Ceylon. The rock, felling a man he might have seen one forgotten day on the roads or at Diwali. They might have greeted each other.

"Thank you, Eligius. You may go."

He ran from the room. In the hall of paintings, he saw his mother. Catherine's throaty sobs rang in the air.

"I heard," Sudarma said. "And the maid. Was it the men?"

He nodded dully.

"Was there anyone that we know?"

It was hard for him to find the woman she once was. Her face was tanned to a rough hide from too much labor in the sun.

The bones of her chest no longer made it possible for him to see the crib that she used to be for him. Someone had balled her up like one of the sa'ab's discarded writings. Wrinkled, worn, ready for the fire.

"If they were there," he told his mother, "I didn't see them."

"I'm glad. I cannot think of mere boys like that."

"But if any one of them were among the men who took down the colonials' servant, can you doubt they would have joined in willingly if it meant the other men would accept them? Like Chandrak. You brought him into our home and look what he became. Did you know this about him? How easily he could become an animal?"

Sudarma took him by the wrists. She turned his palms up. They bore dry map lines of blood where the rock had sloughed off skin.

"I know this about all men," she said.

Remembrance

THE KNOCKING CAME URGENTLY AGAINST THE FRONT door. It pierced Catherine's grogginess and sent her fumbling for her clothes. No one in the house had slept. Now dawn, come too soon.

She'd spent much of the deep night listening to Julia cry and watching the mist gather itself to leave the sea. *The sea isn't enough for it,* was what her mother once said when as a girl she'd wondered about London's constant shroud. *So it comes to land, hoping to find what is missing.*

She reached the door ahead of Eligius. Governor Wynfield stood on the porch, hat in hand. Soldiers waited in the road. "Catherine, their carriage was found in a ditch eight miles from here. They're searching–"

"Where?" Eligius blurted.

"I will not be questioned by a servant about this matter. If something befell him, it's you who deserves blame. How can we know you didn't come across him out there, you and the other thugs–"

"I want my husband back." She touched Wynfield's arm as if it were the thing that had spoken. "Tell him."

Were he here, Eligius thought, the old lion might finally believe in her love for him.

"South of here. Outside Devampiya."

"On the Port road? The trade road?"

"The dirt path. The one your kind takes to the valley below the mountains."

Eligius was running before he realized that he had moved at all. Wynfield shouted for him to tell his servant where to go. The soldiers swiftly mounted their horses. He scrambled onto Wynfield's carriage and seized the reins. Panic extinguished everything in him save the sound of sobbing, the quiet cloud-bursts that he'd walked away from three nights before.

"You will not be alone this time."

Catherine climbed next to him and clasped his hand. The air, thick with rain, fell atop her. The clouds and steel sky followed, and the stars somewhere above it all in the black vastation. It all plummeted down on her.

She heard the carriage door close, felt Wynfield's weight settle in the compartment below her, but it was all so far away.

Wynfield's servant took the reins from Eligius. "Where? Are you listening? Where do we go?"

"The valley of the children," Eligius said.

And one man, Catherine thought.

AT THE EDGE of the valley, where the low clouds brought merciless storms that quickly liquefied the ground, they came upon Ault's meager cart upended in a ditch. Eligius told Wynfield's servant to stop where the trees parted to reveal a walking path overgrown with vines. His skin prickled at the kiss of the cold rain. Mud sucked his feet under when he stepped down to steady Catherine.

"Which way?" she called above the storm.

"Into the valley. I know a path."

Wynfield's soldiers followed them, but the governor remained on the road. "You're sure of this?" he asked from the shelter of the carriage.

"I thought I heard someone. I cannot be sure."

"Then undo the damage."

Soon the road was gone behind them. The going was slow

and treacherous. Gradually, he and Catherine pulled ahead of the soldiers, whose heavy boots mired them.

Without Eligius as a guide, the soldiers would quickly lose their way, but their welfare didn't concern Catherine. Too much time had gone by already. She feared for what she might find; she feared finding nothing at all.

Water. Its sluicing rush rose above the rain. Eligius knew where he was now. The apex of the valley's gentle bow towards the sea. The rain had all but eclipsed a path of footprints along the right bank. "There were two," he told Catherine. He remained on the right side of the water. She took the left. Even a few feet away, they were like clouds to each other.

After what seemed like hours, they reached a part of the valley that years of weather had scrubbed down to rock. Something fluttered from a low branch ahead. Catherine fought her way to it on aching legs.

Eligius saw her path and followed. Exhaustion made a terrible jest of him; he teetered like Chandrak.

A man's torn and bloody shirt wafted above a shape lying in the pooled water. On stumbling feet they ran to Charles' side. Charles' face was swollen. He was naked to his sodden undergarments. His flesh could be read underneath, like words through glass.

Catherine touched him. She pulled the storm from his beard. Leaves and mud and the drowned husks of insects.

A gurgling moan left the old lion's mouth. "I've come to take you home," she told him.

The soldiers began to ford the brown floodwater. "Is he alive?" one of them cried.

"Yes!" Eligius called. "He's breathing!"

They lifted Charles out of the water. "Is the missionary with you?" one of the soldiers shouted, as if Charles was already too far away to hear them. He got no answer. Charles' body drained water when they stood him up. He burbled pain and collapsed.

Lead us back, one of the soldiers told Eligius. Your master shouldn't die here.

Charles was whimpering.

"Save your strength," Catherine whispered, and he quieted. Taking his hand, she told him to close his eyes. She would fight through the rising wind for him.

BY THE TIME they reached Dimbola, the rain began to ease. She cradled Charles in the rear of the carriage. His breathing made her wince.

Eligius helped them out of the coach. The front door of the house opened. Ewen and Julia ran down to the grass.

The air outside smelled of sweet burning wood despite the rains. Soon, Eligius thought, we'll hear the pops, and they'll be closer.

Sir John came from the foyer holding a thick chamois, which Catherine used to wrap Charles. As they brought him into the house, Julia remained on the porch with her brother. They stared without comprehension at the specter entering their home.

Don't look for your father, Catherine wanted to say to her children. *He's hardly there.*

Julia watched her mother through the open door, struggling to keep Charles upright but waving off assistance from the soldiers. "They found the missionary," she told Eligius. "He took a terrible blow to the head. He was wandering the road incoherently. They're treating him at the church."

"I am glad he is alive," Eligius said.

Sudarma built a fire under the cover of a tree and set a pot of water over it. She stared at him, not comprehending his English. Yet her eyes could read him all his life. He turned away from her.

Julia folded her arms against the wind. "I didn't think you'd come back."

"Then there would be no one to carry your writing to and fro."

"You're an insolent boy." She was crying. "I saw my portrait. George brought it here while you were gone."

"Did he do the subject justice?" He couldn't help the fever taking the words from him.

"Do you see love when you look at it?"

"I do. However regretful a thing that might be."

He forgot his mother's eyes. They fell away with the rest of the world.

CATHERINE LAY CHARLES in his bed. When the soldiers left she undressed him, dried him, built a fire, and stoked its heat until its radiance reached the far corners of the room. Sitting at his side, she placed her hand atop his chest and felt it rise and fall, felt the flutter within.

He opened his eyes and looked at her. The lion of old, gathering strength he no longer had.

"There are things I am aware of, Charles."

She went to the door and closed it. Outside, Sir John nodded in understanding.

"Our time is leaving us," she said. "There is only time for me to tell you, I have ever loved you. For you, there is time to tell me what I do not know of you. You must remain at least that long."

She cradled him. After a while, the rain slowed, became mist. By then, Charles had closed his eyes and begun to speak.

AT THE LATE hour of the garrison doctor's arrival with Wynfield, the sky bled smoke and embers above Dimbola's turned fields. The winds swept small immolations over Wynfield's carriage and out to sea.

Eligius led them to the house. Ruby flakes of ash withered and fell. He trod over them, wondering what lives these had been.

The doctor's arrival only confirmed the family's fears for

Charles. A funerary presence, the doctor wore an expression of weary resignation, as if he'd failed before his first ministration to Charles had begun. After ordering a freshened fire in the hearth, he pressed the flat end of a rubber tube against Charles' chest. "His heart is terribly weak," he said to himself. "It may have been better to leave him where you found him."

"Surely there's some medicine," Catherine demanded. "Some poultice to take the cold from him."

"There is nothing, madam."

Governor Wynfield stood near the fire, warming himself. "Things have come to a regrettable point."

"Keep him warm." The doctor repacked his things and accepted payment from the governor. "Give him what he asks for should he wake again. That is all I can offer you. That, and make arrangements."

"The question of location must be addressed," Wynfield said.

"Outrageous," Sir John snapped. "Must such a thing be discussed in front of his children?"

Wynfield waited until the doctor could be seen from the bedroom window, crossing the yard. "We've no time for the luxury of manners. Or have you somehow been spared from what is happening across the countryside? I cannot offer protection to you indefinitely. I need every available soldier to put down this uprising, and more yet. Another full garrison sails as we speak, but they are still a week away. I can't spare a man to act as chaperone so you may all continue living here as if nothing has changed. Everything has changed."

"Is every colonial being told that they are alone in this?" Catherine said. "Or is this only for us?"

"I resent whatever imagined skullduggery lies beneath those words, Catherine. I'm only concerned with the safety of children I have watched grow up and a woman who, whatever our differences, is wife to my friend. Yes, to answer you. In good conscience I cannot allow any of us to remain in Ceylon. All

must go until matters are settled here, myself included. I will
return as soon as I can. The Court must not lack a voice."

"And when matters are settled?" Sir John asked.

"The Court shall be reestablished, of course. Laws will be
drafted and instituted to prevent this happening again."

"I see," Sir John said quietly. "In your image, as it were.
Who will speak for Charles?"

"I will, as I always have. We were in agreement on all matters of importance. Not that such things concern you."

Catherine sat on the edge of her husband's bed. She stared
out the window. "Where shall we go?"

"England, I expect," Wynfield said. "Unless you have friends
or family elsewhere – "

"We have nothing."

A landscape of wonderment lay before her. The thought
had only just found her. *I stand atop nothing at all.*

"I am aware of that," Wynfield said.

A terrible quiet took the room. She and Wynfield glared at
each other while Charles' breath rasped. "There are places
for you in London," Wynfield finally said. "You could become a
portraitist. I will be your patron. I shall sit for you at the first
opportunity."

"I'm not my husband. I do not wish to be in your debt."

"And yet you are."

Wynfield took a poker from its mount on the wall and
stirred the fire until sparks danced against the bricks. "It seems
that Julia is to marry George, and so our families shall be
bound to each other. You and I. And I assure you, she will have
every privilege, and does that not fulfill your every hope for
your daughter? Yours is a successful motherhood. Do not end it
in ashes. Come to London. I will help you place-hunt. A nanny,
perhaps."

"Bastard." It was Julia who spoke.

Wynfield stared at her, his smile harsh and fixed. He went
to her and cupped her face in his bearish hand. "You will be

welcomed into my family," he said, "but I fear this habit of speaking beyond your place must stop now."

Eligius tried to catch Julia's eye. She didn't look up, even after Wynfield left.

Catherine ushered all of them out of the bedroom. She drew the curtains together and shrouded the room from light. She told her eldest to get some rest, that things would be clear with rest. Then she carried her son to his bed in her arms, like a baby.

Eligius had never seen her do that, in all the time he'd been at Dimbola.

He heard the memsa'ab whisper to Sir John in the hall outside Ewen's bedroom, to begin packing his maps and compasses, his telescope and the chemical casks.

Leaving them, Eligius went to Charles' bedroom and poked the fire back to life. Charles' eyes were open. He stared at Eligius with impossible composure. His lips parted, but no sound came. His fingers plucked at the air.

Eligius went to his side and listened. Then he left, to fetch what the old lion had asked for. He found the key in Charles' study, unlocked the cabinet and brought every last paper. At Charles' whispered request, he took the old map of Ceylon out of its frame and turned it over. There was a second map hidden behind the first.

"He has come to see you as I do."

Catherine stood in the doorway. "Read it, Eligius. All of it. But first, give me your word. Tell me you won't remember him this way."

The Madness of Farewells

WYNFIELD'S SERVANT OPENED HIS MASTER'S DOOR.
Eligius peered into the Wynfields' home. Their interior was a
grand expanse of marble and walls washed with a color like goat's
milk. George's paintings covered almost every available square
of space. They portrayed men of importance sitting in lushly
quilted chairs, surrounded by birds of paradise arranged in deep
crystal vases.

Wynfield descended his curved staircase, binding his
black robe. In his broken repose he looked curiously small. "Is
it Charles?"

"Yes."

"Has he passed?"

Eligius thought of how Charles looked now. His limbs
swimming atop the covers. His eyes rolling like balls in water.

"Soon," he told the governor. "But not before he sees you
one last time."

THEY JOURNEYED SEPARATELY. Wynfield's servant followed
Eligius' carriage back to Dimbola. When the air began to burn,
Eligius saw terror on the servant's face.

He dismounted at Dimbola's gate and surprised the servant
by opening Wynfield's carriage door before the servant could
climb down. "Your name," he said to the servant in their shared
language. "You never told me."

"Rajadi."

Eligius smiled at the ridiculous lineage of his name. "Your village?"

"Kilkerry."

"It's gone, like mine."

"I know."

"Did you know what was happening?"

"I don't allow my servants to speak in that tongue around me," Wynfield said. "It's treacherous to do so, boy."

They entered the house. It was quiet but for the mumblings of the missionary. In the dining room, Sudarma waited against the wall to be called.

He led Wynfield down the hall to the bedroom, where Catherine sat at the foot of Charles' bed, surrounded by her family. Wynfield entered and bowed his head. "A terrible time. My deepest condolences. Lady Wynfield succumbed to her fear of the roads, but she is here in spirit."

Catherine went to the window. "Charles has something to say, but no voice to say it. He wishes it to be read in your presence. He wants to hear from you on it."

Wynfield folded his arms. "Very well."

She spread Charles' documents. From the stack she selected one sheet and handed it to Eligius. A slight smile tugged at Wynfield's lips as he began to read.

Andrew,

I have requests of you, and reasons.

My requests: Relieve my family of my debts to you. Take them out of Ceylon, but leave Dimbola in my name and lineage so that it may pass to Catherine and our children, should they ever return. See to their happiness. Provide them a home and means in London. Then join them there. Do not return to Ceylon. Step out of the way of those who will reconstitute the Court when Ceylon ceases her bleeding. It is my sincere hope that they will divide all seized lands equitably between the Crown and the natives, as we should have done.

My reasons:

I have in my possession every piece of paper ever drafted for your aims. They demonstrate beyond doubt your complicity and profiteering, your manipulation of the governorship and the Company Charter to bring about the seizure of villages throughout the southern provinces. I have evidence of the accounts you maintain in England, filled with the revenues you have sent back. I have the map you drew of the territories to be identified and targeted for our taking, and the colonial patrons these seized properties would be granted to. I have these documents because I wrote them for you. I advocated your desires tirelessly until any hint of opposition was removed. Did I ever really believe that what we did, we did for the good of Ceylon? Did I think ours were the best hands to hold this country until its children were grown and ready? In truth, I don't know what I believed anymore. Only that my gift of gab, as you oftentimes promised me, would see my way back from poverty, loss of station and the purgatory of place-hunting I so dreaded. I have chased that spectre since my arrival in Ceylon. I believed these things mattered above my honor, to my shame. I believed you.

Do as I ask, Andrew, for the sake of my family. Nothing need be known of the terrible wrongs we have done. Only when you see my family, when your eyes meet theirs, will anything of this be shared. My family will keep their end of this silence in exchange for freedom from my bankrupt influences. I have watched over you all, and I know your ability to live with unspoken regret. My life, I fear, has been spent teaching this very thing to the ones I love most.

I am so sorry, my wife. My children. I could not face you as a man of no means. In the name of money and standing, I agreed to do these things. I see now, when I am fading from the memory of all but a pitiable few, that I will forever be a part of the destruction of Ceylon. I am lost. Whether I can hear you now or not as this is read, I am further away than I

have ever been from the man who arrived in Ceylon to make
for himself a notable life.
   Yours,
   Charles Hague Colebrook.

Eligius gave the paper back to Catherine. She set it atop her husband's documents. Her son came to her and she put her arm around his waist and held him close. She beckoned Julia and took her in as well; there was room.

The old man's breathing came infrequently. His face grimaced in pain and concentration, as if by indomitable will he could make whatever world he floated through better than the one he left.

"It seems we are all in debt now," Wynfield said.

"Speak to my husband's words while there is still a chance he can hear you. And know that anything you do for us does not absolve you. Either of you." She raised a bony blackened finger at him. Her chemicals would never leave her.

"What I did," Wynfield began, his voice thin and lacking its sonorous authority, "what Charles and I did, I would do again. Perhaps I would augment the garrisons against the lack of civility in these people, but that is all. We took a country that at its best could scarcely sustain villages built from mud, and made them estates that offered the Indian man a living wage. Where is the wrong? That we accelerated the inevitable failing of a backward people? That we sought to reclaim some good from that failure? Were I to tell it to the queen herself, I would be rewarded. Perhaps I will tell her myself.

"But I will honor my friend's wishes. Do you hear, Charles? I will do this for you. Your family will be seen to with the earnings from all our endeavors to improve Ceylon's lands. What do you say about that, Catherine? Do you object? Are your morals inflamed? Or in the name of your well-being and that of your loved ones, do you say to yourself, there is a greater good met. None of us are different. Indeed, we belong together. And Charles, should I decide to come back and serve Ceylon, I will do so with no one's permission. Speak of my work to your heart's desire. Find someone who will care."

"Then why leave?"

All my life, Eligius thought, I shall remember his expression, that a kutha could ask such a thing.

There was plain hate in Wynfield's eyes, shorn of class or race. Hate between men. "Because I do not want to die here," Wynfield said, "with the likes of you."

He stayed only long enough to issue orders to Catherine. There was a steamer, the Royal Captain, that had veered into Colombo to avoid Calcutta's sand banks lest it run aground in the Hooghly River. The steamer was due to leave soon, and there was little room left on it. Servants who were English were welcome.

"And Eligius," Julia said.

"I cannot speak to that." Wynfield took his jacket and threw it at Eligius. Turning, he waited to be robed.

Eligius held the jacket open for the governor. "Be sure of your choices, kutha. If by some chance you leave here, there will be no returning for you, no matter the circumstance. Your own will not take you back."

"I shall earn my own passage to England, and back again if I choose."

"London will teach you a hard lesson. Think on it." He stormed out without so much as a token touch of Charles' hem.

Catherine held her husband's hand. Her expression was unknowable. Eligius had never before seen a woman gaze upon her mate in such a way. Even his mother, pulling a thin blanket over a drunken Chandrak when he fell into an indifferent sleep, even she tended a small ember of affection. This was something else the memsa'ab sent to Charles as he drifted further away.

"I don't know what sort of life you'll have, Eligius," Sir John said. "You're a good fellow. You certainly will make a good husband and father, and even help your country get back on its feet. These are not options for you in England, I'm afraid."

Catherine tried to coax Ewen back into her lap, but her son would have none of his mother's attention. "I don't care if he comes or not," he said angrily while staring at his father.

A man emerges, she thought.

Footsteps, dry and scuttling, trailed away from the bedroom and down the corridor. "I must speak with my mother," Eligius said.

"Be under no illusions," she told him. "There is no way to make right what has been done. Do not spend your life in search of such a thing."

Charles' stirrings had slowed to nothing. His mouth opened and remained.

"I am aware," Eligius said.

HE FOUND SUDARMA in his room. She held the feather print as tears filled her eyes, but he was already trying to forget the sight of her crying; the flush of silence it brought to the world. He wanted his blood to turn cold and indifferent. Then he could begin to forget Dimbola. This place he belonged to.

"How do you even consider going with them?" she asked. "Is it her? The daughter?"

He tried to walk away from her. She grabbed his shoulder and spun him roughly. "Do you think I'm stupid? I see a man's coveting in your eyes, but don't be so foolish to think that the likes of you will ever have the likes of her. You'll do nothing but move your servitude from one place to another."

"The servitude you wished for me."

"Yes. I was wrong. Is that what you need to hear from me? Very well. I was wrong and selfish, thinking only of my belly. How much more punishment do I deserve? And what about Gita? Should she be abandoned by her only brother?"

"What does it matter, to leave or stay? I've seen how their people and now my own people look at me. I am hated equally. There is no life left for me."

"With them you'll have nothing! Here, at least you have your family."

"We have no family left. Only what we remember."

He sat on the floor and let his head rest against the cool wall. It trembled with the storming of feet in the halls. Julia's wailing rose. "I have to go. There is one thing to do yet, for the sa'ab. Come. I want you to watch."

"I've seen all I want to see of them."

"Perhaps, amma. But you've seen nothing of me."

THEY FOUND EACH other in the hush of Dimbola, in the quiet corridors and darkened rooms, and that was how they told each other. One at a time, gentlest with Ewen, who grew still more sullen with the word that his father had died.

Everyone gathered in the bedroom. Charles lay in his finest suit. His hands were clasped across his chest. One eyelid remained stubbornly ajar, enough to see the lightless mote behind.

Catherine placed flowers in an unbound garland around his head. She stepped back to study the scene as tears rolled freely down her face. Eligius whispered in her ear and she sobbed, nodding. He left and returned with Charles' map and documents. She stood motionless, so he took the liberty of arranging them for her. The documents under one of Charles' stiffening hands. The map above his head, with the artist's warm stencil lines facing out.

"Mother, my tunic."

Sudarma brought the tunic without a word. Eligius put it on and knelt to the side of Charles' bed. To let the memsa'ab see.

"Yes," she said, weeping.

She arranged candles in a ring around the bed. Eligius removed the glass from Charles' map. Using the small pane, he caught a sufficient amount of the candles' flickering glow to direct a golden cloud across the old man's face, filling it with a false radiance. Then he took up his position at the side of the bed.

She stepped beneath the camera cloak. *Never could I have*

done what I have done if you were not with me, guiding me straight
and letting me wander. You never prayed and you never believed
enough that I loved you, and you will remain with me.

She opened the shutter. "Oh, my husband," she wept
from beneath. "You have torn my heart from me."

Julia knelt on the other side of the deathbed. She laced her
fingers together and muttered silent words over her father.

So did Eligius. He closed his eyes and found something to
pray for that was his alone.

What you did, you are damned for. But it is not how I see
you now. Should I ever view this photograph again and follow
it back to this moment, I will not find the man who would save
Ceylon. I will not find a worthy man. I will find a father who
brought into the world a girl with pools of light in her eyes.
A husband who stood back and let his woman find what had not
been found. It is not a bad way to be remembered.

Catherine emerged from under the cloak. Her face was
salted with tears and sweat. She washed the glass. Leaves of
silver and shadow rode the water to the floor.

Eligius took the plate from her and left it to the light.
Charles came soon, with the two-hearted map of Ceylon above
him. On either side, Eligius and Julia knelt reverentially, their
heads bowed.

Sudarma approached the plate. The candles behind
the glass formed clouds on the image. She clutched her sari and
knelt before it.

"What shall it be called?" Sir John asked. He watched
Sudarma's quiet reverie before the glass.

"Ceylon remembers him," Eligius said.

Catherine cradled her husband's head. Next to her, the
image of her husband bled and froze on the glass. "So it does,"
she said.

BY SIR JOHN'S calculations, they could take five crates' worth
of possessions on the ship before running the risk of leaving

their clothes and collectibles behind, to face the ignominy of being picked through by Ceylon's unfortunates. Their furniture and books, all save Charles' most prized legal tomes and treatises, had to stay.

They set about packing what remained. Julia's writings and implements, her favorite dresses. Ewen's calliope, into which a candle could be set to spin the shadows of exotic animals onto the walls. Sir John's maps. For Catherine, her camera and all the plates from the portraits she'd made.

Sir John guessed the ship's captain would forbid her chemicals. "We'll find new ones in London," he told her. "Or we'll create our own. Think of the resources we'll have there."

Eligius told his mother to bind the Colebrooks' possessions with sheets to protect them. In the morning, he would ride to the Galle Face to give the vicar word of Charles' passing. "I want him to be buried here," Catherine said. "Behind the Galle Face. I will grant him his love for this country, but he will rest in the shadow of a Christian God's house. As for whatever else remains here, to hell with all of it."

Eligius offered his help to Ewen but the boy refused. There was a hint of recrimination in Ewen's dismissive wave. It disturbed Eligius to see the boy behave in such a way, but he gave Ewen wide berth.

Sudarma was in Catherine's bedroom, wrapping Charles' photograph. A sheet lay over Charles' face. Eligius could make out the contours of Charles' beard and nose.

"I've lost you already." She held the plate to her chest.

A noise startled him. He lifted the winding sheet. Gita played guilelessly under Charles' bed. She cooed with pleasure at being found.

"I showed her what you did," Sudarma said. "You made the dead stay in the world. I told her, we are watching him sail to a strange place and we are happy for him. A boy who can make light do as he wishes can surely find a way home again. But I ask you, meri beta. If you go, take Gita. She'll be safer with you."

"She would become a servant, amma. A woman without a family in a strange place."

"She would be worse off if she remained. I don't want her to live like this. Like me. A mother raises her children to leave home and not look back. Let me say I succeeded at just this one thing."

He put his arms around her. "You did," he told her.

AS THE NIGHT deepened, the activity of packing paused for sleep. Eligius stood on the porch, considering Sir John's mapped sky. He saw Julia emerge from the gazebo and followed her to Holland House. Inside, she opened the camera's legs and stood it upright.

"I have to pack this," he said.

"And you will. Is there a plate and some of that dreadful water you need?"

"There is. But – "

"Can you make a photograph alone?"

He thought about this. The breaths between the opening of the camera eye and its closing. The amount of chemical needed to wash the exposed glass. The light. "Yes. I can."

"Then make it of us."

He set the candles in a circle around the chair and placed more in a cluster across the floor. Outside were the far sounds of guns, as Ceylon cut deeper into its own throat. Yet the cracks came to him as if he lay under deep water. The lights he set loose rippled in her eyes. There was nothing else to know.

She sat in the chair and watched him prepare the glass. "One night, mother spoke of you to my father. How you wanted to refashion the camera's glass to reach the stars. I think they were discussing mother's desire for knowledge. For accomplishment and a lasting place. Yet she spoke of you as well, in the same breath.

"I kept my father company more so than my mother or brother. I understood his treasury of quiet more than they. I knew how to hear him, and I expected no response from him to mother's idle chat. But to my surprise, my father said that every night he would gaze at the photograph of me with the light in my hand. He spoke of it as the portrait you both made, Eligius. He said you made me beautiful."

Eligius slipped the new plate into the camera. He gazed at her as the camera would. "You were beautiful before I ever saw you."

He opened the camera's eye, then went to sit next to her. Her arm pressed against his and remained. Around them, the night cooled. It tasted of winter. She would not be under the next rains. Where he would be could no longer be seen.

How strange, he thought as her skin's warmth joined with his and became indivisible from him.

He counted his first breaths. "What to call it," he murmured.

Her hand found his cheek and turned him. "We must be still," he said.

"We are."

He felt himself becoming woven into the air, into her. When their lips touched it was like the silver on his skin, replacing his flesh with what they'd stolen out of time. They would never die. They would always be here.

Soon he told her that enough breaths had passed. He took the plate from the camera. "Now," she said, "pack it all. Tomorrow will be as it is. By week's end we'll be on the sea. My father will be buried here. To make sense of all that's happened is a farce. I don't understand any of it, but there is tonight. I wish life could stand still, here in this moment."

He told her he would make the photograph. She asked that he pack the camera quickly so her mother wouldn't be angry. "I will think of what to call it," she said. "Without a name, it's an orphan."

After she left he washed the plate and himself. The nitrate of silver cascaded over his hands. He set the plate to its light and himself with it. Their faces came to glass and skin. An amniotic haze enveloped them; a pigment of refracted candlelight that they seemed to float in like stars behind milky clouds.

He lay down, weary from the packing. Every second of the last days radiated through his legs, but he wanted to see the tide of them come.

The stain on his hand began to arrange itself. A little mote of pale – her eye, in profile, gazing at him. In the dry crease of his palm, their kiss. She'd asked that life stand still here and he'd lit a candle and burned the two of them into permanence.

"Of course, you know what you've done."

Catherine stood in the doorway, regarding the coming image. Julia and Eligius must have wanted that moment above all, she thought. To be free. To burn down all that held them still.

"You kept your promise. You made a portrait sitter of a star."

"Not yet, memsa'ab. But I will. And you. You tied light to the sa'ab as he departed."

"Perhaps."

They were quiet a while.

"It is a marked improvement over mine," she said. "Clearly, I need your hand with me. Your light. The English sun can be as capricious as Ceylon's."

"Is it your desire that I come?"

It surprised her, to cry in front of him. "You have become a part of my life. I cannot allow you to simply leave it. There's so much we've yet to do. You found the way to me. This cannot be meaningless, that you have remained."

"No."

"I've always wanted more of the world than I am meant to have. I cannot imagine my life with another hole in it. I cannot imagine not knowing you. And Julia …"

"Memsa'ab, what do I do?"

"About loving her."

"About wanting to belong where I do not."

"I am acquainted with that problem myself."

They laughed, content, while the cottage filled with the sounds of their twinned voices.

"I don't know what will become of you and her, Eligius. It would be hard. But if it matters at all, I think you belong with her."

He moved to be next to her. "It matters very much."

"May I tell you of things? Of London?"

"I cannot create a picture in my mind to equal what it must be."

"May I tell you of Hardy?"

"Yes."

"I don't think I've spoken of him. Not to anyone."

"Look at every image you make. Each time, you speak of him."

She talked about the child she never knew. She described the lights of London. She told him of people they might portray. Poets, scientists, seers, divines. She told him of the day his father died, of his shadow across the Court floor.

By then the moon had dipped below the trees. He could hear the weariness in her softening voice.

"Look at her," she said. "Look at you both. Like one of Sir John's double stars."

Memsa'ab, you should sleep. The image remains. It will still be here in the morning. So will I."

"Tomorrow, then."

She kissed his cheek and left him. He lay down next to the photo and closed his eyes. Exhaustion consumed him, but the plate and paper hadn't finished with each other yet. When the candles burned down, it would be done. Then he would pack the camera and sleep.

There must be as many candles as stars in London, he thought. I can live among them. I may grow old and be wretched in strange rooms, but I will always have this night. We all wish we were better than we are. It won't matter where I do the wishing.

Before he could stop himself he was still and dreaming of the John Company's Court on Chatham Street, at six degrees

294 | DAVID ROCKLIN

and eighty degrees below the southern hemispheric orbits. He was in the lobby, watching Julia make her bauble's lights dance across the wooden floor while the memsa'ab tried to arrest it all. Her lights grew brighter and brighter. His eyes stung the way they did when he stood too close to his mother's cooking fires. The room grew fiercely hot. The lights ignited the floor, the walls, everything was burning—

Life Stood Still, Here

ELIGIUS LEAPT TO HIS FEET AND WENT TO THE DOOR.
The stars shimmered sickeningly through the heat and smoke.
A sea of flame erupted in the Colebrooks' field. Then they came.
Shapes of men emerged from the burning rows. Their hair
and clothes trailed tendrils of gray smoke. Some of them carried
spent torches. Others carried machetes.

They left the field and moved towards the main house.
Flames followed them, engulfing Dimbola's eastern fence line
and twisting angry red veins into the cracking wood. Drawing
a breath, he broke from Holland House. The men didn't see him
as he raced up the porch steps and pushed against the front
door. Locked. He ran around to the servant's entrance, picked up
a rock and threw it through the window, then scrambled in as
glass teeth raked his skin. He screamed for Dimbola to wake up.
Trailing blood, he pounded on doors until Julia stumbled into
the hall, clutching at her dressing gown. "Don't go near your windows. They're setting fire."

She went to her brother's room. Sir John opened his door,
holding his gun in a trembling hand.

Glass shattered somewhere else in the house.

He moved to the memsa'ab's bedroom, terrified. Smoke
lacerated his throat and eyes. He pushed the door open. She was
on the bed next to her husband's body, cradling his head in
her lap. A hail of stones burst the window behind her, showering
the floor with glass. Hands took hold of the window frame.

She kissed her husband goodbye.

Sir John appeared in the doorway and cried that the back of the house was on fire. There were men already inside, taking everything they could carry.

"Go to the front of the house," Catherine told them. "I have to find my children."

She pushed them toward the dining room, then ran towards the rear. The hall was full of burning black clouds. In the sooty smoke she heard the cries of the men. Lost as well, they clawed at everything on the walls. They tugged violently at the carpet beneath her feet. Bodies pummeled her as the men careened past without recognition. A gauntlet of hands swept the air, looking for purchase. The sounds of hoarded glass and metal made a terrible music.

Already the smoke was gathering at the front of the house. She found her children and led them there, where Eligius and Sir John waited. Opening the door, she peered out as Dimbola came apart behind them.

"I see Sudarma," Sir John said. He pointed to the gate, where Sudarma stood, gazing out at the sea.

Catherine wrapped her arm around her children. Julia's eyes were vacant. She held her writing pad to her chest as if it would save her. Together they stumbled out, sobbing and screaming down the porch steps and across the lawn. Men carrying paintings and furniture continued to stream in and out of Dimbola through its open wounds.

"Take them to the carriage!" Catherine cried, and left them for the yard.

Eligius brought them to the barn. The old horse whinnied pitiably as he harnessed it and pulled it to the door. Swarms of embers spewed from the field. Some landed on the gazebo. Its roof began to curl as new flames rose.

He pushed Ewen into the carriage and climbed to the seat above.

"Mama!" Ewen screamed. He pointed towards Holland

House. Catherine was running from the cottage, her arms full. She reached the carriage and climbed in next to Ewen. "Is everyone all right?"

Ewen sought refuge in her arms. She held him, her living and dead child, his features stained from the heat of the fire.

Thrusting the reins into Sir John's hands, Eligius slapped the horse into motion. In an instant the carriage was across the yard, taking them into the veil of smoke.

They pulled up at the gate. Sudarma handed Gita up to him, then withdrew the stake holding the gate closed. Eligius folded Gita into his arms and made room for his mother.

"There was never a time when I did not love you," Sudarma said. She backed away from the carriage, shaking her head. "But I must go where I belong."

"Amma!" He stood, ready to leap from the carriage. But his mother looked at him as if he were better than he was; the boy who took her from home and broke her over Dimbola's wood and stone. He couldn't move.

"Catherine," Sudarma said. The English word trembled in her mouth.

This was the amma he'd known, whose word was heeded, whose love was infinite.

"I know she hears me," Sudarma said. "Tell her."

Eligius translated.

"Yes," Catherine said.

"Finish what I began. Raise my son to be a good man."

Eligius said the words.

"Yes."

"Do not make a secret of him."

Ewen touched Catherine's hand. He began to cry. "Bleed."

Childish words. She raised her palm and marveled at the permanence of all she'd become. Mauve and apparition, inter-stitched with the skin whorls across her palm. She saw what alarmed Ewen. A trickle of blood from the cut across her hand. She'd gripped the photograph too tightly as she'd fled Holland

House. Now the cracked glass had struck back. There would be a scar, ever. She would look at it one day, under a different sky.

Her cupped hand filled with blood. She listened to Eligius as he translated, then wept. "I will never make a secret of him. Never."

The world Sudarma turned and walked into was blackened and quieting. They waited until she entered the remains of the house. As Sir John took the reins and guided the carriage out onto the lane, Dimbola creaked in capitulation to the insistent fire. Pieces of the roof crumpled.

In the murk, Catherine saw the last of Dimbola fall away. A curtain of ash and umber. Flames leapt high into the air, then down to the invisible earth. Over it, she heard the sounds of the wheels.

She took her children into her arms. Ahead there was a ship, and the sea, and a city men crossed the world to glimpse. They made their way to the port, the last of the colonials to depart their lives.

FROM THE HILL above Queen Street the Galle Face appeared to clasp Ceylon's jungles and the colonials' dock together in a grid of interwoven color. The jeweled sea washed against the gunmetal of the Royal Captain. A swath of crimson soldiers held a crescent line against the massed knot of crinolines, cashmeres, silks, and cottons of the colonials, who dressed as if decreeing the fires in their once-country contrivances.

At the far end, the hues of saris and dulled white servant smocks, blackened from unwashable labor and uprising. The servants were not moving forward with the mass intent on reaching the ship. They remained behind, near the green carpet of jungle and the seams of fire inching in every direction.

Eligius steered onto a path that narrowed as it descended. Before Ceylon opened to afford them a glimpse of the sea, they saw empty fields, streams of char where the flames had traveled, processions of people.

They arrived at Queen and Chatham. The roads trembled with so many pressed onto the dock. An impenetrable queue of carriages stretched from the Company's receiving gate back into the road and to the foot of the solemn clock. He brought the carriage alongside another and tied the horse to its brethren.

They took what they could carry and left their horse to whinny amongst its own. Satchels of clothes, a trunk filled with Catherine's photographs and Sir John's celestial map, the camera itself, folded like a dead bird; they dragged their belongings to the foot of the dock. There they clambered over a fallen retaining wall and joined the hundreds. In the pall of smoke and the rattling of fearful voices, they gathered together and braced against the relentless surge of the crowd.

Water washed against the shoreline. Voices at once close and at odd distances drowned all else. The crush of so many made their progress hot and oppressive.

Catherine smelled the bereft odor of ash, sweat, flight. Ahead, the Royal Captain blotted the horizon. She felt the insistence of the sea beneath her feet. It moved under the dock and back again. She could see it in the slow sway of the ship. All around them the men of each family frantically waved bills of entitlement. They shouted at the cordon of soldiers. Men unaccustomed to begging begged uniformed boys for permissions and favors. One more crate. One place ahead in line. Pleas on behalf of sun-poisoned children and wives made mad with close quarters. Promise of tobacco, coin, glowing letters to superiors, introductions to London firms.

She saw Andrew at the ship's rail. He looked old as men approached him and spoke into his ear. He nodded assent to what they said and they scurried off to be replaced by the next.

"He cannot see us," Sir John shouted.

Eligius brought the bauble out from under his tunic. He held it towards the smoke-blighted sun and twisted it until it found what little light could be sent towards the ship.

Andrew looked up when he saw the light burst from the

crowd. For a moment he was still. The distance was too great to discern his expression.

Somewhere behind them, a roar went up. A great collapsing into the fire. Trees, maybe, dried to splitting, or the collective shudder of falling structures traveling across Ceylon's air like the light of a far sun. Old by the time of its arrival, the remains of something already gone into history.

Eligius heard the dirge of prayer. He felt eyes on him. Faces interspersed among the colonials. They gazed at him with recognition. As the English bodies passed, they held their ground.

Julia took her mother's arm. She clutched Gita to her chest. Like everyone, she turned at the sound. Now she pulled Catherine close. "Mother–"

Catherine grabbed Eligius' hand and pulled him next to her, so no one would mistake him for anything but hers. She'd seen what alarmed Julia. Ahead, the colonials' transit from the dock to the gangplank and safety. Behind, the Indians who had lived among the British. None of them moved forward. They didn't beg the soldiers for passage. Some silent message had already been conveyed.

On board, Andrew raised his hand. He gestured toward her. She saw soldiers break free from their cordon and wade into the crowd. Three uniforms moved toward her family like droplets of blood trickling into the slopes of an upheld palm.

Closer to the Royal Captain, servants still holding their employers' goods handed them over to English porters, then turned and left.

"Hold me tightly," she shouted. Locked together by hands, they surged forward to meet the soldiers.

She saw Ault on the gangplank, waving them on. Above him, Andrew watched implacably.

They converged near the front. The soldiers took their belongings and handed them to the porters, who spirited them away. Ault led Ewen and Julia onto the gangplank. One of the porters took Gita.

A soldier laced his fingers around Catherine's arm. Another took hold of Eligius.

The porter placed Gita on the dock and walked away.

Andrew nodded. The soldiers set about the task of prying Catherine and Eligius apart.

"No."

Above the roar of the fearful hundreds, Eligius heard Catherine's protest.

"They can't come," Ault cried above the din. The rest of his words broke into stones. Rebellion. Consort. Suspicion.

"How will I know you live?" Julia screamed from the entrance to the ship. Sir John put his arms around her and sent her up. More soldiers emerged from the dark mouth of the Royal Captain and brought her inside. Sir John turned back to watch helplessly.

Catherine shook free of the hands holding her. She waded forward through the hot amber air and took hold of Eligius as voices rose in strata of sound. Orders to leave, to stay, to get aboard, to clear a path, to go back. Cries of disbelief came from everywhere and were quickly stolen by the hot winds blowing out to sea. People hurried past, awkward under the unfamiliar weight of their own possessions. Children pulled by the arms with kerchiefs pressed to their mouths and eyes, as if Ceylon's collapse could lodge within them like an infection.

She pressed the folded camera into Eligius' arms.

"Listen," she said.

The word rose above everything.

It was no longer a port and a murmuring ship, but the world, reduced to one thing.

Somewhere, Andrew cried that he would leave her to Ceylon, so help him.

Eligius counted breaths.

Catherine felt his hand tighten around hers. The world

fell away. *The one who will make portrait sitters of the stars*, she thought. *We promised each other*.

He could feel his fingers go bloodless with the effort to remain in hers. He pulled her close; no words would be lost.

"We promised," and her fingers curled in his hair, her lips against his ear, "Oh my child, we are not still. We will always move towards each other. Swear to me –"

"I swear. Swear to me –"

"We will find each other again –"

She was gone. A curtain of uniforms cut him from her, and the ship, and Sir John and Julia. He heard only what he thought was her voice. Disembodied, floating above the sea of hands like nothing in the world.

"Remember me," it said.

He held the camera. Gita sat alone on the dock, crying as the world emptied around her. He went to her and stood over her protectively. It wasn't enough, to stand. He crouched and made a shell of himself over her and the camera, turning away from everything.

"HOW WILL I know he lives?"

Catherine stood at the rails. She held her children to her.

"I don't see him." Sir John scoured the departing colonials still clogging the dock. They could see the end now. The receiving bay and Chatham were empty but for the natives wandering away from the port.

"None were allowed," Andrew said. "Not my doing. These were directives from Parliament. Too much to sort through, the loyals from the seditionists."

He stood to Catherine's left, hat in hand, his wife behind him. To onlookers down below, he might have passed for a suitor.

"He's a resourceful boy," Sir John said.

"And Catherine left him with means," Andrew said.

Below her, the rest of her fellow countrymen came forward to meet their new life. She closed her eyes, counted breaths,

yearned for old days, waited for the world to turn back to her.
She wanted to be stronger than she was, in front of them all.
She wanted to be mother enough to answer her daughter's plea.
How will I ever know?

The hope that he wouldn't be alone, that someone would
break open the secret of him and love him, was too hard to
hold now that the *Royal Captain* pulled away from Ceylon and
met the coming sea.

"Wait. I think that's him."

She gazed in the direction Sir John pointed. A lone figure
arrived at the entrance to the port, almost at the street. A tod-
dling child stumbled alongside. There was a length of wood in
the figure's arms. At one end, a box that caught the light and
sent it back to her as a mote. A brilliant brief glimmer that disappeared when they turned the corner.

She felt the sudden plummet of her heart. Facing Andrew,
she slapped him hard enough to bring a shocked cry.

Taking the hands of her children, she walked away.

GITA PUT OUT her arms. "Up."

Eligius lifted her. Around them, the mad flights of the colonials could be read from the road. The wheels of their carriages
split the dry dirt open and stripped the closest trees of bark.
Clothes, furniture, even casks of good brandy littered Chatham.

A faint breath of white ship's steam rose at the horizon.
Gita pointed to it.

"Yes," he said.

FOR HOURS THEY heard nothing, saw no one on the roads or
in the estates. With each step, it was as if they were descending
deeper and deeper into a black bottomless well.

When Gita saw a fallen doll that made her smile, he put it
into her arms and told her that now, beginning right now, she'd
have to learn to care for her own things.

This is what it is to be alone, he thought. To be driven to the ground by silence and dead space.

Dimbola was dark. He placed Gita in the gazebo's remains and told her to keep her head below the broken trellising in case any more men came. Then he went to the main house to see what might be salvaged. Closing the front door behind him, he held himself until his body stopped trembling. There was a little girl to be fed and clothed.

In the scullery he found some blackened potatoes and a bit of bread, some lard and a few stray morsels of lamb. The water his mother had collected from the rains now reeked of ash. He poured the buckets out of the scullery window and set them in the doorway to be taken to the well.

It was almost a year since he'd first come. If this winter was like the last, the rains would find them soon.

He brought the food, some linens and blankets and some clothes to the front room. The fire had eaten his modest quarters down to the frame. A pile of soot marked his sleeping corner. There was nothing left of his possessions. Everything was dust. The feather shadow was gone.

He walked down the corridor. The paintings had been stolen. The walls were pockmarked with cavities from the men's crude bludgeoning at the gas light fixtures. Scorched shadows adorned the ceiling where the flames had journeyed through the arteries of the house.

He opened Charles' door.

The window wall no longer stood. Glass littered the floor in a glimmering trail out onto the grass. The room had been stripped of everything he'd come to know. Curtains, books with spines that crackled like split coconuts when opened, the fronds and step stool and every other trapping of her photograph, all gone.

Charles' burnt remains had been left to rot atop the debris. He was so bereft. Age and illness had already begun to shrink him, then three nights lashed by the valley's bitter rains. Now, finished by fire. Only a hand, upturned like a gnarled root, marked the blackened thing for the once-lion it was.

He closed the door softly, and wondered where his mother fell.

Gita helped him carry everything to Holland House. He ushered her inside with a promise of some bread and lamb. Sitting her atop a folded sheet, he told her to be still while he swept broken glass from the ceiling window into a corner. While she ate, he set up the camera on its legs. Next to it, he lay Sir John's telescope. The telescope's curved eye reflected the room.

He saw the image reflected in its glass, of a gracefully carved wooden frame jutting out from its hiding place under a drop cloth.

He brought the painting out from its alcove, set it against the wall and let the cloth fall away. *I asked, do you see love when you look at it?*

In time, he thought, I will know every detail of this. Her lips, apart as if captured in the creation of a word. Her hair, her skin, her eyes like submerged pearls. George had painted light into her eyes, remaking the soft glow cast by the lit diya which she held near her heart.

I do, you said. However regretful a thing it may be.

He stayed a long time with her, staring at his diya in her hands until the light drained from the world. But not from her, nor from the memsa'ab's house. The light stood still, here.

4.

Dimbola is dark now. Its feverish life and bustle are stilled as are the lights which shined there. Servants, scientists, disciples, painters, astronomers and divines, all those who came to her in hopes of burning themselves into memory are gone. Silence is the only tenant left. But I have seen their faces across this land and others, and I say they live.

SIR GEORGE WYNFIELD
Portraitist to the Royal Family, on his memories of Ceylon, 1902

Departing

ELIGIUS PICKED DEAD PETALS FROM THE TAMARIND
growing near the broken wall. He'd planted it in an effort to
pretty up what remained of their hut, but it had gone to pulp in
only a few days, a victim of the unrelenting rains. He rolled
the petals into his palm, using his thumb as a mortar until a fine
rust smear remained.

Gita's laughter at this distraction filled the bones of Matara.
Four years and as many monsoon seasons had passed over
his old village since the soldiers felled it. Little remained to mark
the place. Yet this burial ground was where she chose for her
reading each day.

It was the colonials' June, in their year of 1842. His sister
no longer remembered her own mother's face.

It had taken him many days of scavenging before he'd
found Sudarma at the rear of the house. She had fallen in the
memsa'ab's sacred room; he found her lying on the floor,
covered in the smoke and ash she'd breathed until no air was
left in her.

He could see the neglect tattering away at Gita's memory
of her mother and he let it happen. Let her fill the void with
a woman of her own fashioning. A perfect union of doll parts.
Sustainer, beauty, angel, ghost.

Gita no longer cried in outrage that her brother's hands
tucked her in for the night. Yet something in her yearned for her
old home and he had long since given up fighting with her about

her desire to sit outside the hut she'd been born in and hear of
Gretel slipping beneath the waves.

Gita began kicking through the mud. Her four-year old's
attention span had reached its limit. "Very good today," he said.
"Your pronunciation is much better."

She shrugged. Progress in the colonials' language mattered
little to her.

"Let's start back." He picked up the book. "I'll make you
rice with curd."

"Stay."

She took such joy in chasing her shadow among the banyans. When she was ready, she smiled and then ran without
waiting for him, down the rain-carved road towards the jungle.
It was the long way back. But it was the only route she tolerated.
She loved the sea.

He gave in, as he always did. He'd come to perceive
unexpected things in her childish tantrums. He needed to give
her everything she wanted. Safety and certainty above all,
because in her outcries he heard his own death, and the void
after him, and how she would fill it with memories of him.

Let them be worth keeping, he thought. I can give her so
little else.

The wind was with them. The journey was not so daunting
to her little legs. They found the road and followed it back to
Dimbola, where they saw a carriage waiting at the gate. Its doors
bore the ornate crest of the Galle Face.

Gita's face darkened. When the vicar's messenger stepped
out, she dropped her eyes as she always did around others.
Even ones she saw often enough to know, soldiers and colonials
and this boy. She refused to make eye contact at his awkward
pleasantries.

Her poor eyes, Eligius thought. Always expecting to see
the worst.

"We need to speak," the vicar's oldest altar boy said.

Eligius told his sister to mind the church's horse. He led

the boy to the main house. The boy – he never did see fit to give Eligius his name, and Eligius never asked – seemed more comfortable there. The colonials liked their formalities.

"There is a family."

There always is, Eligius thought.

The boy covered familiar terrain. Address, societal position. None of it mattered much. Eligius knew his role, and what it was worth. "My fee."

"They will pay you when you arrive. You may meet the servant's gaze only. The master of the house will not have it."

Again, he thought, familiar terrain. "A favor, of the vicar. May Gita stay at the church until I am finished?"

Starchy indignation crept into the boy's eyes. "It's harder for her when she's alone." He paused, letting the lie settle against his tongue. "She finds peace at the church."

"Very well. But you should go before the light fades."

"I make my own."

"It is not so much to light a candle," the boy said haughtily. "We light hundreds each evening in the church and we are not prideful. It's unseemly for anyone, let alone such as you."

"Then you should have no trouble finding someone else to attend to this family's needs."

There were but a few others in Ceylon who had taken up the art. He'd heard of them. Colonials who came to shore in the months following the violence to stake claims on the abandoned estates. They brought a new crop of tea that they hoped might circumvent the blight that had taken such a toll on the coffee plantations, and another garrison of soldiers who kept troublemakers at bay. They brought as well new cameras that were smaller than his, with lenses like prisms, and new ways of coating the glass plates. But they were prisoners of their new world and its capricious light. None knew its ways like he did. None were willing to bathe in poisons like he was. Hobbyists, that was all they were. Effete portrayers of fox hunts and christenings. No one save he went to the families needing their darkest moments arrested. Only him.

Sometimes he wondered if those families were behind the odd peace he'd come to know in Ceylon. Perhaps they kept Matara's roaming boys from the one who made death a portrait sitter.

He chose not to belabor the point. There was no need. On the church's behalf, the boy had performed this minuet many times. Never did these people feel closer to their God than when they unleashed their contempt.

"I am grateful to you and to the vicar for thinking of me," Eligius said, "and for taking Gita. Of course I will go shortly."

The boy left Eligius for his carriage. Gita was dutifully petting the horse. Eligius gave her the book. Its page was bent to Gretel's tale. "Practice your words one more time before you go to bed," he told her.

"I don't want to go."

He hushed her. "They are always nice to you. They cook good food and keep you in a warm room. There is nothing to object to. I will look in on you tonight, when I am done." The church carriage propelled forward with a sharp jerk. Her face appeared in the window, quietly disconsolate. She had grown to be obedient. Too much so. He could put her in anyone's hands and upon his word, she would do whatever was asked of her. Hers was a life too easily ruled.

She thrust her hand out of the carriage window and waved.

She had four years of memories, and he'd done what he could to make something tolerable of them. *Will you have room for one more, Gita? Just one, just a goodbye. And from it, I hope you will make something like forgiveness.*

He waved back.

THE INDIAN GIRL who answered his knocking was young, with luminous eyes and smooth skin. Eligius touched his camera. "I have been sent for."

She stepped aside for him. He brought the camera in and leaned it against the wall. Slipping his rucksack off, he checked to make sure the glass plates survived the journey. Giggles drew his attention to a doorway across the tiled foyer. Three small boys covered their mouths and jostled each other. Maybe Gita's age or younger.

The servant girl rushed up the curved stairs to the master of the house waiting at the top. He whispered to her and walked away, letting a small velvet satchel fall from his fingers to the floor just outside an open door. The girl came to the banister and waved. Eligius brought his tools upstairs. "Close the door," he told her. She obeyed.

He set down his camera and spread its legs before considering the room. The curtains were open in the mistaken belief that every available drop of light was required. He asked the girl to close them, careful to keep his voice low and his gaze averted from the master standing in the corner, mumbling words into the silence. She did as he asked. The room sank into a murky haze.

Eligius lit the first candle. He dipped a taper into the bobbing light and brought it to the others.

"Are there enough?" the girl asked him.

It was always good to hear something like his own language in these places. "Yes. You did very well."

The room was oddly shaped. Like an oval, but with one end smaller than the portion with the bed. That end would require more light. He brought candles to surround the bed and gazed upon his subject for the first time. *I remember you, memsa'ab Pike.*

Her family had surrounded her with pieces of themselves. A tiger figurine fashioned from the husks of coconuts rested in the crook of her arm. Satin cloth embroidered with her family crest made a cloak around her head. A garland of hyacinth crowned her dry hair. A crucifix hung on the wall above her. The Bible – there was always this book, he thought, closer at hand than it likely ever was in life – lay open across her midsection.

She was to be remembered for her children, he saw, and for flowers, and piety. Her once-spoken dream of a song that could bring tears was nowhere in the room. Nor was his memsa'ab's photograph. Perhaps her husband could not look at the sculpture of his wife's secret life. Maybe he'd never known of it. Here then was the spouse and mother they would rather remember. The other would simply be buried.

He surrounded Mrs. Pike with candles until her loose flesh radiated something like sleep. Positioning the camera, he treated the plate, readied the paper, and slipped under the cloak. There you are.

While the image developed in his light box, he accepted a mug of spiced black tea from the maid. In a small, sweet voice, she told him her name. Navneet. Punjabi. She was fourteen. Her family came south before she was born. The master's boys called her Nan. Her village, Tutakoreen, was one of the first to fall. She remembered the sounds of hammers against her walls, but little else. Two nights before her memsa'ab died, she heard the woman's moaning and the doctor saying that her stomach had burst. Later, the sa'ab left his wife's side, came to her room and raped her. She knew it would happen again.

Eligius glanced at the master. He was reading from his own Bible. Occasionally he looked up at his dead wife as if she were a slumbering child drifting away on a story.

He wanted to tell Navneet to leave, but life wasn't like that. Only the fighting had gone away. Everything else had remained, with new faces manning the old ramparts. "Take kunch or suarnalata," he told the girl. "It will end any baby that begins from him."

She smiled.

He put the imprint into a simple frame fashioned from detritus Dimbola wood. Setting it next to the body, he took his rupees and left. The plate, with Mrs. Pike's image seared into it, bounced at his side as he walked to the carriage. Later, he could use the glass to make photographic copies of her to sell at the bazaar. The colonials never went there and didn't know how highly pictures of dead Britishers were valued. He'd taken many of the dead and sold them twice, to the grieving and to the pleased. Soldiers who'd died of their wounds, or old sa'abs whose cholera came with the droughts, those were the easiest to sell. He'd even sold Charles' photo to the colonials. It touched them, the new directors especially. How they went on about the inspiration this old patriarch had kindled, compelling an Indian boy to such a Christian display of bedside mourning, like an angel at the Nativity.

He counted his rupees. Added to the others, it was finally enough. Some would pay for the post. The rest for the return of the *Royal Captain*, due into the John port four months hence.

He counted them a second time while passing the Galle Face's lamps. It was late, and Gita was no doubt asleep. She'd still be asleep when he returned.

The Colebrooks' old horse wobbled drunkenly by the time he arrived back at Dimbola. The animal had never recovered from the night Dimbola was attacked. He hadn't been badly injured. Just a few surface wounds that healed like engorged blood worms at the horse's haunches and across the bunched muscles of his shoulders. But something had broken in the beast that night. Now his nostrils flared at the least bit of work. He sought the darkness of his stall at every opportunity.

"Not too much further," Eligius told him as he dismounted the carriage.

When the time came, he'd take only a few things. Nothing of value to anyone. Some clothes; he had nothing warm and wondered whether a servant's attire would see him very far. He would take Sir John's telescope, the camera, glass plates, paper, a cask of chemical. There would be room for Julia's painting. He would insist upon it.

He'd wrap them carefully and place them next to the faded slip of paper Mrs. Pike had given the memsa'ab once. A gallery, where her photographs might be seen by the wider world.

Before leaving, he took a last look around the house. Ceylon had begun to reclaim it. Creeping flowers crossed the broken threshold into the sa'ab's bedroom. The house smelled of rain and rot. He didn't like it inside and never stayed longer than necessary. Holland House was far preferable. Their moments still lived inside its walls. He felt them each time he entered.

It was there that he took the photograph he'd made, wrapped it in cloth, marked the gallery's address across it and below, her name.

There were still months yet before the ship came. But today felt like the beginning of his leaving. He sat down to write his note to the vicar.

> *I thank you for all you have done for us and for watching over my sister as I know you will. I will send for her when I've raised enough money for her passage. I hope that will be soon, but I can't be sure of what I will find. Tell her I love her. I've never been certain that she knows. Teach her to be a Christian, if that pleases you. She won't oppose you.*

When it was time, he would rub the paper with a bit of tamarind. Gita loved the scent and would take some comfort in being thought of that way.

That will be the last thing I do at Dimbola, he thought. Already, it was slipping away.

He closed the door to Holland House and walked to the carriage.

DAWN WAS STILL some hours away. There was only one priest in the Galle Face sanctuary, making his preparations for services.

He found Gita's room. She slept peacefully in a loose cinch of covers. Her window opened onto the stone garden. He crossed the room quietly and peered out.

There were many stones now. Charles' was among them. The church had commissioned the port's finest mason to craft an elegant marker with dates, the names of Charles' family, and a place where his role on the court was remembered. A few nights after Charles' remains were interred, he'd slipped in and buried the sa'ab's beloved map next to him.

But only that one; the map of Wynfield's handiwork rested in his rucksack between glass plates. Perhaps he'd have need of it.

Gita turned in her sleep. He kissed her forehead. She made a face and curled her fists against her cheeks but didn't wake. She rose early, most days. Sleep was too filled.

He left. Outside, the air grew cooler despite the coming morning. Clouds blocked the hint of light at the far horizon. They were fat, cottony, and so weighted with water that they threatened to pull the sky down.

He sat on the hard wood and took out one more sheet of paper, to compose his letter. Together with the parcel, it would find the gallery first and go from there.

He tried to imagine its path through London, to her. Around him, the air took on a sheen of green gray from the coming storm. Another monsoon, on them so quickly.

At the horizon line where the water and the sky met, he saw a light. He counted breaths and watched it grow like a diya returning home. The postal ship would be here soon. Then it would turn around again not long after. It would take his parcel away from here.

He envisioned how the sea would look from the ship's rail, sweeping into the great hull and back again. Months from now, when they were close enough, he'd use Sir John's telescope to see the lights of an unimaginable city.

He spared a look for the clock on Chatham and the lush jungle beyond, and found that they were difficult to watch for very long. The ship's mournful whistle roughened the air. When it blew a second time, it was much closer.

The memsa'ab would say, photograph all this so it won't be lost. No one possesses anything for all its life, she would say.

Yet we persist, he thought. We pin time down by the wings. Our patrons ask only that we make them better than they were in the living moment before, but all the while, memsa'ab, we are after something else. We always have been. We have requests of the world, and reasons.

He began to write.

The Luminist

"REALLY, CATHERINE. IT'S ENOUGH THAT I'M MADE TO sit stock still for these interminable hours, robed like a dirty monk. Must I stare at that photograph, of all the images I might behold? It's not appropriate and should be put away, out of proper sight."

Catherine smiled at the familiar lament. Lord Tennyson was far from the first to complain at the discomfort caused by the photograph hanging on the cottage wall. Sin made permanent, he'd dubbed it upon seeing it for the first time, bringing his considerable poetic gifts to bear. Others had been less graceful in their remarks. Abomination, Carlyle had said. Against God's plan, the Archbishop had declared as he departed. Almost all who made the journey from the great cities to her cottage at Freshwater, Isle of Wight had something damning to say on encountering the photograph.

Lady Wynfield had surprised her with the delicacy of her condemnation. Andrew had broken his minor promise and had sent his wife in his stead to be the first portrait sitter. She and Lady Wynfield had said little to each other during the exposure time. As Lady Wynfield was leaving, she'd looked at the photograph. "Sad," she'd said. "Unnecessarily so."

When Catherine had delivered Lady Wynfield's portrait to their estate across the Isle, a maid took it without a word. No thanks ever came by card or visit. Only more portrait sitters, money in hand.

Lord Tennyson was one such patron. A great man, among London's eminent. Yet he was no different in his sensibility regarding the photograph on the wall, and deserved no different response from that which she always gave.

Touching the image of Eligius and Julia, she said, "this moment shall never be made a secret."

"Very well. But must I sit much longer?"

"Not long."

Her attention drifted past the cottage doors, past the sweep of January's falling rain, past Julia playing with Ewen as if no drop touched them, and Sir John making his notes under the safety of a gazebo. The gazebo had been the only architectural addition she'd requested after seeing the property she would receive pursuant to Charles' final compensation from the John Company. All these things that composed the simple drift of her life.

At the fence, she saw the postal carrier step off of his cart. He held a shabby parasol over the parcel in his hand. He opened the gate and walked to her.

Behind her, a great man burned in glass and light.

She went to the cottage doorway. The rain moved across the visible landscape.

The postal carrier greeted her. He brought her the expected letters from Reijlander and Talbott, then lay the parcel in her hands. "I brought it fast as I could, madam. You can see it went to a gallery in London first. I guess they had your address. See how far it's come? At sea for seven months, since Ceylon."

"Catherine," Lord Tennyson complained. "Please –"

His words fell away with the parcel's threadbare cloth. There was a letter, and a photograph.

Outside, Sir John and Julia, and even Ewen, who was young yet but understood that the simple act of a post had changed the shape of the day, all came to her, to see.

Ceylon was the world now.

She gave in to the onrush of moments. The liturgic

breathing wind through its jungle. The painterly light. Dimbola. The boy, counting breaths.

She opened the letter.

I am not of Ceylon anymore. Gita will never know me, for all my promises. I don't have a trade and could never serve another colonial. I have no home and only enough money to starve on a different shore. I've had too many faces on my hands to remember them all. My own kind thinks of me as a monster. Maybe I am, but one with the power to burn dreams onto the world.

So I bring the camera and some ideas for cutting lenses that will make true portrait sitters of the stars.

I'm leaving everything I know for you, and for Julia. I do what I must. Cross oceans. Live amongst the Wynfields of that city. The light and the love I want are only with you. And if not with you, if I'm wrong, then surround my head with strange flowers and open the Christian book over my chest. I will not live where I can't be seen.

Memsa'ab, the Royal Captain *will be here for me soon. They say we will sail by storms. Such a thing, to pass a storm at sea as if it were just another traveler making its way.*

I've learned. I've become your disciple in tying light to the departing. It is the 22nd day of your June, here at six degrees latitude, eighty degrees longitude. The stars are the same everywhere.

I have found the way to you. I am coming.

Her heart came wondrously undone.

She studied the photograph. He was in Holland House. In the chair, in the open doorway. There were candles all around him, and behind him there was the cloudless night sky, and there were more stars than lay atop the sea at the holiday he once spoke of, when burning lights made a celestial map of the black waters. This was the moment he'd kept safe, until he found the way to send it across oceans and years to her.

The rain diminished. The veiled day emerged. She held the photograph up, into the returning light.